Blues in the Night

Max Maxwell Mystery #6

Paul Sinor

Print ISBNs
Amazon Print 9780228622208
LSI Print 9780228622215
B&N Print 9780228622222

BWL Publishing Inc

Books we love to write ...
Authors around the world.

http://bwlpublishing.ca

Dedication

To poker players everywhere. Never go all in with pocket Jacks or an Ace Queen. They are the Devil's hand.

And as always, to Jewell.

Chapter 1

Amsterdam, the home of Anne Frank, was also the home of three of the largest and best-known red-light districts in Europe. The largest of the three: the Singelgebied was usually crowded with not only men and a few women looking for a few minutes of no-commitment sex, to busloads of gawking tourists taking photos of the prostitutes in the windows as they openly solicited their next customer. Negotiations were made on the spot with the customer on one side of the window or door and the hooker on the other. Agree on a price and a curtain was drawn and the act was consummated mere feet from the people strolling on the sidewalks who had not yet made a purchase. Sex was legal in Amsterdam as were drugs. Both were readily available, but they were regulated. Cafes were where one bought and enjoyed drugs. The red-light district was where one bought and enjoyed sex. Like the variety of available drugs, there was a veritable smorgasbord of sex awaiting anyone ready to pick out the provider, name the act and pay the price.

Jacob Dirksen was just such a customer. He preferred to do business in De Jijp, the smaller of the three red-light districts. He recently heard of a special house catering to his needs that had just opened in the Sigelgebied.

He took the tram from his apartment to the Amsterdam Central stop and left it, and the car filled with Saturday night fun seekers and tourists behind, as he exited the station and headed for his night of fun. He walked a few minutes and stopped once to purchase and drink a cup of tea at one of the many cafés that were found on every block. As he sat at a small table outside, he wondered how many of the men passing him were going to the district and if any of them were going to the same house he planned to visit.

Jacob walked down Monninkenstraat, turned on Gordijenstreeg and took another turn on Bloedstraat. His destination was in a small three block area bordered by Monninkenstraat and Bloedstraat. He knew the area well as he came here at least twice a month. He was not a wealthy man, but this was an indulgence he allowed himself. Once he was on the right block, he slowly made his way past several open windows where the women, who often referred to themselves as models, were on display. Unlike many of the other customers who strolled the streets, he could not be swayed by a sales pitch. He knew what he wanted, and he had a good idea where to find it.

Finally, he got to the right address. It was the one he had been told about and he was not disappointed. His preference was a tall, leggy blonde with large breasts. He did not ask, nor did he care if they were natural or enhanced. The windows were rented to the models by the hour, so in a day as many as five or six different faces and bodies would be on display. If what you wanted was not behind the glass, wait a few minutes or ask for someone else and it was delivered. The first model was a stunning brunet with hair cut to accent a moon-shaped face, a tiny nose and eyes that almost sparkled beneath the lights in the window. Dressed in a bra that barely covered the nipples and a thong that was little more than a patch, Jacob knew this model would not be on display much longer before a deal was struck, and the curtain was closed.

The next window was filled with a model that looked like a special order for Jacob. A blonde with straight hair that ended at shoulder length, smiled and turned slowly to allow Jacob to see everything on sale. Breasts were large and hardly moved as the model turned from side to side. Long, slender fingers with bright red nails slid easily into the band on the thong that appeared to be more paint than cloth. Slowly it was peeled down in the back to reveal ass cheeks as smooth as those of a newborn child. That was all it took for Jacob to make a purchase.

*   *   *

Professor Jacob Dirksen was known throughout Holland as the country's, and perhaps the world's most knowledgeable horticulturist dealing with tulips. His office at the University of Amsterdam was a part of the largest agrarian in the country. Hundreds of tulips in every variety and color grew year-round in the controlled environment of the room. His classes were always filled with waiting lists for seats and any lecture he gave was standing room only. That was to be expected in a country known for its tulips and with an economy that depended on the flowers and the tourists brought to see them. In his twenty years at the university, he had developed almost a hundred new colors and varieties of the bulbs from which they grew. Only one strain eluded him. For over ten years he had been attempting to develop a new shade of blue, the most popular color in the tulip fields that surrounded the university and much of the open land in the entire country. He tried everything he could think of for the first seven years. He was successful in the eyes of some of his colleagues, but he had a shade and style in mind. He could see it. He dreamed about it. He saw it for fleeting seconds in clouds and in the ocean when he was at the seashore, but he could not describe it to anyone else and he could not duplicate it. For him, it was the Holy Grail. It would be a Nobel Prize in his mind if only he could make it happen. It was an obsession that his colleagues were familiar with and a subject they rarely allowed to come up in conversation, lest they were ready to sit for an hour and listen to the same dissertation they had heard in the past.

Never married, when he got home, he spent hours on his computer researching new formulas, reading articles about new strains produced around the world by universities and home growers alike. He had a habit of reading aloud from the screen and most of the time it was only heard by a small dog he found with an injured leg in front of his apartment one day. He took the dog to a veterinarian and once the leg was well, the dog had a place to live. On occasion, he spoke aloud to one of the overnight guests with whom he shared his life for a few days at a time. The guest was usually someone who was recommended to him or someone he found in one of his favorite houses in the red-light district of Amsterdam. Unlike sex workers in most other cities and even those who worked outside the district, those whom he selected were disease free and would do anything he required if he was willing to pay for it.

Once he was alone in his apartment, no matter the time of day or day of the week, his mind was consumed with his work. He had been working on a new variety of tulip bulb for over five years. He had tried almost everything he could come up with and many of the ideas recommended by colleagues, but his goal to produce a new variety of tulip with the color of blue he envisioned still eluded him. Blue was the most popular color of the tuber, and a new strain would not only give him the added status he sought in the academic community but would come with a very nice reward from the Dutch government, but that was not enough. As a reward for all his hard work, he felt he deserved more...much more than the Dutch government was willing to give. A patent on the new bulb would be worth millions to the right people.

The tulip business was so important to the Dutch government and their economy that there was a government agency that dealt with them. Secret formulas for the colors, the methods of growing and preserving the bulbs were guarded as closely as the gold in the national treasury. Several years earlier, a man had been arrested and tried as a case of espionage for stealing several pages of notes on a new strain of bulbs from the agency. He was a foreign national and the Dutch government considered a declaration of war when he was caught.

Two years previously, due to an accident in the lab, Dirksen had a bulb that produced as close to the color as he had come. By forcing the growth of several genetically reengineered bulbs, in another two years he finally had the bulb he wanted. He was able to duplicate the bulb and the color as easily as a casual gardener did by planting bulbs in a flower garden in the front yard of their home. By the time he had sufficient bulbs and the corresponding research to ensure that he alone could reproduce them, he was ready for the final chapter in his search for his just reward. All he had to do now was find a buyer and he had several leads on them. It would be a difficult and selective move on his part, for once the Genie was out of the bottle, it would be impossible to put it back in. He did not want to introduce it in Holland, so he planned to do it at the next best place.

For almost a year, Professor Dirksen had been considering a visit to the United States, particularly to the Skagit Valley in the state of Washington to attend the annual Tulip Festival. If anyone was a likely client to purchase his new bulb, it would be one of the growers there who grew more tulips in numbers and acreage than in his native Holland. It was scheduled to start in two weeks, and he was already packed.

9

Chapter 2

Even as a fully tenured professor, Jacob Dirksen was not a wealthy man. He lived comfortably within his salary and had a modest savings account, and the university had a retirement plan that would allow him to continue to live just as if he was still working. He spent his discretionary money on the things he liked to do. He went to a little village in the Bavarian Alps where he took a ski vacation each winter, usually with a person with whom he shared his week and his bed. He made it a point to never take the same person twice, so once the week was over, they had nothing but memories.

His main job at the university was research when he was not lecturing a class, so he was very good at finding out what he needed to know. After he was satisfied that he had sufficient data to put his new color of blue on the market, he researched the most likely buyers. From all indications it was one of four growers in the Skagit Valley of the state of Washington in the United States. He had never been to the United States, so he further researched the state and especially the city of Seattle which he saw was not only the largest city closest to the tulip fields but a major metropolitan area as well. He felt certain that between the fields and the city he could find everything he wanted.

When he researched the flights from Amsterdam to Seattle, he made an interesting discovery. The least expensive way was not non-stop. He had arranged for a sabbatical from the university, so all he wanted was a one-way ticket. He did not want to be on a time crunch when he found the right person. A non-stop was over fifteen hundred dollars, but if he selected one that had a two-hour layover in Dublin, Ireland, he could save almost five hundred dollars. In searching the flights, the most expensive connecting flight was between Amsterdam and Frankfort where he would have a fourteen-hour layover. He selected Dublin, since he had been to Germany many times. Due to the trip being during a sabbatical, he was paying for the ticket himself. He was not a cheapskate, but he had other plans for his money once he arrived in the United States. Like most people in Holland, he spoke German and English, so there would be no language barriers once he arrived in the United States.

The flight from Amsterdam to Dublin took less than two hours. His seat companion was an Irishman who had been to the Netherlands on a business trip. He said he worked for an international chemical company and was attending a convention in the city. Dirksen listened for most of the trip while he was regaled with stories of the incredible night life of the city. All he did was nod his head occasionally and agree that it was a most unusual city.

When the flight finally landed, Dirksen reached in the overhead compartment and pulled down the small bag he had brought with him and secured in the space above his seat. Once on a trip to Madrid his suitcase had been lost and he had nothing with him, save what he was wearing and had in his pockets and a small briefcase. He had to purchase everything he needed for his stay, and to his dismay, he was told the airline was not responsible for the amount he claimed for the suitcase and contents that was never found. From that trip forward, he always packed a small bag with a change of clothes and enough personal items to last until a piece of delayed or lost luggage could be located.

The Dublin airport was a massive array of airline counters, security checkpoints, restaurants and shops catering to any need a traveler may have. As he left the arrival gate, he found himself near a large café that appeared to specialize in chocolate. He quickly passed by that operation, since he knew that Dutch chocolate had no rivals anyplace on earth, especially in an airport in Dublin, Ireland. He looked down the main area that was dominated by a large hanging sculpture made of metal that appeared to be a representation of an atom. His interest was directed more to a large restaurant where the ever-present sign indicating the Irish national beverage of Guinness was featured. He made his way to the seating area and selected one of the small tables which were surrounded by four straight-back white wooden chairs. Behind him at one of the high-top tables a man who appeared to already have had far too many pints was trying to explain the innerworkings of the European game of football to a younger man who was wearing a jersey with the name of an American football team on it. Dirksen took his time with his pint, occasionally directing his attention from the conversation behind him to the rows of computer monitors mounted overhead in the corridor, but visible in the seating area to check the status of his flight.

With a two hour lay-over he had enough time to enjoy his pint and then take a quick stroll from the restaurant to the gate where he was to board the flight to Seattle. Outside the windows of the lobby the gate area was filled with planes featuring names and logos from countries around the world. The majority of those he saw were the green and white planes from Aer Lingus. Beyond the runways the clouds were banking up and turning dark. He checked his watch, hoping his flight would be called, boarded and lifted off before the weather became a consideration.

Across from the checkpoint leading to his departure gate was a shop selling books, magazines and newspapers from around the world. Most of the publications were in English, but there was a scattering of others, mostly newspapers and popular magazines in German and French. He selected a murder mystery novel printed in English, paid for it and tucked it in his carry-on bag. Almost as an afterthought as he stood in line to pay, he selected a roll of mints and a pack of chewing gum. He had no idea who his seat companion might be for the next leg of his flight, but there was no sense in taking a chance on having bad breath if it was a woman who wanted to talk.

Dirksen had seen everything he found of interest in the airport when his flight was finally called for boarding. He was flying against the clock, so he was careful not to eat too much or allow himself to sleep any more than was necessary or unavoidable on the flight from Dublin to Seattle. He knew from the digital map on the seatback screen in front of him that he was flying across the vastness of the United States. He wished he had thought of landing in New York and taking a train across the country just so he could see it. Perhaps on the return to Amsterdam he would do that...if he returned.

After what seemed to be a lifetime, he heard the pilot announce that they were making their final approach to land in Seattle. Instructions and directions were given for customs and where to pick up their checked baggage. He patted his pocket to make certain his passport was still secured where he had left it upon re-boarding in Dublin.

Finally, he felt the bump as the wheels touched the runway, and the pushback in his seat as the pilot applied the brakes to slow the plane once it was on the ground. He was in the United States and if everything went according to his plan, he would soon become a very wealthy man.

It always amazed him anytime he flew, no matter the country or the airline, as soon as the seat belt light went out, it became a push and shove contest to see who could get off first. Unless he was changing planes or had to make a phone call, he kept his seat until the line in the aisle moved forward. Once it did, he felt safe in standing up and getting anything he had stored in the overhead rack. If there was one thing that made him crazy, it was passengers who refused to check their bags and came on board with more than they should and then attempted to store it in the overhead by their seats. Many had to search up and down the aisle for a vacant spot when they found the one over their seat was already full. Naturally, they were one of the first to stand and they then had to push in the reverse direction to retrieve their bags.

He pulled a small bag he had placed in the overhead rack and moved with the line until he was out of the plane and into the terminal. All the passengers were arriving on this flight from outside the United States, so everyone had to queue up for customs. After a quick few questions and a check of his passport, he was directed to the baggage claim area.

He had made reservations at a hotel in downtown Seattle while still in Amsterdam, so all he had to do was grab his checked bag, follow the signs to the taxi line and have a taxi take him to the hotel.

"I notice an accent. German?" The driver asked when Dirksen gave him the name of the hotel.

"Close. I am from Amsterdam, Holland. Many of us speak German in our daily lives."

"Amsterdam, huh? I've heard some pretty wild stories about that place," the driver turned sideways to speak to Dirksen.

"From your passengers?" Dirksen watched as the taxi made its way from the taxi stand to the road outside the airport. It was after sunset, so the streets were ablaze with neon and lights advertising all the businesses along the way. There were as many signs in the short drive to what Dirksen recognized as an Autobahn as he normally saw in the entire city of Amsterdam.

"Yes. I've gotten a few people who have been there and none of them had a bad time...if you know what I mean?"

"I do indeed, and I have heard that your city of Seattle is able to give a visitor some of the same...entertainment. Is that true?"

Before the driver could answer, the taxi made the crest of the hill leading into the city. Anyone who has ever seen Seattle at night for the first time on a clear night agrees that it is one of the most beautiful cities in the world. The only problem is seeing it on a clear night, with the number of rain and fog days the city has it is a crap shoot to see it. Tonight, it was sparkling in its glory. The lights of the city and the Puget Sound behind it were the perfect greeting for a visitor.

The driver took the Spring Street exit from I-5 and made his way to the hotel. When he stopped and got out to assist Dirksen with his baggage, he handed him a business card. "When you get ready to leave, give me a call and I'll come pick you up." He leaned closer so the bellman who came out to load the bags on a cart could not hear him. "If you want to explore some of that entertainment you are looking for, give me a call and I can help with that as well. I know some places the Chamber of Commerce don't put in their visitor's brochures."

Dirksen paid with a nice tip and took the card. "I'm sure I will be calling on you for both services."

Chapter 3

After breakfast in the hotel restaurant, Jacob asked the concierge to assist him in renting a car. He had an international driver's license and a letter from his insurance company saying he was covered world-wide, so after a few minutes at the hotel desk with the rental agent, he had a map marked with the route north on I-5 to the Skagit Valley and the Tulip Festival. He had driven on autobahns in Germany, so the speed and carelessness of Seattle drivers was of no concern after about ten minutes on the road.

Leaving the Interstate to take the surface roads to the fields was nothing like he expected. Two minutes after he turned west on Highway 725, he was surrounded by fields of tulips and other tubulars in every color he could imagine. The pallet of color for each variety stretched to what he imagined were hundreds of acres. He slowed as he neared a field of blue. It was the first one he saw, and it was stunning. It was a field of blue luster tulips, one of the most popular and purest shades of the color. It would remain popular until he introduced his new bulb which he still had not named.

A driver behind him blew his horn indicating Jacob was driving too slowly and looking too long. He responded by speeding up until he came to the entrance to the farm where the blues were.

After pulling into the parking lot and finding a place to leave his rental, Jacob went to the building that was overflowing with people who were purchasing bulbs, tee shirts, candy and drinks and anything with a tulip pictured or printed on it.

"May I help you, sir?" A young woman in her mid-twenties stood behind a counter and spoke to him.

"Uh, yes. I'd like to see the owner of these fields." He spread his hands out indicating the fields surrounding the building.

"I'm afraid I don't know who that is. I think it's a corporation out of California, at least that's where we get our pay checks. The manager is in his office if you want to talk to him." She pointed. "It's right over there by the soda machines."

By the end of the day, Jacob had visited more of the operations and found out which ones were locally owned and which ones were owned by corporations or conglomerates. At the last field, he asked about a good place to have dinner and he was directed to a small water-front restaurant nearby. He had salmon cooked on a redwood plank, grilled asparagus and a glass of sauvignon blanc. Dinner was the last thing on his mind. He was simply killing time until sunset and the departure of the tourists and the workers at the various tulip fields. If his information was correct, there would be enough moon for him to see when he went back to the fields.

He left the restaurant and went to a field where he saw at least fifty acres of blue luster tulips. Once he was at the field, he made certain there were no other cars or people around when he parked and left his car. Like he did in Holland, he went into the field and walked the rows. It was always the blue tulips that drew him to them at night. His passion was the blues in the night. He loved the way they picked up the light from the moon, and like the fields in Holland these were far enough away from cities so that the only light they got was natural. Three fields and two hours later, he got into his rental and headed south on the Interstate.

Jacob spent the next day in the fields as well. His first stop was meeting with the actual owner of one of the farms. The man had agreed to meet with him during this, the busiest time of the season, only because he had heard of him and his work in Holland. He knew that would be his entre to getting to meet the men or women who would be interested in his new bulb. Finding the right person and making the right financial deal would take some time, but he had prepared to stay as long as necessary. Prior to leaving his hotel, he had called a real estate agent to talk about a short-term rental. He picked the agent from a booklet he found at the airport. If the photo in the booklet was accurate and not one that had been taken years earlier and photoshopped, she was a very attractive blonde. If he had to spend time with a person trying to get him to spend money, he wanted to make it worth his while.

He pulled into the parking lot of the farm and found a space near the office and away from the acres of tourist's cars. It was late March, and the weather was incredible. The sky was a clear blue, and it was almost the blue of his tulip. He noticed when he was walking to the entrance to the office, that a nearby field was planted in blue tulips. Next to it was one with deep red and beyond that was a field of yellow. The blue field was the largest of the three which added to the fact that that was the most popular color here in the United States as well as in Europe: a fact that he planned to build on with each meeting.

An elderly lady was sitting behind a large metal desk that looked like something found in an office shared by adjunct instructors at the university. "May I help you sir?" she asked when she looked up and saw him.

"Yes. I'm Professor Jacob Dirksen to see Mister Richardson." He felt using his professional title opened more doors than introducing himself as a mister.

18

"Oh yes, Professor Dirksen, he's expecting you. You can go on in. His office is over there." She pointed to a door while she remained seated.

If she was that casual, Jacob was inclined to enter the office without first knocking on the closed door, but he did not want to lower himself to the level of the hired help, so he knocked twice and waited.

"Come in," he heard from inside the office, so he pushed the door and entered.

"Sorry if the place is a mess. I don't get many serious visitors during the festival. Mostly tour groups who have a complaint about something." The man stood and came around the desk and extended his hand. "I'm Frank Richardson and I understand you're the Professor Dirksen that I've read about." He pointed to a sofa and a clear spot where catalogs and other books and magazines had been pushed aside. "You want a cup of coffee or something. Tea maybe?"

The man was at least five inches taller than Jacob's five feet ten and, although he was dressed in working man's clothes, Jacob estimated his weight to be over two hundred fifty pounds.. His pants were heavy with cargo pockets and mud smears at the cuffs. Dirksen estimated his age to be mid-forties, give or take five years. His hair was a little long indicating he either did not care or had not had time to get a haircut recently. He had on a light jacket over a sweatshirt with a tulip logo and an advertisement for the festival. He looked at his watch when Jacob took a seat. "You picked a good time. We don't have a tour for the next two hours, so it'll just be the normal pain-in-the-ass tourists." He laughed. "I hate to describe them that way since they keep this place going, but hey..." He selected a chair across from the sofa and took a seat.

Jacob held up his hand. "I understand. We have tourists at the university as well."

"I gotta say, you have quite the reputation in the tulip field, no pun intended. I think everyone in the business knows your name."

"I'm flattered that you say so..." Jacob stopped and cleared his voice. "I think because of my research that I have developed a new strain of tulip that will revolutionize the industry and will certainly enhance the reputation and bank account of those who have access to it."

Richardson leaned forward. "I imagine you did some research before you came out here and know that I represent the largest operation that is owned by a single family, so decisions can be made around the kitchen table...so to speak."

"That is precisely why I chose to meet with you today." Jacob opened a folder he had with him and pulled out several photos. "The photos do not do the color justice but short of seeing the actual tulip, this is the best I can do at the moment. Of course, if you are interested, I do have everything you need." He handed the large color photos to Richardson.

"I...I don't think I've ever seen a blue quite like this one. It's hard to describe. It looks different in each photo...the color I mean."

"You're correct. Depending on the light and the source, it takes on a different shade. It reacts to the light."

Richardson held the photos and went through them again, much slower. "We order bulbs from other sources based on the color and description in their catalogs, so...but...I'm sure the owners will want to have a field of these as soon as possible." He looked at Jacob. "That is why you're here, isn't it? To sell the bulbs?"

"It is, but this will not be an ordinary purchase like one would do from a catalog. It will get a bit more involved." Dirksen hesitated for effect. "Have you ever heard of the Semper Augustus bulb?" For the next thirty minutes Jacob Dirksen explained to Richardson what he had in mind.

After Jacob left Richardson's office, he drove slowly through several adjacent fields and found the other two operations that he had selected. He did not want to just drop in on them, so he noted their location and planned to call and make an appointment. In the meantime, he had to find a business with a telephone so he could make another call. He was almost to the Interstate when he spotted a combination gas and convenience store. He stopped and went inside where he asked the woman behind the counter if she had a phone he could use. "You're lucky. We have one of the only pay phones in the area." She pointed to a pay phone hanging on the wall near the back of the store.

He walked to the back and could not stop himself from examining the variety of goods available for sale. One row was filled with nothing but candy, much of it chocolate. He was tempted to purchase a bar just to compare it with Dutch chocolate, but he knew it would never make the grade. The next aisle was chips of every variety and style imaginable. A large cooler covered the entire back wall of the store and was filled to overflowing with beer, wine and sodas. He recognized many of the brands of beer and sodas but none of the wines.

He lifted the handset, dropped a coin in the slot and looked at the business card he had removed from his wallet. It was the one he got from the taxi driver who brought him from the airport. When it was answered, he identified himself and asked if the driver remembered him and the offer he made to show him some of the things not seen in tourists brochures?

Once he was certain it was the same driver, he continued. "I have some very specific needs and if you can assist me in fulfilling them, I will be most grateful. To begin with, I want to retain you and your vehicle for the remainder of the evening. You can

21

meet me at my hotel in two hours. I will come out front, so you can park and wait. I will give you further instructions at that time." When the driver agreed, Jacob replaced the handset and left by walking down an aisle filled with oil, transmission fluid and other automotive accessories. He was still shaking his head when he got back into his car.

Chapter 4

It was a little after ten when he pulled into the driveway of a building set to the side of a massive field of multi colors where tulips and daffodils were in full and radiant bloom. No matter how many times he had seen such fields, Jacob always stopped to admire them. Seeing them gave him almost as much pleasure as he had gotten the previous night. He smiled to himself thinking how fortunate he had been to select just the perfect taxi driver for his time in Seattle.

The building had a sign indicating it was the offices of the Stately Tulip Farms. He was further impressed when he saw a parking spot reserved for Mr. Hardie and a large car sitting in it.

After checking in with the receptionist, he was told to have a seat and Mr. Hardie would be out in a few minutes. He did not like to wait, but he often asked people who came to see him to wait. Even if he was free now, he had them wait in order to make them think his time was more valuable than theirs. If this was a game, he knew how to play.

After a wait of less than five minutes he heard a buzzing sound on the receptionist's desk and she rose and led him to another door which she opened for him.

The man behind the desk was more to Jacob's liking. He was dressed in a pair of pants that were a part of a suit with the jacket neatly hanging on a coat rack near the entrance. He wore a starched white shirt with French cuffs adorned with a pair of cuff links that appeared at a quick glance to be gold with a stone of some sort set in them. His tie was silk and sported a perfect Windsor knot.

He extended his hand when Jacob entered. "Professor Dirksen, it's a pleasure to meet you." He pointed to a large leather chair. "Please, have a seat." He introduced himself as Ed Hardie. "I almost met you several years ago when I was in Holland. I came by the university, but you were out of town." He took a seat in a matching chair facing Jacob.

"From what I have seen, you have a very impressive operation here," Jacob said.

"We're the largest family-owned operation in the state and we intend to keep it that way. I don't have to tell you, but this is a volatile business. Most of the operations here in the valley sold out to corporations that wouldn't know a tulip from a coconut. My family has been in the business since bulbs were selling for a nickel each."

"That was a very long time ago." Jacob sat a little taller in his seat. "Which brings me very nicely to the point of this meeting."

"I'm all ears, as we say."

"Good, let your ears hear this. How would you like to be in sole possession of a bulb that would sell for dollars? Perhaps several hundreds, even thousands of dollars initially, with the right marketing plan?"

"The bulb or the flower?"

"The bulb. The flower would bring even more." Jacob sat back and let his comments sink in.

Hardie went to his desk and pressed a button on his phone. "Hold all my calls and no visitors until I finish my meeting." He turned to Jacob. "How about if I order some lunch for us so we can have sufficient time to talk about this bulb of yours?"

"Are you familiar with the famous Semper Augustus?"

24

"Famous or legendary? I don't think it ever really existed, do you?" Hardie got up and went to a cabinet where he poured himself a cup of coffee and offered one to Jacob. "Coffee is the best I can do in the office, but I'm inviting you to dinner tonight so we can talk over a bottle of wine." He came back to his seat. "So, what's this new bulb got to do with the Semper Augustus legend? Have you re-created it?"

"It's not a legend. It did exist but it was a freak of nature created by a strain of virus that was unheard of in the seventeenth century. The only evidence of its existence are some period paintings. We only know of it by way of those paintings and I'm sure they don't do it justice." He opened his folder and pulled out several photos. "Just as these photographs do not show the true beauty of the bulb I call The Blue Jewel." He handed them to Hardie.

He sat and looked at each photo several times. "I don't think I've ever seen a blue quite like this one. You may have recreated the Semper Augustus. That will be something very…uh—"

"Valuable? I like to think so."

"So that's the purpose of this meeting. You want to make a deal to sell the bulb?"

"I want to make a deal, but not to sell."

*   *   *

It was a little after eleven when Jacob returned to his hotel. He went to his room, took a quick shower and shave and met his taxi driver who was waiting at the curb in front of the hotel. The driver got out of the car and opened the rear passenger's door for Jacob. "That was quick, Mister Holland," said the driver. "I saw you walk across the lobby when you came in. I was in the coffee shop getting a cup."

Jacob often used the last name of Holland when he was out of town. It was convenient and easy to remember. "Yes, I did not want to waste any time if you found what I asked you to."

"I did. I had to call in some favors, but like I told you the night I picked you up at the airport, this is Seattle. You can find anything you want if you know where to look or who to ask. And are willing to pay," he said as he put the taxi in gear and pulled away from the hotel.

He turned slightly to the right to speak to Jacob as he drove. "I found just what you wanted. Tall, long blonde hair, big boobs...I even said you wanted a short leather skirt and six-inch heels." He caught a red light and tuned to face Jacob. "You gonna go back to your hotel, or you want me to take you someplace else?"

"I have a room reserved at another hotel. You can take us there. After that, you're free to go."

"What about tomorrow night? You want the same one or do you want me to start looking again?"

The traffic in Seattle at midnight was almost as bad as it was at rush hour. The Interstate was moving at half the posted speed limit through the city and the surface streets were not moving any faster. The clear sky over Seattle the previous night had given way to a massive fog bank that floated across the city obscuring everything above the twentieth floor on some of the buildings. A few were tall enough that occasionally, Jacob could see the top of the skyscraper punch through the fog and stand like the topping on a frothy sundae.

"I want to try something different tomorrow night. I want one of your African Americans."

"You want me to find one who's a blonde, too? We got some who dye their hair and you can't tell—"

"No. No blonde. This one must be small. Short but fully developed."

They were slowing to make a turn off Broadway into a street of mixed usage. Several of the old, large houses had been converted to offices for lawyers or doctors and a few businesses were scattered about, mostly on corners. "How about the dress and shoes? Same as tonight?"

"No. A black cocktail dress, with stockings and a garter belt. Black heels and a pearl necklace."

The driver pulled up to a large brick building and stopped. "This is the place where we meet. You want to go in, or you want me to do it?"

"You go in and take care of it." Jacob could feel his heart pounding in his chest. He had made similar arrangements on his travels in the past, but he had great expectations for this, his first trip to the United Stated.

"I'll be right back." The driver opened his door and went up the brick walkway to the front door of the house. Jacob watched him push a button on the side of the door and wait for the ring to be answered. It took less than a minute for the door to be opened. Jacob saw someone standing in the doorway talking to the driver. In a minute the door closed and the two of them approached the taxi.

Walking to him was exactly what he had ordered: a tall blonde with long hair, a short leather skirt and heels that stretched calves to the breaking point. He was more than satisfied that this would be a night to rival those he spent in Amsterdam.

Jacob was not disappointed with his date who did everything Jacob asked and some things he had not thought of. The date ended with them parting ways at nearly six in the morning. He paid the agreed amount, included a very nice tip and ordered a taxi to take him back to his original hotel.

He did not like the idea of having to take his evening companions to a place other than where he was staying. There was a built-in risk, he knew, of letting them know where he lived but that was offset by the fact that he didn't plan to see any of them more than once. That scenario would change starting the next day.

*   *   *

Once he was in the lobby of his hotel, he went to the coffee shop and picked up an early morning cup of coffee which he took to his room.

Back in his room, he pulled out a small notebook he had in a jacket pocket and looked at the three other names he had placed in it as possibly having an interest in the reason he was in Seattle. They were the remaining family operated tulip farms and he planned to visit each one of them, starting in about three hours.

The day dawned clear and cool. It was the kind of day where you went out in the morning with a light jacket and knew by evening you would need a heavier coat. Jacob stood outside the hotel as he waited for the rental car company to deliver his car and planned his day. In the back of his mind was the thought of moving from the hotel into a short-term rental apartment.

His day was spent talking to mostly workers who had no authority for anything other than writing orders or making sales to the tourists who came to the fields. As far as he was concerned, it was a total waste of a good day in America. If all went according to plans, the remainder of his day and evening would be anything but a waste.

He drove back to his hotel in Seattle and called the rental car company and had them come pick up the car. Once he was rid of the car, he could concentrate on his planned evening.

Jacob left his hotel room and walked back through the lobby of the hotel. It was half filled with people either going to their rooms after a day of business meetings, shopping or visiting the many tourist sites in the city, or others who were on their way out to see what the night held for them. He knew what it held for him, and it was waiting in a taxi at curbside.

"Evening, Mister Holland," the taxi driver stood by the open passenger's back door. He watched as Jacob placed his hand on the roof of the taxi and leaned down to look in the back seat. "This is Monique." He waited for Jacob to respond to his initial impression.

Monique was just what Jacob had asked for. Monique sat in the far corner of the rear seat behind the driver. He had requested an African American and Monique fit the bill. Skin the color of warm whipped cocoa, a short black dress rode up above knee high over legs encased in black nylons, crossed daintily. One black high heel shoe dangling from a foot showed toenails pointed a light pink, the same as Monique's nails.

"My friend, you are a master," Jacob said to the driver as he eased himself into the back seat and draped his arm around Monique's shoulders.

"Where to tonight?"

"You pick it but make it someplace where I can show the clientele how lucky I am to have Monique on my arm."

After two hours of showing the city how grateful he was to have Monique, they returned to Jacob's hotel where Monique showed a similar amount of gratitude for being selected for a night of dining, dancing and sex, all of which left Jacob completely drained by the time Monique left after three in the morning.

Jacob slept in and did not get to the tulip fields until almost noon. He made his pitch to a very receptive owner and left with a promise that they would get back with him within the week. All the way back to Seattle, he thought about the idea of moving into an apartment. If he was going to have to wait a week for an answer, he did not want to spend it in a hotel room. He decided to take the plunge and rent an apartment.

As he was walking across the lobby of the hotel, the desk clerk caught his attention. "Mister Dirksen..." He held up his hand. "I have a message for you that just came in. I haven't had time to even ring your room."

Jacob went to the desk and was handed a note. "The blonde from two nights ago wants to see you again. You must have really made an impression. Having one of them asking for a repeat is a first for me. Call and let me know what to do."

After reading it twice, there was no decision to be made. Jacob knew exactly what to do. He went to a bank of pay phones in the lobby and called the number of the taxi driver on the back of the card. "I am available this evening for a repeat."

Chapter 5

When I retired from the Army, I thought I had my life planned out as well as could be expected. But, as someone once said, 'life is what happens when you have other plans," and that's what happened to me. After twenty plus years in boots, I found myself as commander of a recruiting district in the Seattle, WA area. I knew I was on the downhill slope as far as career and time in service was concerned and having no other place in mind to retire to, I bought a house for the family in a little community just north of the city. Three years later, with one daughter in college and the other one a senior about to graduate high school, my wife informed me that although she didn't mean for it to happen, she had fallen in love with someone else and had filed for divorce. Her reason, other than being in heat, was that she really never liked the Army, or for that matter was no longer overly fond of me.

According to the military, if a spouse puts up with the military member for ten years and that person retires, the putting up spouse is entitled to half of the put-up-withs retirement pay. My half pay and a small stipend I get from the VA for being used as a target by the bad guys in Iraq and Afghanistan allowed me to exist. I didn't want to simply exist, I wanted to live, so I used my background as a military police and intelligence officer to get a private investigators license and opened my own business.

Being a private investigator in real life is nothing like the ones I saw on television or in the movies. It was mostly boring, mundane work chasing bad debts for a few banks, loan companies and lawyers, the occasional divorce case where I had to follow a cheating spouse and get photos, and once, finding a runaway. All that changed in a matter of a few months after I opened my office.

The first change was meeting Anna. I was looking into the supposed drowning death of an old SCUBA diving buddy and need a dive partner. The local dive shop recommended her, we did two dives and after the second one she made me an offer I could not refuse by standing nude in front of me when she changed clothes in the back room of my office. Ten minutes later we were making love and have been together ever since.

The second, and probably even much larger change took place when my old Army boss and friend, retired major general Bill Hart called me out of the blue one day and asked me to help him as a "favor." What I didn't fully realize at the time was that Bill was a beltway bandit in Washington, DC and was back in the intelligence business. The favor turned out to be finding out who killed one of his operatives and why. Both answers led me, and Anna to Canada where we found ourselves in between some Koreas smuggling nuclear material, a turncoat Canadian Intelligence officer and another one working undercover as a nun. Since then, he has called on me to work on several other operations for him. Out of necessity, I have included Anna in a couple of them and along the way, I have been shot, Anna has been put on Bill's payroll to cover her activities and we have become more deeply involved than I, and perhaps she, ever thought possible.

The reason she did not think it possible is simple. She is married. I knew it from day one and like a moth to a flame, I could not stop myself. I felt like a slug since I was doing to her husband what my wife did to me. We justified our relationship because he

32

had several women on the side in cities he traveled to for work, and even had a child with one of them. Anna found out about it when a school called and asked about the father's medical history. My guilt was not as strong as my feelings for Anna, and I continued to see her and kept looking over my shoulder for her husband with a gun. After I returned from an assignment for Bill where I met an old love interest and did things I still regret, Anna met me at the Seattle airport and drove me home. On the way, she informed me that she and her husband had agreed to a legal separation. I knew he would never divorce her for financial reasons if for nothing else. The agreement was satisfactory to both of them. She kept the very expensive home they owned on Whidbey Island, just off the mainland, and she got a monthly check for living expenses that equaled the pay of some of the Microsoft millionaires in the area.

It had been two weeks since we last saw each other, and I was beginning to fear that she had come to the realization that she could do much better than a half-deaf former soldier who relived some things he could not talk about almost every night in his sleep.

I was in the office talking to my friend George. George, or Crazy George, as some of the local merchants referred to him was a Viet Nam veteran who had the foresight to purchase a small house overlooking the Puget Sound when he first came home from the war. The place was now worth north of two million. Most days George roamed the city streets doing odd jobs for cash and living life the way he wants. He comes by my place to get a cup of coffee or to have me pay for him to go to a latte stand and get us two cups. No matter what kind of bill I give him I never see any change. It's always tucked safely away in the old Army field jacket he wears no matter the weather.

He was in my office sitting across from me, cup of coffee in one hand and eyes staring at something a million miles and a million memories away when the phone on my desk rang. Unlike me, he did not give any indication to include blinking his eyes when he heard it rang.

"Max here," I said, not giving the name of my business or my last name. I figured if they called, they knew who they were calling regardless of if it was personal or professional.

The only word I heard or wanted to hear floated from the handset.

"Hi."

It was Anna.

"What a very pleasant surprise," was all I could manage.

"What's so surprising? You didn't think I was going to call you again?"

She had a way of putting me on the spot with a few words. I never knew if she saved those responses up and pulled them out at the appropriate time or if she just knew what to say.

"No...no. Of course not. I mean...I knew, or at least I hoped you would call." I looked at George and pointed to the phone. He took the hint and left me alone. "It's just that—"

"It's okay. You don't have to say anything. I know what you've been thinking, and I've been doing the same myself. We are in a completely different situation now than we have been in the past and I'm not sure how to handle it. That's what I want to talk to you about, but I don't want to do it over the phone."

She hesitated long enough for me to ask, "Would you like to meet for dinner tonight?" Anytime she came across the Sound to the mainland she had to take a ferry. Getting here was no problem, but since they didn't run all night, she had to be back at the ferry terminal to catch the last one if we were not spending the night together. I wanted to see her and if we spent the night together, just holding her in my arms would be a sufficient reward for not seeing her for so long.

"Do you want me to pick you up at the dock in Mukilteo?"

"No, I don't want to come there. I want you to come to me."

I had only seen Anna's house once when I had to be on Whidbey Island when I was attempting to collect a bad debt for a local attorney, and I drove by the address. Even seeing it in passing from the road, I knew it was more house than I would ever be able to afford. It saw on a bluff overlooking the Puget Sound and the Straights of Juan De Fuca. I slowed as I passed and saw that the grounds were obviously professionally landscaped and kept that way by a gardener or a company on the payroll on a regular basis. Large bushes that I assumed were rhododendrons, like every other bush in the state, dotted the yard. I am severely flower deficient in that there are only one or two I recognize by sight, roses and tulips being at the top of the list. The house sat close enough to the Sound that it had to have a sea wall between the property line and any amount of waterfront beach they had at low tide. That was all I could tell from my drive-by and I expected at the time that it was all I would ever know of her home.

Chapter 6

There are only two ways to go from my office to Whidbey Island. One is by taking the Mukilteo Ferry to Clinton or taking a very long drive across the Deception Pass Bridge to the island. I did not want to take the time to make the land route so as soon as I ended the call with Anna, I closed my office and went home to shower and clean up. Not that sitting in my office all day can get me dirty, but even though my hair is light brown, as is my beard, my beard is very rough and on occasion Anna had remarked that it was causing an unnecessary rash on various parts of her body. I had great hopes that I would come into contact with her body tonight and I did not want anything to cause her to stop me.

After a quick shower and a very close shave, I dressed in a pair of charcoal pants, a light blue button-down shirt and a navy-blue sports coat that I recently purchased. I was in DC and out of clothes and about to be sent God-knows-where for Bill Hart. He had a propensity of calling me to DC and then telling me he wanted me to go someplace and do something and then hand me a credit card and tell me to go buy some clothes, knowing I only brought enough with me to stay in DC for a day or two. If he kept sending me out of the country, I would soon amass a very nice wardrobe.

Before putting on the jacket, I sat at my kitchen table and did a quick shine on a pair of black shoes. After brushing them, I pulled out a pair of lady's panty hose and polished them with the hose. It was an old

Army trick to get a decent shine in the least amount of time. I remember once after my divorce I was friends with a lady I met here in town. We were sitting in the park next to the waterfront one day when I asked her if I could have a pair of her old panty hose. At the time I did not realize just how perverted that sounded and after stuttering and stammering an explanation, she laughed and promised to give me a pair. As it turned out, the pair she gave me was one she removed later that night after we shared a very nice dinner and a walk along the Seattle waterfront. Unfortunately, the panty hose lasted longer than our relationship. Soon after that, she got a promotion at work that included a transfer. Had that not happened, she might have been a keeper. Anytime I need a new pair for my shoes, I buy them, but I have filed that incident away as a possible opening line to use again if the timing is right. So far, I have never had the opportunity to try it again.

Satisfied that my appearance was as good as it was going to get, I left and headed for the ferry. There are so many ferries in the Seattle area that most locals keep a current schedule for them in their car's glove box or behind the sun visor. The more progressive, me not being one of them, keep the schedules on their phones. As I drove toward the ferry dock in Mukilteo, I pulled the latest schedule from behind the sun visor and checked the time for the next crossing. After looking at my watch, I realized that if I hurried, I could catch it.

The parking lot for the ferry was half-filled as the cars were already loading when I arrived. I got in line and pulled up to the ticket booth, paid the toll and followed the car in front of me onto the deck of the ferry. Like any large city with an Interstate, the ones around Seattle were filled with drivers who seemed not to care for anyone or anything except themselves once they got on them. It was every man or woman for themselves. That was not the rule on the ferries.

Here there was a system, and drivers had to follow it. Cars were stacked in long rows, trucks and campers went in another direction and everyone followed the rules. Once the ferry docked on the other side and the ramp was lowered and the vehicles hit the parking lot, the drivers forgot all about the rules of the road once again.

Since the ferries loaded and unloaded from both ends, the first cars on were also the first off. I was close to the back of the ferry, so it took me almost five minutes of sitting with the engine running to be waved forward to exit the cavernous giant bobbing at the dock.

I followed a large SUV off the ferry and through the parking lot. It was only a ten-minute drive from the dock to Anna's home, so I was in good shape as far as time was concerned. We had not set a time to meet, but I was getting to her house at about the time the sun eases its way west, leaving the Sound in a glow of reds and oranges, colors meant for sitting on a deck or patio, drink in hand, watching them turn to the purple of night. I hoped that Anna had a place to do just that.

Her house number was displayed in large, carved wood numbers placed on the stump of a large tree that had been cut or fallen during a storm leaving enough of the tree for a chainsaw artist to carve it into a bear. The bear was on its hind legs, the house numbers held in its hands. On previous trips to the island, I had seen other such carvings in front yards. I imagine the chainsaw artist on the island is kept busy, and well-paid, especially after a storm.

I pulled into the driveway and stopped in front of the house. For a minute I wondered if I was being set up. Was her husband waiting inside the door with a gun? Had he forced her to call, to lure me over after finding out about us? I had a pistol in the console, and I considered the merits of tucking it in the small of my back, but quickly rejected the idea when the door opened and I saw Anna standing there framed by the massive wood around it. The smile on her face assured me there was no one behind the door with a weapon.

She pointed to the detached garage standing to the right of the house. She raised her hand and for a fleeting moment when I saw the large black object she clutched, I thought I had misjudged, and she was the one with the gun. She pointed to the garage and one of the two double doors rolled back and up into the building. I hesitated because if it was like any garage I ever had, it would have been filled with boxes of stuff that I probably would never need or want again, hadn't used in years but thought it too good to discard, and had no room for a car. To my surprise the garage was almost bare. Her gold Jaguar was parked in the other side and the only clutter I saw was on a work bench that ran the length of the side of the building. Peg boards on the wall held a variety of mechanic and woodworking tools, all neatly hung and clean. The workbench had several battery chargers with batteries in them, their lights blinking green indicating the batteries were fully charged. I cautiously pulled in and got out of my car.

Anna met me halfway between the garage and the house. When I saw her, I wanted to take her in my arms and hold her, but this was her house and her neighborhood, so I did not want to do anything that would cause her any trouble or embarrassment. She solved my dilemma by giving me a kiss on the cheek and taking my hand in hers to lead me to the front door to her house.

"I'm so glad you came," she said as we entered the house.

"Was there ever any doubt that I would?"

We were inside the massive living room when she turned to me. The room was almost as large as the house I grew up in. One wall of nothing but windows overlooked the Sound and the evening sunsets. A fireplace the size of a pick-up truck dominated the opposite wall, and I could see a large dining table that could seat a football team at the end of the room. The table was some type of dark, highly polished exotic wood from the way it shined. A chandelier hung overhead in the middle of the table. The remainder of the room, from what I could see, was professionally decorated as everything matched. Even I could tell that. I turned my attention from the room back to Anna.

"You have a lovely home, but it's just what I would have expected," I said as I continued to hold her hand.

"Why? Because my husband is wealthy?" There was an edge to her voice.

"No, because I can imagine you telling someone what you want and how you want it. This has you and your taste all over it." I hoped that was enough to get me off the hook.

"That was a good try, so I'll let it go...for now." She tugged at my hand. "Come with me and you can fix us a drink." She led us to a space I had not noticed between the two parts of the room.

It contained a wet bar. Behind the bar was a fully stocked shelf with any kind of liquor one could want. Bar glasses were lined up overhead and four large, padded stools stood in front of the bar.

"I think you'll find everything you need," she said as she took a seat on one of the stools.

I pulled down a bottle of gin and opened the refrigerator to find limes cut and waiting in a bowl. A bottle of champagne was already opened, so I removed the silver stopper and poured her a glass. After fixing my drink, I placed both on the bar and came around to take a seat beside her.

She picked up her glass and touched it to mine. "To what shall we toast?"

As my glass touched hers, I looked around. "That depends. Is there anyone here who could hear my toast?"

I watched her smile and stifle a laugh. "Is it going to be that bad?"

"Depends on your definition of bad."

"You're safe," she said, "there's no one here but us, so go ahead. Live dangerously."

"I heard an old navy senior chief petty officer once make this one in a bar one night in a place I can't even remember now---"

"Can't remember or can't tell me?" she quickly asked.

"Yes," I said as I held my glass up. "To seas un-sailed and mountains un-scaled. May they both fall before the sunrise."

"I like that," she said as she took a drink. "It has lots of possibilities."

We sat for a silent moment, each lost in thought as to what to say or do next. Finally, Anna stood. "Come with me. I want to show you the rest of the house...if you'd like to see it."

The guided tour took me through the kitchen with at least two ovens and refrigerators, a gas stove with enough burners to open a Waffle House and a view of the Sound. Along the way, she occasionally took my hand or led me by my arm. Each touch was firmer than the previously one. We passed by her husband's office with its closed door with the explanation that it was 'just a typical office' and I wouldn't be interested in seeing it. The second floor had a balcony overlooking the large room below and the windows extended to ceiling height so the view of the Sound was visible from here as well. The next five rooms were three bedrooms and two baths. Two of the bathrooms were en suite and connected to their adjoining bedrooms.

Finally, we stood outside a closed door. It did not take a rocket surgeon to realize that on the other side of the door was Anna's bedroom. I did not know if she had shared it with her husband until they separated, but I had the feeling it was a sacred place for her.

Anna placed her hand on the doorknob then hesitated. She turned to face me, reached up and pulled me to her for the kiss I had been waiting for. When she broke it, she put her arm around me and led me away. "Maybe later."

She took us to the kitchen. "I had my housekeeper prepare dinner for us prior to her leaving tonight. We can eat on the deck if you like." She pointed to a table set for two outside on a large deck that appeared to run the entire length of the back of the house.

"Sounds like a great idea. What can I do?" I asked.

"Fix us another drink while I take everything outside."

Five minutes later we were seated on redwood patio furniture enjoying a cut of beef that needed nothing more than a fork to pick it up. It was as tender as anything I had ever tasted. Anna served us from a cart that held all the food and a bottle of red wine, the name and type I did not know and did not ask.

Two gin and tonics, three glasses of champagne and a glass of wine each and it was time to just sit and watch the sun as it headed for the open waters of the Pacific. Anna stood, "Why don't you put a couple of pieces of wood in the fire pit while I take care of all of this," she said as she loaded the serving cart with our dinner dishes.

A large stone firepit was situated next to a round, wood hot tub that was giving off a steady cloud of steam as the night got cooler.

I put wood in the pit and was looking around for matches or a fire starter when suddenly a flame leapt from the bottom of the pit. By the time Anna got back to the table, I realized she had activated a gas lighter and it was working very nicely as several of the pieces of wood were burning. I also realized that she had changed clothes and now wore a large white robe. I didn't know if it was because she was getting cold and wanted to go back inside or not. If she was ready to go inside, I expected her to tell me.

"Can you control everything from inside the house?"

"Not everything," she said as she walked to the hot tub. She tested the water and looked at me. "Remember the hot tub we shared in New Orleans? This one is not as large so we will be closer." She untied the belt of the robe at her waist. Once it was untied, she shrugged her shoulders and let the open robe fall to the deck. "Care to join me?" she asked as she eased her naked body over the edge and into the steamy water.

I did not have to be asked twice as I undressed and got in the tub with her. For the first few minutes we sat and stared at each other, touching hands and playing footsie, then it got serious when I leaned forward and kissed her. I wanted to make love to her in the tub, on the deck, on the redwood table or anyplace she desired, but she had other plans. She placed her hands on my chest and pushed me back.

"Not now. Later, I promise, but we have to talk first."

Chapter 7

When I returned from the last debacle that Bill Hart sent me on, I had enough excess emotional baggage to fill a freight car. I had met and renewed a relationship with a woman I had worked with when I was stationed in Europe. She was an agent with the French DGSE, and was assigned to assist me while I was on the mission. We found ourselves in Iran and while there she shot me. This was after we had renewed both our personal and professional relationship to the point that we had slept together all over Europe. She was the first and only woman I had slept with since meeting Anna and I felt terrible about it, more so on the way home than while it was happening, I hate to admit. I did not want to lose Anna, but I didn't want to tell her about my indiscretions either.

If I was ever going to tell her, now was probably the best time to do it. "I think that's a good idea. I need to tell you something---" She stopped me.

"No. Don't. I have an idea what you were about to say, and I don't need to hear it. I don't want you to clear your conscience, by destroying mine."

I felt her tighten the grip on my hand beneath the bubbling water of the hot tub as she spoke. "We are in a completely different situation now and it's going to have some new rules and responsibilities.

I tried to say something, but she placed her finger against my lips to silence me. "Just listen and don't say anything till I'm through. Stuart and I have agreed to a legal separation. I'm sure it will never lead to a divorce unless he is willing to part with a very large portion of his business and assets. I'm not a gold digger, but we have a very specific pre-nuptial agreement, and I will hold him to it if it ever comes to that." She took a long look at me, and I saw something in her eyes I had never seen in the past. "And…I hate to say this but under the circumstances, I feel it's necessary. I have no interest in supporting a man who does not make an effort to pull his own weight." She stopped and took her time before continuing.

"The more I learn about you, the less I know. You are a complete mystery in some ways and the most open man I have ever met in others. I find it both intriguing and frustrating, but I want to learn more and that means I have to keep you around.

"I have never felt about a man…even my husband…the way I feel for you, but I must now think with my head as well as my heart. I said I love you and I meant it. You don't have to say it unless you mean it. As far as I am concerned, what happened prior to tonight and this conversation is history. And that was never one of my favorite subjects."

She leaned forward and pulled me to her. "Now, kiss me and take me to my bed."

*   *   *

I awoke the next morning in Anna's bed. It was a massive, probably custom made king-size or perhaps even bigger, but I had no idea what to call it, if it was. Without moving I felt her soft, warm and nude body next to me. One leg was thrown over mine as if she were trying to keep me from leaving…a thought that never entered my mind. I felt a little strange in her bed in her bedroom. I didn't know if she had shared it with her husband until they separated or if they had decided on two beds and two bedrooms prior to that. It was a generally accepted fact among most of the

45

men I knew that if a woman who was married and having an affair or a lover on the side ever took them to her bed, it was revenge, or as most men called it "a grudge fuck." It was to mark the bed with another man's scent. On the other hand, men never did that as the scent of another woman in the bed he shared with his wife would be picked up like a bloodhound on an escaped prisoner's trail.

I didn't feel this fell into that category. Stuart was out of the picture and she was free to do as she pleased. I was still running that through my mind when I felt her snuggle closer.

"Hi," she breathed. "I'm glad I didn't dream last night, and it really happened."

She could not possibly have been happier about the last twelve hours than I. Since coming back home after my last mission for Bill Hart, I had thought of nothing else but Anna. I wasn't sure what to call what we had: was it a relationship? Were we friends with benefits?

Lovers? Not to make light of it, but were we just two needy ships passing in the night only to drift apart at the dawn? Whatever it was, I did not want to lose it without talking to her about it. We had started the conversation last night and I planned to finish it today.

"I've got a great idea," I said as I cradled her in my arms.

"Umm," I felt her snuggle closer. "I can hardly wait to hear it...no I want to see it."

"That'll come later." I eased up in bed not anxious to break our contact. "I want to cook breakfast for you...for us."

Anna let the sheet slip down to her waist as she sat up in the bed. "You're kidding? I didn't know you could cook. What other secrets are you keeping from me...that you can tell me without me losing my life?"

"Breakfast is my specialty, although you may lose your life eating it, but I make killer eggs, pancakes, bacon and all the trimmings. Believe it or not I can make biscuits that don't come from a can that you must demolish to get, and gravy that'll make you want to slap your grandma…as you would say in Georgia."

Her laugh was hearty when she spoke. "Okay, chef. I think we'll find everything we need in the kitchen." She pulled the sheet completely off and was ready to swing out of bed.

"Oh, no. If I cook, it means I don't need help. You stay here, take a quick nap and I'll bring you breakfast in bed." I got out of bed and slipped into my pants as Anna stared at me with an 'I don't believe this' look.

I rambled through the kitchen, opened cabinets, drawers, looked into pantries, and finally found enough to make eggs, hot biscuits, sausage gravy and several types of jams and jellies. I put all of this on a tray and carried it to the bedroom. While I was busy in the kitchen, Anna was busy in the bedroom. She had put on a dressing gown, freshened her make-up and worked magic on her hair. She could have posed for an ad to sell just about anything. I placed the tray on pillow she had put across her upper legs after sitting up in bed.

"I don't remember the last time I had…" she stopped as she was about to tell me the last time her husband had served or ordered breakfast in bed for her. It was either a memory she did not want to recall or one she did not want to share.

"Where's yours?" she asked as she put jam on a biscuit.

"Like all good cooks, I sampled my work as it was cooking. All I need is this cup of coffee," I said as I held up my cup.

Thirty minutes later, I had cleared the tray, put the dishes in the dishwasher and was back and sitting on the edge of the bed. "What now?" I asked.

"I think we should do something completely out of character for us." She was holding a nearly empty second cup of coffee.

"We've done so many things, I hesitate to ask what you have in mind?" I quickly ran through some of the things we had done since we met and especially since Bill Hart came back into our collective lives. We had ferried a sailboat across the Puget Sound to prove a dead man found aboard had been murdered, gone to New Orleans and seen a voodoo ceremony and perhaps helped elect the next president of the United States and helped keep the most dangerous secret remaining from WWII from falling into the wrong hands. With that as a backdrop, she was going to have to really get creative.

"I want to go to the Tulip Festival. I haven't been in years." She waited for my response.

"I went years ago and all I remember was it was just a lot of flowers."

"Spoken like a man. They're not just flowers...well, actually they are, but it's more than that. It's beautiful. Tulips of every color in bloom for as far as you can see, and besides I know for a fact that the only flowers you recognize are roses and tulips...you said that yourself."

I knew I was fighting a losing battle, but I had to put up a little bit of an argument. I couldn't let her win too easily. "You're right, but just because I know that they look like doesn't mean I want to spend all day looking at them."

She clinched the deal when she eased out of bed. "I'll make it up to you when we get back."

Chapter 8

The first farm we came to was only about three miles from the Interstate. The area was crisscrossed with county roads, all of which were packed with cars and tourists' busses. Leaving the Interstate and joining the caravan of vehicles meant we were committed to going at the same speed as the car in front of us and only leaving the line to turn into a farms parking lot. "Do you have any specific place in mind?" I asked as we rolled pass the first farm.

"No. Just drive. I'll tell you when I see a place I want to stop." She leaned back in the seat and relaxed. As I glanced at her, I think it was the first time I had ever seen her completely at ease. That alone was worth all the effort I was making to enjoy myself.

We drove, or crawled was more like it, for another thirty minutes before she spotted a place she wanted to stop. I had no idea why she picked this one as they all looked alike to me, but this is what she wanted, and this was what she was going to get. I broke from the pack and found a place in the gravel parking lot. I left my seat, went around and opened Anna's door. I had done it so often now that she waited for me and did not get out without my having opened the door. Between us and the building where all the bulbs, souvenirs and other tourist things were sold was at least fifty small plots of tulips in full bloom. Each plot was a different theme. Some were in circles, a few were planted in farm wagons, windmills were a popular theme as was old cast iron bathtubs, all of which were available spots for the visitors to take photos.

Anna surprised me when she pulled out her phone and pointed to a nearby windmill. "Stand over there. I want a picture of you."

She noticed my hesitation. "Don't worry. I'm the only one who knows how to see the photos on my camera."

With that reassurance, I stood to the right of the spinning blades of the six feet tall windmill. I have never liked having my picture taken and my family always accused me of posing like I was standing in a parade line.

"Relax," she said as she snapped the first one. She was about to take another one when a lady came up and stood beside her.

"Would you like me to take a photo of both you and your husband?" she asked.

That was the first time I had been confused for Anna's husband. It was a strange feeling and I wasn't certain how to respond. Anna had no problem.

"Yes, I'm certain he would appreciate that very much," Anna said as she handed her the phone.

We spent the remainder of the day going from one farm and field to another. I have to admit the colors were spectacular but after a couple of hours, even spectacular gets a little boring. We stopped for a late lunch at a roadside stand selling a limited menu of hot dogs and hot dogs. The only good thing about that was that I knew Anna would be ready for a real meal by the time we left the fields. It was almost five when she finally said she had seen enough, bought enough and taken sufficient photos to last until the festival next year. I promised myself that I would find out the dates and call Bill Hart and volunteer for something at that time, although I knew that if Anna and I were still together all she had to do was ask and I'd be right back up here again.

We took I-5 south and stopped at a local seafood restaurant near the Mukilteo ferry dock. In the Seattle area if you don't eat seafood, you don't eat. Seafood restaurants are as plentiful as latte stands. I had a bowl of clam chowder and gorged myself on about half a loaf of warm, buttered sourdough bread which all the restaurants served. One gin and tonic for me, a salmon entre with dill and two glasses of wine for Anna and dinner was over. We made our way to the ferry parking lot and got in line. I parked, turned the engine off and waited for the signal to load. The first thing Anna did while we waited was to call her maid and tell her she could take the remainder of the evening off. Anna had already called and told her she did not have to prepare dinner. She ended the call and turned to me. "You must be gone before eight thirty tomorrow morning. I haven't explained to her what is going on with me and Stuart."

* * *

I set my internal clock for six thirty and it worked. I woke about six fifteen and lay without moving as I held Anna who was cradled next to me. I didn't want to wake her, but I knew I couldn't slip out of bed without her knowing it, so I waited as long as I could before I moved.

"Don't," she said as she held on to me. Her eyes were still closed but there was a smile on her face.

"Okay. You convinced me," I said to see what her reaction would be.

"Not yet, but soon. I promise." She opened her eyes and pushed back against the headboard, so she was half-sitting.

We had spent the night together with the first half of it just lying beside each other, hardly speaking, holding on to each other and what we had. "Make love to me," she whispered about midnight and those were the last words she spoke till just now.

I got up, went to the kitchen and found a coffee maker. After putting all the ingredients together, I went to the shower and by the time I finished, the coffee was ready. I poured a cup and took it to Anna who was still in bed.

"I think I'm getting used to this. I may want to keep you around," she said as she took her first sip.

"A fate worse than death, I'm sure," I said as I slipped into, my pants and shirt. Fifteen minutes later I was in my car and on the road to the ferry. I was only passed by four cars heading in the opposite direction and only one was being driven by a woman, so I assumed it was her housekeeper and we were both keeping good time.

After a wait and a ride on the ferry, I was back in Edmonds before nine. That was about the time I normally get to my office, so I went straight there and pulled into my parking spot next to the building. Most of the retail operations in the city open at ten, so there were few people on the street. The exception was George.

I saw George as I was pulling into my parking spot. He was walking slowly down toward the center of the city on the other side of the street. I knew he saw me, so I waved and made the motion for him to come to the office. Once I got inside, I'd give him a couple of dollars and send him across the traffic circle to a latte stand where he'd buy two cups of coffee, a sweet if he felt hungry and keep whatever change was left over from any size bill I gave him.

If the WWII veterans were referred to as Americas Greatest Generation, George and many men his age were America Forgotten Generation. George had served in some capacity in Viet Nam during the war. I never asked what he did, but at times I saw him return to days and times he could never forget any more than he could explain to anyone who did not share those days and times. He got a monthly disability payment from the VA and worked at day jobs in the city for anyone who would hire him and pay in cash. The one constant about him was the old, green Army field jacket he wore no matter the time of year or weather. I could usually see the outline of a pint bottle in one pocket, and I was certain I had seen him pull out a pistol from the other pocket one day in the office while he was searching the jacket's pockets for something. George was always good for a short conversation on sports, the weather or a subject of his choice.

"Mornin' Colonel," he said as he came into my office. I have two main rooms that I rent in the building. The larger of the two I use for a waiting and reception area, although I rarely have more than one person in the office at a time, so nobody has to wait, and I have no need for a receptionist. The smaller one is where I have my office. I have a small alcove between my office and the bathroom. I keep a coffee pot brewing most of the time on a table in the alcove, and if I have coffee made, I drink it from there. There's also an upstairs area that I have used as a place to sleep on occasion. It is also the place where Anna and I made love for the first time.

"Come on in, George." I reached into my pocket and the first bill I pulled out was a ten. I handed it to him. "I'll buy. You fly. Get yourself a donut or something if you want it." He took the money and left. My chances of seeing him and the coffee again, were fifty-fifty . The chance I'd get any change was zero. From the first time we met, George had always called me Colonel. I had never tried to explain to him that the Vice President of the United States had promoted me to Brigadier General after one of my operations for Bill. It was to keep me in line and to have a strong leash on me in case I ever divulged any details of the situation that resulted in the promotion. For George and me, Colonel was good enough.

* * *

53

While I was waiting for George to maybe return with our coffee, Jacob Dirksen was leaving his hotel heading for the next possible buyer on his list. Like his previous visit to a farm, he called ahead and this time he refused to speak to a manager. If the owner was not available, he did not want to waste his time on anyone who could not first, appreciate what he had to offer, and second, make the deal he wanted.

*   *   *

No thanks to me, Anna was getting used to being alone in her house and for the most part, in her life. Her husband had been almost an occasional visitor for the last year or two prior to his securing a legal separation. I didn't know and did not plan to ask much about her married life.   First, it was none of my business unless she wanted to make it mine. I could not shake the thought that even though they were legally separated, she was still married, and I was doing to her husband what another man had done to break up my marriage.   The guilt built up when we were apart but seemed to disappear the minute she and I were together. I called it my situational morals.

I don't know how much Anna's maid knew or suspected of our relationship, but she seemed to be the only one that Anna gave any thought to when she spent the night with me or had me come to her for an occasional overnighter. She always planned for the maid to have the evening off on those times. Only once did she mention Stuart coming back to her house to retrieve something from his home office. He had the courtesy of calling a day ahead of when he planned to be there, "in case you've already replaced me," he said when he called.

I was settling into a routine in my work.   An attorney in town asked me to appear in court as an expert witness on the subject of piloting small aircraft.

He felt a commercial pilot would talk over the jury's head and cloud the issue of the insurance claim he was defending. His client had survived a crash which he claimed was caused by the manufacturer and dealer of the plane not fully explaining the intricacies of a small aircraft. I had flown the same type of aircraft and had gotten a full briefing and a check ride from the dealer when I considered but did not purchase the same model. Had his client gotten such a briefing and check ride, he would not have crashed was his defense, and he won. He paid me a very nice fee for the three days I was either on call or in the courtroom.

I wanted to see Anna that evening after court, but I had committed to attend a City Council meeting where the city was attempting to change the rule on street-side parking. For as long as anyone could remember, all parking spaces were free. There weren't many in the downtown area and a driver usually had to circle a block or wait until someone left a space to get one, but when it became empty it was free. A proposal to put in parking meters was brought to the floor and soundly and very vocally defeated. After the meeting, I stopped at one of the local taverns, had beer and shot a game of pool with a local hustler who let me win the first two games at two dollars a game and then wanted to raise the stakes to ten dollars...so he could maybe get his money back. This was an old trick called "hustling the hustler." I refused his offer, pocketed the four dollars and left. I could hear the not-so-very-nice things he said about me and my family behind my back as I left.

Chapter 9

One of the things I like best about being my own boss is that I am the one who makes the rules. I work the days and times when I want to. As a private investigator I have the luxury of only accepting the cases that interest me. I like helping a family find a missing child and finding out who's stealing from a small business owner who is barely making it and can't afford to have a thief dipping his or her hand in the till. For those reasons, I have only had two clients at the same time twice since I opened. I don't count the work I do for Bill Hart, since he's not exactly a client, since he considers himself my boss. Technically he is when I work for him, which I seem to be doing much more often than I originally thought I would when he came back into my life.

I was at my desk, finishing up the daily crossword puzzle when I looked up and saw something on the street outside my office that I did not like. For a moment as the man got out of the car parked in one of the three street-side spaces in front of my office I wished the city sanitation department's street sweeper would suddenly appear and roll him up in the brush and dump him in a steel container someplace. With the normal reflection on the glass between him and me, I didn't know if he could see me looking at him or not. It was too late to put a sign on my door saying I was in Africa learning to become a holy man and would not be back for several years.

He stopped at the rear of his car long enough to take two final drags from the cigarette that he had in his mouth. Once he let the last bit of smoke escape into what is otherwise the clear air of the Puget Sound, he dropped the remaining piece of the cigarette and ground it out with the toe of his shoe. He pulled the sides of the wrinkled brown suit coat he was wearing to the side and grabbed his belt and hiked his pants up. Satisfied that he was as presentable as he could get in the wrinkled suit, off white shirt and blue tie that was pulled down revealing an open collar, he stepped up onto the sidewalk and came to my door.

When he got inside, he took a quick look around the room that serves as a lobby for me, saw no other person in the room and walked directly to my open door. As soon as he saw me, he smiled. "Hey, Max. I see I ain't disturbing you from a client." He laughed at his joke and came in.

"Remind me to change my open-door policy," I said as he took an uninvited seat.

"Now, that ain't no way to treat a potential client." He pulled another cigarette from a pack in his jacket pocket and held it up as if he were asking for permission to light it.

"No smoking in here. You know the rules, and what makes you think you are a client, potential or otherwise?"

Byron Getz was an insurance agent who had hired me once to help expose a woman who wanted to hire a hit man to kill her husband who had a million-dollar insurance policy with a double indemnity payoff if his death was accidental. I was to convince her I was the man to do the deed and make it look like a robbery gone bad, thus the accidental death since he had nothing to do with the incident. I met the wife at her exclusive home and as soon as I introduced myself, she led me to the back deck where she said we should discuss the job while sitting in her hot tub. In order to convince her I was legit and not wearing a wire, she insisted we both get naked before getting

57

into the tub. After convincing her that I was the real deal and not a plant, she noticed I had risen to the occasion and offered to take care of the situation. It was hard in more ways than one to turn her down as I carefully climbed from the tub. The set-up worked and she was arrested, Getz and his company saved two million dollars, I got paid a nice fee and, it seems, I have become an asset for Byron.

He took his time putting the unused cigarette back in the pack. I was certain he was using the time to gather his thoughts before he asked me to do something, he would know instinctively that I would not want to do. "Lots of things have changed for me since the last time we worked together."

I did not interrupt by reminding him that the work I did meant I was the only one naked in the hot tub with a lady willing to have me kill her husband.

When I did not say anything, he continued. "I started out selling insurance for just one company. I even had to go door-to-door for a while until I built up my client base. That lasted a couple of years then I got tired…and smart. I've branched out and kinda like you, I'm my own boss now. I started my own independent insurance agency. We'll talk about your insurance needs later, but right now, I have something more important to discuss with you." He leaned forward in the chair he selected across from my desk.

"You see, as an independent I can write all kinds of insurance, like personal and commercial, and I can get the client the best deal 'cause I have access to so many carriers. He hesitated and then continued. "That's the larger companies that underwrite the policies that independent agencies write."

"I really don't need a lesson in Insurance 101, so get to the point."

"That's one of the things I remember about you. You just want people to cut to the chase, so I will. I've had a rash of house fires...three of them, recently involving clients of mine."

"And?"

"My old man used to say that if the same thing happens more than once it is not a coincidence."

"Smart man, but you need the fire department and not me."

As soon as I mentioned the fire department, I heard the distinctive sound of one of the city trucks pulling out from the station a few blocks away. Good timing or bad karma? I knew I was about to find out.

"I wrote the policy on all three of them from one carrier. I've been doing business with them since I opened my own agency. So far, they're honoring the client's policy and not questioning our relationship. But if they think I'm a bad risk for them they'll pull my ability to use them. They're one of my best carriers and I can't afford to lose them."

"I hate to ask, but where do you think I fit into this little scenario?"

"The three policies were all were all taken out by corporations for property they intended to use for rentals. That's not a problem, since I write commercial as well as personal. All three were owned by different corporations, and all were vacant when they burned. No single insured, but with a corporation, who knows who owns what. I'm convinced it's an insurance fraud scam and I have three more properties with corporations as the owners. One of them is a multi-unit apartment. If that thing goes up a lot of people could be hurting."

"Especially you?"

"No, not just me. It's a low-income property so if it goes, the residents will lose what little they have and then many of them will have no place to live...assuming they don't die in the fire."

He took his time leaning back while he left me on the hook.

I took my time to answer since I knew anything I said would be something he could use against me to convince me to work for him again. "Okay," I said, "let's just say for the sake of clarification, that I might have the slightest interest in this little escapade of yours. What are you asking that I do?"

He gave me a "gotcha" grin before he spoke. "When you helped me out the last time, it was for the company and not me personally. The company authorized me to hire you. Now that I am like you, as in my own boss, I have to take care of all my insured. I need you to be my fire investigator and talk to some of the owners of the property that burned. I think they're all connected through a corporation. If I, or we, can prove the claims are fraudulent, my carrier doesn't have to pay, and I don't get my ass handed to me for writing bad paper. I don't have the resources to ferret it out."

"And you think I do?"

"I don't know about that, but I think if you begin digging through the ashes, so to speak and talk to some of the owners you'll find out a lot more than I can. If you find out that the corporations I wrote are owned by another, larger one and they didn't disclose that, it could be fraud. They may own other properties that I am covering that they plan to burn. If they think you are on the take, they may talk about the next one they are going to torch."

"You've got this all figured out, don't you?" I said as I contemplated what he wanted me to do. "And what if I refuse. You have a back-up plan?"

He hesitated, pulled out another cigarette and held it for a minute before putting it back in the pack. It was a classic stalling technique. "I haven't really given it much consideration after I thought of you." He stopped and looked me in the eye. "You may not believe this, but I think you do a hell of a good job and I know you can pull this off if anybody can." He stood

60

and paced the small space between my desk and where he had been sitting.

"I know you think I'm a pain in the ass...most people do, but I'm just a guy trying to make a living the best way I know how. I had the opportunity to go out on my own and I jumped on it. If I lose my biggest carrier I may as well start flipping burgers at the Burger Doodle." He looked at me for a reaction. "You don't want that to happen, do you?"

We were at a standoff. I knew if I was the first to speak, I'd lose, but for some reason I felt...what...sorry? for him and knew that I was going to at least find out more about what he wanted. "I know I'm going to regret this as soon as you drag your ass out of here but tell me more. I know you have it all figured out."

"Why don't you let me buy you lunch, and we can talk...one businessman to another." He looked at his watch. "It's almost two so the main lunch crowd will be gone, and we can talk in private."

"The things I do for a free lunch," I said as I stood up and prepared to leave the office with him.

The summer, or what passes for summer in the Pacific Northwest was almost to an end. We had gone through the usual heavy rains around the middle of July and the intermittent sun and clouds for the rest of the month of July and August. School was about to start back for the fall and some of the shops in town were advertising back-to-school specials on clothes and shoes. I slipped on a light jacket to ward off the possibility of an afternoon that suddenly turned chilly if I got cold while we were out.

The city had maintained several trees along each block, and they were in the first stages of their leaves changing colors. All things considered it was a very nice day to be out of the office.

"I'll drive," he said as he pulled out a remote key fob and pushed the button to unlock the doors on the car he had parked in front of my office.

Once we were in the car, he did a U-turn and headed for the waterfront. "Place on the water okay with you? Last time I was here I had some great clam chowder down there." He looked to his right to see my reaction. "If you're tired of seafood, they have red meat as well."

One of the things I like about living in the area is the abundance and variety of restaurants and their menus. "No, that's fine with me. I'll find something I like no matter where we go."

"That's right," he said, "you were in the Army so I guess you've eaten just about anything and everyplace one can imagine." We got to the railroad crossing just as the gates were going down, blocking traffic as the train running up the coast to Vancouver, BC Canada passed through town. Ten minutes later we were being seated at one of the three restaurants that lined the waterfront.

Getz ordered a bowl of clam chowder and a Caesar salad. I skipped the salad and had the chowder and some of the warm sourdough bread that was served at almost every restaurant as soon as an order was taken.

I took my time as I pulled a slice from the round half loaf and buttered it. "Okay, start talking," I said as I put a piece of the bread in my mouth and began to chew.

"Insurance scams and frauds are a multi-billion dollar a year loss for the industry. Nobody is immune from it, and unfortunately the general consensus is the companies can afford it." He reached for a piece of bread. "And they can as long as they keep raising rates but at some point, the consumer is going to drop their insurance, and then we're all in deep shit." He took a bite. "You have a car accident, and the other person doesn't have insurance, so you have to look to your carrier. Next year, higher rates. Get sick and go to the hospital with no medical coverage? They have

62

to treat you, but who pays for it? The person who still has a policy which will increase the next year."

I held up my hand to silence him. "I got it. I told you in the office that I don't need Insurance 101. Cut to the chase. How does all of this affect you and what do you think I can do to stop it?"

Every table in the restaurant had a view of the water. Ours was positioned so that we not only looked over the water but were able to see the Edmonds/Kingston Ferry as it slowed to ease into the dock on the Edmonds side of the Sound. The ferry was usually filled with vehicles and passengers who walked on board for every crossing no matter in which direction it was traveling. I stared at the ferry as the captain cut its engines and let the forward momentum allow it to slide gently into the large wood dock. I lived a short distance from the dock, and I could see the ferry from my front room and if the wind was blowing in the proper direction, I could hear the horn as it docked or loaded.

A waiter dressed in black pants and a white shirt with a black bow tie brought us our lunch. He held a grater and asked if we would like fresh ground parmesan cheese. I had a liberal sprinkling on my chowder while Getz had his salad literally covered in it. We waited until the waiter had finished and then we resumed our conversation.

Getz spoke with his salad laden fork half-way to his mouth. "I'm sure all the fires were arson, but the owners were very slick. The fire investigators only listed one as being suspicious, the others were declared accidents and I processed the payments." He finished the trip with his fork and began to chew.

Before I could even take a bite, the waiter came back to the table. "Is everything all right, gentlemen?"

One of the many things that make me crazy is for the server to return to the table before I have even tasted the food and then if I have a problem, I never see them until it's time to pay. Getz just nodded and waved him away.

"Let me get this straight. If the fire inspector said the fires were accidental and you paid, what's the problem? What do you need me for?"

By this time, he was digging into his chowder. "Good question. I can't prove it, but I'm almost certain the same person or persons owned all three of the properties and burned them to collect the insurance. Fortunately, none of them were occupied at the time, but I just wrote a policy on an apartment complex that is almost full of residents."

"So?" I asked as I took my first spoonful of chowder.

"So, you will act as my associate and meet with the person who I deal with that represents one of the corporations. He's a sleazy little bastard and I don't think it will take much to get him to roll over on anyone who pays more than he's getting now. If they're all tied together, he may know it and will cut you in for some of the action if you can keep the insurance payments coming in." He looked up to see, if I was paying attention. "I don't think it will take much to convince them that you can make sure that any future fires are fully covered, and the insurance will be paid very quickly. If I'm right, they're in it for the money and couldn't care less about the possible loss of life or property involved."

The ferry had emptied and was awaiting the first line of cars moving from the parking lot to the entrance ramp and the two decks on the ferry when he finished explaining what he wanted me to do. Despite my earlier trepidations, I found the prospects of investigating, or at least pretending to investigate some probable arson fires interesting. When I was on active duty, there was a suspicious fire at the quarters of one of the men on base. His wife was severely burned in the fire and during her hospitalization, she indicated that she suspected him of setting it. As the senior military police officer at the time, I had to investigate it. I found out she was right. He was having an affair. The fact that he was married was getting in the way. I think he may still be in the Federal Penitentiary in Leavenworth, KS.

Our waiter was watching us, waiting for us to leave so he could clear the bill and get his tip. Only two other tables were occupied, and it appeared he was responsible for them as well. I finished my chowder at the same time Getz placed his fork on the salad plate indicating he was finished as well. He motioned for the waiter to bring us the check, which he paid in cash, leaving a tip larger than I would have expected from him. I thought of the old book and cover analogy. He placed his cloth napkin on the table and stood. "Why don't we go back to your office and work out the details?"

Chapter 10

Just as I suspected, by the time we left the restaurant, a stiff, and much cooler breeze was blowing in across the Sound, and I welcomed the fact that I had a real jacket with me. The parking lot for the restaurant was almost empty with most of the remaining cars belonging to employees of the three establishments connected to the eatery at ground level. The restaurant was on the second level of a space that was designed to look like a waterfront dock. Large pilings were spaced throughout the spaces to give the impression they were supporting the second floor. The walkway in front and between the two ground floor businesses was made of heavy, weathered boards that extended to a pathway that connected the long city dock where one could find fishermen and tourists at almost any time day or night.

Getz pushed the remote fob and I heard the locks on his car pop up, unlocking the doors. I got in and he drove us back to my office. It was nearing election time in the city so there were signs on almost every yard indicating the choice of the resident for a candidate for one of the local offices. Our current mayor, Valentino was running for his third term and for the first time, he had a serious opponent. His efforts to get every possible vote was evident when we got to the first intersection in town. Valentino was standing on the corner waving at passers-by. Those who supported him seemed to be giving him a "thumbs-up" signal as they passed by him. Those who obviously were for his opponent give him another digit from their hand as they blew their horn to make sure he saw them.

When we got back to my office Getz and I worked out some of the details of what he expected me to do, and what I was looking for. After an hour, I felt that I could probably help him or at least get enough information to start a criminal investigation into the fires. I was still on the fence until he told me about the apartment building he thought was a part of the arson scheme. Burning a vacant house is one thing but putting families with children in danger was a whole 'nother story. Furniture and possessions could be replaced but lives lost were permanent. We agreed on a fee based on time and results and we signed a contract. I made two copies, gave him one and put the other in my files. I suppose I could have kept it on my computer, but I'm still old fashioned enough to want a paper trail of documents.

It was near happy hour when he left, so I began to wrap up a few things in the office so I could leave and go home. I had spoken to Anna earlier in the day and found out that she was going out to dinner with one of her lady friends on the island. She went out of her way to assure me that it was a woman, and she was not seeing another man for dinner. That was the first time we had a conversation like that. I had no hold on her that was not emotional, since although she was now legally separated, she was still a married woman.

I made the short drive through town and parked in front of my place. The sun had long since disappeared and was probably somewhere between Seattle and Honolulu when I opened the front door and went inside. I usually always kept the television in the living room on. I sometimes sat on my sofa and had dinner or breakfast and watched the news, but mostly I kept it on just for the noise and I often had no idea what was on. The station was giving a local weather report and the woman read the teleprompter off-screen while she deftly pointed to the greenscreen map behind her. I heard her say the next day would start with fog and end with showers. It didn't take a rocket surgeon to come up with that forecast as it could have been almost any day of the year.

A friend once gave me a Seattle Weather Stick to use to determine the weather. He said hold it outside and if it gets wet, it's raining. If it stays dry, get back on the plane and come home. You're obviously not in Seattle.

I don't usually like to drink by myself, I sometimes make exceptions when I can think of a good reason. As I poured a healthy slug of gin in a glass and opened a fresh bottle of tonic, I rationalized it by thinking that I would be eating alone since Anna was with one of her friends.

Outside my place in back is a small porch where I have a gas grill. It's connected to a large bottle of propane gas, so I fired up the grill to let it get hot while I went inside and pulled a steak from my freezer. I had to place it in my microwave set to defrost before I could place it on the grill. Thirty minutes after coming home I was seated at my table, steak, a small array of vegetables that had rested frozen in my freezer until I fired them up, and a second gin and tonic in front of me. I finished and put my dishes in the dishwasher, picked up the bottle to make another gin and tonic, then thought better of it and fired up my coffee maker instead.

I was in my bedroom changing into a pair of jogging pants when I heard my cell phone play a tune indicating an incoming call. I have several different ring tones or songs to let me know who is calling. I have a different one for each of my daughters, one for Bill and one for Anna. As soon as I heard Pretty Woman, I forgot about changing clothes and went back to the table where I had left my phone.

"Hello, Darlin'," I said as I pressed the green spot on the front of the phone.

"What if I was a bill collector and you answered like that?" Anna's voice was the dessert I needed after a good meal.

"I'd hope if it was a woman, she'd be impressed and not pressure me to pay what I owed."

"And if it was a man?"

"Maybe he'd think I was crazy and not responsible for anything I might have done in the past."

"You are the eternal optimist, aren't you?"

"I think I'm more of an optimistic pessimist. I hope for the best and expect the worst and I'm never surprised."

"I'll bet I could surprise you," Anna said.

I could almost see here smiling as she kept the banter up. "Have you finished dinner with your friend already?" I asked when I heard what sounded like road noise.

"Yes, I'm on the way home now. Too bad the ferry is not running. It wouldn't matter which direction. I could come to you, or you could come over here."

"You really know how to hurt a fellow, don't you?" I said as I thought about how nice a night with her always was.

"Rain check. I'll let you make it up to me later this week."

"You drive a hard bargain, but I'll take it." I hesitated. "Call me when you get home and let me know you made it safely." She agreed and we broke the connection. I finished changing into my jogging pants and went into the living room and turned my television on to a poker tournament coming in from Las Vegas. The buy-in was over three hundred thousand dollars and several of the winning players were destined to walk away with over a million dollars each. The most I ever paid to enter a tournament was three hundred dollars and I had to think about it for two days before I shelled out the money. I can't imagine what it would take for me to put up a third of a million dollars and take a chance on losing all of it.

The tournament was going to be televised over three days, so I set my television to record it and promptly fell asleep sitting in my recliner. I woke after about an hour when my cell rang. It was Anna telling me she was home and safely tucked into her bed. She quickly added that she was alone and missed me. After getting that image out of my mind, I slowly made my way to the bedroom where I fell into bed and slept until my alarm woke me eight hours later.

After a trip to the Tree Topper for breakfast and a quick read of the morning newspaper, I headed for the office. I had made a commitment to help Byron Getz find out if he was getting played by some of the people whose property he was insuring, so I wanted to get to the office and try to determine the best way to help him. I had some ideas, but I needed to do a little research to make sure I was not crossing a line that could get me fined for impersonating a whatever it was that I was impersonating or have Byron lose his license to do business.

Edmonds began years ago as a bedroom community for Seattle and since I decided to retire here, it has grown to a thriving city in its own right. Like most communities in the Seattle area, home prices have gone through the roof and the locals make enough money to afford them. There are quite a few "Microsoft millionaires" who call the city home. The infrastructure is sufficient to handle any problems that may arise and I have become friends with most of the police and first responders. I was banking on that friendship when I called the chief of the fire department and asked if he had time to see me.

I learned years ago that there are two almost sure-fire ways to get information from people. I stumbled on it by accident when my oldest daughter was in seventh grade, and we were living in Virginia, and I was assigned to the Pentagon. She was writing a report and needed some information from the local police department. She was afraid to call and ask them, so I did it and after explaining I was calling for my daughter, they told me things I probably could not have gotten, if I told them it was for me. The second way I found to get information is to tell the person that I am writing a book and I need their expertise. I can't remember the number of books I am supposed to have written using that ploy.

When I explained to the chief that I was thinking about writing a book and I needed his help, he was quick to invite me over.

We talked in his office over two refills on coffee and I found out a little about what an arson investigator looks for and some of the ways he has seen them stumped for a while and outright fooled in the twenty-five years he has been a fire fighter. When I left, I knew more about some of the things I should not do and not so much the things I should do. I figured if I avoided the bad, the good would fall into place. I was ready to give working for Getz a try.

Chapter 11

I got to the office and went inside to start the first step, or at least what I assumed would be the first step in finding out some of the answers to what Getz had hired me to do. Since opening my own agency, I have become much more adept at using the Internet. I'm convinced that someplace on the world wide web is a site that guarantees they know the whereabouts of Jimmy Hoffa's body and the name of the mysterious man on the grassy knoll when President Kennedy was assassinated in Dallas, and they're probably right. I didn't need to know the answers to state secrets, but I did want to know the names of the principals of the corporation that owned the two properties that had burned.

The state has a website that lists all the corporations and gives the names of the officers. After checking the two, I did not find any matching names, but they were both using the same law firm to do their incorporation paperwork. At least that was a start. I printed out the information and sat for a minute wondering what I was going to do with it. If I started at the lawyer's office, I felt certain that I would hit a brick wall and possibly let the corporate officers know that someone was looking into the fires.

My second choice was the Seattle Fire Department that had answered the calls and determined that the fires were accidental. The first house that I wanted to talk to them about was in the Green Lake neighborhood. The station that responded to that fire was located only six blocks away, so their response time was great. It was only a twenty-minute drive from my office, so I headed out to see what I could find out.

The station was in the middle of a block of mixed-use buildings and a few houses. When I got to the station, several of the men were washing one of the pumpers. I parked well to the side of the massive, open doors at the front of the station. Both men nodded to me as I passed by them and entered a door to the right of the main area where they kept the vehicles. The office had a large glass window facing the street and an even larger one overlooking the bay. I didn't knock, since it seemed to be an area where anyone could enter. After getting the door half open, the man behind the desk looked up and asked if he could help me.

"I'm not sure who to ask for, so maybe you can." Before leaving the office, I had printed out some business cards identifying me as M. Maxwell with an occupation of Insurance Liaison. I had no idea what an "insurance liaison" would do but it sounded innocuous enough that I could make it up as necessary. I handed him one of the cards and gave him a moment to look at it. "I'm working with an insurance company that had a loss in the area a couple of weeks ago. Your station answered the call, and it was ultimately found to be an accident."

"And?"

"And I would like to speak to the person who made that determination."

"You don't think he didn't do a good job, or you have information to the contrary?" He had put down the papers he was going over when I entered, and I now had his undivided attention.

"No, nothing like that. I'm kinda new at this job and I want to get some background as to what constitutes and accident and how does one tell the difference between an accident and arson." I felt like I should add that I was either writing a book or my daughter was doing a report for school.

"We just hose 'em down and let someone else determine why they were on fire in the first place." He opened a drawer and pulled out a book. After opening it, he took a small piece of paper from a sticky pad on his desk and wrote down a name and number. "These are the folks you need to talk to. They do the investigations, but I can tell you from experience, unless the person had his or her shit together when they torched the place, it's not difficult to tell the difference between arson and accident." He handed me the paper and gave me a look that said unless you have something else, this conversation is over. I took the hint, thanked him and headed for my car just as I heard a very loud phone ringing.

I was just outside the open doors when I heard a sound from inside that I didn't have to ask what it meant. In less than ten seconds, men were streaming out and putting on their fire gear. I stood aside as the first truck rolled out and onto the street. The traffic light at the edge of the driveway turned red and all traffic was stopped until the units were on their way to a fire or another type of emergency.

Once in a conversation at the bar in an officer's club in Iraq, I was drinking and talking with a civilian contractor who was working with the Baghdad fire department training new recruits. I told him I had been in Iraq and Afghanistan, shot once and gassed by the bad guys one night, and with all that the US government didn't have enough money to get me to intentionally run into a burning building for a living. He laughed and said he had never been shot while fighting a fire or gassed with anything stronger than fumes from a fire once in a plastics factory. We decided we were both crazy for doing what we did and ordered another round.

I took the names I got from the station and decided to go back to my office and try to come up with some workable plans. I learned a long time ago in the Army that a poor plan properly executed is better than no plan at all. Right now, I was behind door number two. I didn't have a plan but with a little thought and enough coffee or perhaps a gin and tonic or two, I'd come up with something.

By the time I left the station and headed back toward Edmonds, it was approaching noon. I had eaten breakfast, but for some reason I felt a hunger pain as I drove up I-5 leaving the city. The greater Seattle area is a mecca for different kinds of food. With little effort, one could find any cuisine that they wanted. I had a craving for Mexican and I knew just the place. I had eaten there several times in the past and I always referred to it as El Sleazo. From the outside, it looked like a place you would not go without being well armed, but the look was the most deceiving thing about it. The food was excellent, the waitresses attractive, the prices right and the beer ice cold. What could be better? I went in, ordered and an in less than ten minutes I was munching on chips, salsa and washing it down with a Mexican beer.

I got back to my office by mid-afternoon. On the way back after I left the restaurant, I stopped at one of the many shopping malls that dot the Seattle area. I found a parking spot near the entrance by the food court, parked and went inside. My intent was to buy a new pair of shoes. I knew what I wanted and had a good idea of where to get them. Like most men, I don't shop. I buy. If I need something I go to where I can get it, make the purchase and go home. Today was no exception. I wanted a new pair of dress black shoes. My requirements were simple. They had to be black, had to have laces, had to fit, be comfortable when I walked around in the store with them on, and they had to look nice. The second pair I tried on, checked off all the blanks so I was in and out of the shoe store in about fifteen minutes. As I passed one of the stands in the food court, I couldn't resist treating myself to a chocolate chip cookie. They were just taking them out of the oven, and I smelled them long before I reached the counter. I didn't realize one cookie was the size of a hubcap from a '57 Pontiac. As I walked away, I did realize that if I made that reference to anyone behind the counter, they wouldn't have a clue what a Pontiac or a hubcap was, and for them, 1957 was ancient history. When I got to my 4 Runner, I broke the cookie in half, thinking that I would either save one half for later or give it to George since I felt certain I'd see him prior to ending my day.

When I got to my office, I fired up my coffee pot in case I was forced to eat the other half of the cookie. While it was brewing, I got on my computer and went to the site for the Secretary of State for Washington. I had to dig a little but by the time my coffee was ready I had a list of the principals for both corporations and the partners in the law firm they used. The law firm was the only thing connecting them that I could find, but I was beginning to formulate a plan. I don't like coincidences, and it seemed too far-fetched that two corporations had the same law firm, the same insurance company and properties that accidently burned.

Next, I went to the tax records and found out what they paid for the properties. Getz had already given me the amount of the payoff for their fires. By comparison, they made a nice chunk of change with the increase in value of the houses from when they bought them and when they cashed the insurance checks. Seattle real estate is some of the best in the country as far as increases in value in a short time and people all over the area take advantage of it by purchasing a house, doing some minor improvements and then putting it on the market for a profit which they almost always get. Burning down the house was a much quicker way and didn't require any repairs. All it took was a nice insurance policy, a shill corporation and someone who knew how to make a fire look like an accident. My poor plan was coming together. The next thing I planned to do was visit the law firm and ask a few questions. The downside was that I didn't have a clue as to what kind of questions I wanted to ask.

I was mulling it over when George pushed open the door to my outer office and came inside. He could see me sitting at my desk and without hesitating, passed through the outer office and came into mine and took a seat. "Afternoon, Colonel. You doin' okay?"

Occasionally George went a day or two without shaving and when he did, his stubble of a beard came in grey. His hair had already begun to turn the same color and from his appearance, he had not visited a barber shop in a few weeks.

"Come on in, George. Coffee's ready if you want a cup." I pointed to the alcove where the pot was sitting on the burner keeping warm. "I got half a chocolate chip cookie if you want it." I passed the bag containing the half cookie across the desk to him. "It's way too big for me to eat the eat the whole thing." He took it without a word and went to get a cup of coffee.

When George came back with his cup of coffee, he took a seat and pulled the half cookie from the bag. The way he placed the flattened bag on his lap and put the cookie on it, I thought he was preparing a feast, and perhaps in his own way he was. I never asked George what he saw or experienced in Viet Nam. I'm sure if I did, I'd get an answer similar to the one I give when people ask me what it was like to be in the war in Iraq or Afghanistan. My stock answer was hours or days of boredom interrupted by periods of sheer terror. That was enough to satisfy them or confuse them enough that the subject passed. I once got into a conversation with my late uncle who retired from the Army as a two-star general after having served through World War Two as a paratrooper in

Europe from D-Day until the end of the war, and then at the Pentagon until the early stages of the war in Viet Nam.

His war was a foreign to me as mine was to him. The only comparison was that people were shooting at us and occasionally hitting their targets. He had three Purple Hearts and I only had one, but that was enough for me. I knew about Viet Nam from studying history and talking to the few veterans who had served there and were still on active duty when I was commissioned.

My understanding of George's war in no way was sufficient to compare his with mine. I only knew he was in the infantry and had been wounded. Beyond that, his story was secured deep within his mind.

He ate the cookie without speaking until he was finished. He folded the bag, being careful not to let any crumbs fall to the floor in the office. Satisfied that it was done, he looked up. "You know, Colonel, I really like you. I ain't never been too fond of officers but I think you's a good one. Wouldn't have minded going to war with you."

I knew that he had just paid me the ultimate compliment. I waited to see if he had anything else to say, but he just stood up, returned his cup to the table with the coffee maker and walked out.

I sat quietly for a minute and drifted away to a time years ago that I usually only go to at night. The sound of my cell phone playing the ring tone I had for Anna brought me back to the present. As soon as I placed it to my ear, I heard her say, "Hey, soldier, buy a lady a drink?"

"I don't know. What's in it for me? I can't be wasting my time or my money if there's no return on my investment."

"Buying me a drink and maybe even dinner would be an investment like buying Microsoft stock for a dollar a share the day it was issued."

78

"You sure drive a hard bargain, but I'll take you up on it." I leaned back in my desk chair and listened.

"I'm in Seattle. I had to come to the city for some business today and if you play your cards right, dinner and drinks will make it too late for me to catch the last ferry to Whidbey."

Anna and I had spent many nights together but most of them had been out of Edmonds. Since she was now legally separated it was a little different if someone saw us together late at night or early in the morning, but I still have a fear that at some point I'm going to run into her husband and he's not going to be very pleased with me. "I think I can arrange some place for you to spend the night after I wine and dine you."

"Somehow I thought you'd say that, and that's why I brought an overnight bag."

All we had to do now was work out the logistics of when and where to meet. "Do you want to come to my place and change before we go to dinner?"

"I've got another hour of things I need to do, so why don't I meet you at your office and I can leave my car there. In the meantime, find a place with a good steak. I'm in the mood for some red meat tonight."

"I can do that. I'll see you when you get here." I ended the conversation and opened my computer to look for a steak. There was a place on Lake Union that was supposed to be one of the best restaurants in Seattle and they specialized in steaks as much as most restaurants in the city did in seafood. I called and made reservations for eight. That would give Anna time enough to finish her business and get here. If we got there early, we could sit on the dockside patio they were so proud of in their ads.

I killed the next hour by sending a long email to my daughters. I still had a very good relationship with both of them. It had been rocky when their mother and I divorced. They both realized the marriage had been over for some time, but we were staying together for some unknown reason. It took the realization that good ol' mom had someone waiting in the wings as soon as she was free for them to realize I was not quite the ass hole they were led to believe. They both decided to live with their mother for a while until they got used to the idea that we were no longer a family. Now both are on their own, one married and the other still in college. I don't ask what their relationship is with their mother as it's none of my business.

I finished the emails just as I saw a flash of gold when Anna pulled her gold-colored jaguar into the parking lot next to my office.

She came into the office and walked straight back to my space. I greeted her in the doorway and took her in my arms. We shared a lingering kiss until she pulled away. "Easy, big boy, you've got to at least buy me dinner before I let you get serious," she said with a beautiful smile.

"I can call the hamburger joint around the corner, and they'll deliver. Would that work?"

"You're kidding, right?" She pulled away, placed her purse on the sofa and took a seat. "I'm glad to just sit for a while. It's been a hectic day."

She didn't volunteer any more information as to why it had been hectic or what made it that way, so I didn't pursue the subject. "Do you want to change or anything before we go to dinner?" I looked at my watch. "We have an hour and a half before our reservations."

"Why don't we just go and sit at the bar...assuming the place you picked has one. We can unwind for a while."

I locked up my office as we left and headed for the parking lot. "Here, you drive," She handed me the keys to her Jaguar. "I want to just drop in the seat and relax." My 4 Runner was a little higher to climb into than her car, so I knew what she meant.

The evening traffic leaving Seattle had dissipated a little as we headed back to the city from the north. Seattle is always rated as one of the cities in the country with the worst traffic. There are only two ways to cross the city from south to north or going the other way. The Interstate runs through the center of the city and Highway 99, or Aurora Avenue runs parallel to the Interstate between it and the Puget Sound. Both are generally clogged with traffic no matter the time of day. We crossed the bridge over Lake Union and took the next exit and then to a number of side streets until we were skirting the waterway.

Find waterfront property in the Seattle area and you'll find a multi-million-dollar mansion or a restaurant built on it. Lake Union was surrounded by both, and it also had a unique community of live-aboard houseboats moored at one of the many marinas on the lake. Some of the houseboats were extravagant in their size and style. I had been on one that belonged to an attorney I did some work for when I first opened my office. He had a party with about twenty people aboard. The top of the houseboat was an outdoor patio where we sat, drinks in hand and watched the sunset. I noticed that everyone there with two exceptions were paired up. They were married or with a date. There was one rather attractive single woman, and me, who seemed to be single.

I took a seat on the patio after visiting his bar and fixing myself a healthy gin and tonic, double lime. I had barely settled into my seat when the single lady pulled up a chair and sat beside me. She introduced herself as Marie and offered a will manicured hand. Even though it was her right hand, I could tell from the way she held her drink in the left hand and turned it toward me, she wanted me to know she was not wearing a wedding ring. We made small talk about the city and our host for about ten minutes while the sun dipped lower on the horizon. She finally placed her left hand on my arm and pointed. "Doesn't that magnificent sunset just make you want to fall in love?"

I wanted to say, "No, actually what it makes me want to do, is finish my drink and haul ass out of here, and away from anyone mentioning the word love," but I held off and mumbled something about how pretty it was, being careful not to mention the "L" word. I was never invited back, and I never saw or heard from Marie again.

The sun had already set when Anna and I were shown to a table on the combination patio and dock. I took the seat facing the main dining area and Anna pulled one closer to me on my right side. I ordered champagne for her and my normal gin and tonic. I could almost see the tension drain from her when she took the first sip from her glass. "I really needed that," she said as she leaned her head on my shoulder.

When our food was placed on the table, she attacked her filet with a vengeance. The first time we dined together I pulled a roll from the basket on the table, cut it open and buttered it for her. I did it without thinking and didn't realize until I handed it to her that she had been watching me. She later informed me that she thought that was an incredibly romantic gesture. I did it with no prior thought, but naturally, I took full credit for it. I held my drinking down to one more gin and tonic since I was driving, but Anna had two more flutes of champagne. We finished with a crème Brule, which we shared and headed back to my place.

I drove back by my office where I parked her car, and we took mine to my place. It would be better for anyone who saw her car in town to see it at a parking lot rather than in front of where I lived.

Later that night as I lay with Anna in my arms, I wished I was an artist or a poet. The feelings I had for her were something I couldn't express in words that I normally use. She snuggled in, one leg across mine, her head in the hollow between my shoulder and my head. She was, at the same time, soft and warm in ways that only a poet or a painter could capture. A soft purr slipped from her as she snuggled closer. I felt her soft breast against my chest. I resisted the urge to touch it and watch her nipple harden. It wasn't until almost daylight when she woke me, that we made love in a physical sense although I had been making love to her all night in my mind.

Chapter 12

Sometimes I felt like I needed to constantly be looking over my shoulder. It had been over three weeks since I heard from Bill Hart, Anna and I were getting along better than we had in a long time, I still managed to work several jobs for a local attorney who needed some papers served on a client whom he had been attempting to find for the last two months and all my bills were paid up to date. I got a call from my youngest daughter, and we had a very long and as close to an adult conversation as we can have. She told me about the things in her life and what was important to her and when she asked about what was going on with me, I found myself at a loss. I did not want to tell her about working for Bill, whom she remembered from my Army days and the things I had recently done for him and by extension for the country. I wanted to tell her about Anna, but I had no idea how to tell her I was seeing a married lady and it was as serious as I had been about anyone since the divorce. Fortunately, we ended the conversation when her phone buzzed indicating she had another incoming message and she told me it was an important call and she had to take it. I wondered just where my calls rated on her important list but did not ask.

I got up and had an appetite like I had not had in a long time, so I decided to head for the Tree Topper, a greasy spoon diner on Aurora where I had breakfast when I had an appetite for a much too-large plate of food. When I walked outside to get in my 4 Runner, I was greeted by a day that was a rarity in the Seattle area. The sky was a beautiful blue, no clouds in any direction and a light breeze coming in across the Puget Sound. It was cool enough to wear a light windbreaker jacket, but I knew that by sundown, a heavier coat would be welcome. Dan, a retired tugboat captain and my next-door neighbor was standing outside his front door. He was a good neighbor. There if I ever needed anyone to sign for a package or letter, but not one to drop by unexpectedly for a cup of coffee or a conversation.

"Mornin', Max. How's it hanging?" He turned to face me.

"Good, Dan. And you?"

"Much better now that I convinced my doctor to give me a prescription for those little blue pills everybody is talking about." He laughed.

"I assume you mean everybody down at the senior center?"

"Hell, yes. Some of the women are even offering to pay for the prescription. I tell you, if they'd had those things when I was a young man, I'd never made it to old age." He crushed the lit end of the cigarette he was smoking between his thumb and forefinger and tossed the butt out in the yard. He obviously had been doing it that way for so long that the skin was tough enough not to feel the burn. Better him than me.

"Maybe I'll ask my doctor for some and come down to the senior center with you one day." I left him smiling at the thought and got in my vehicle.

There were only a few people still seated inside the Tree Topper when I walked in. The regular waitress knew me and simply pointed to a booth giving me no choice in where I was to sit. She got there about the same time I did with a mug of coffee.

"Havin' the usual?" she asked as she waited for a response.

"That'll be good," I said wondering how she could remember not only the customers but what they usually had. I guess that's what made for a good server and good tips.

When she brought my food, she had a Seattle Times newspaper folded up under her arm. "Here, my last customer left this if you want to read it." Without waiting for a response, she dropped it on the table and left to take care of another customer. I arranged the ketchup bottle and the napkin holder in front of me so I could prop the newspaper up and read it while I ate. It was opened to page two, so I started reading there. Most of the columns were devoted to stories that began on page one but there was one that caught my eye. A small heading read: Noted Dutch Tulip Expert Found Dead in Skagit Valley Field. I was struck by the irony of his being a tulip expert and being found dead in a field of tulips in the Skagit Valley. I guess for someone like that, it was an appropriate place to go. I thought about Dan. It would be like him biting the dust in the arms of some widow he met at the drug store when he was picking up his pills.

I continued to read: The victim, Professor Jacob Dirksen, a noted expert on tulips was found dead by several tourists who were walking through a field at the HAZARD FARM early yesterday morning. The initial investigation shows no signs of foul play, and the time of death was put at late night or the early morning hours prior to the field opening for the tourists who regularly flock to the area for the annual Tulip Festival. Dutch authorities have been notified of the death.

When I finished reading about the demise of the professor, I folded the paper so I could read the comics. After the comics came the sports section and since it was still early, I began doing the crossword puzzle. I always did it in ink and not pencil. I was told that is some sort of personality flaw, but I think I have

86

so many that one more that I don't even have a name for won't matter. Half-way through the crossword, my cell phone buzzed. I looked at the screen and recognized Anna's number. I did not have her name on the screen, not because I didn't want anyone to know who was calling but...but I'm not really sure why I have avoided putting it there.

"What a great way to start my day...listening to your smiling voice," I said as I answered the phone.

"I'm glad I bring a smile to your face. You have such a hard life...living alone, not having to answer to anyone, going all over the world on adventures that could get you killed at any moment and charming all the ladies along the way." I could hear the slight sarcasm in her voice.

"Are you sure you have the right number?"

"Oh, I've got your number all right." This time there really was a smile in her voice.

"Guilty as charged, your honor. Isn't this a little early for you to be up and about?" I looked at my watch and saw that it was still earlier than she normally called. I was waiting for her response when the waitress brought a refill on my coffee and took away my dirty dishes.

"Under normal conditions it would be a little early, but a friend called me this morning and made me an offer I hate to refuse, but I won't take it unless you're available."

I'm usually available for anything I want to do, especially if it involves Anna, so I told her to accept the offer.

"Not so fast," she said. "I want to run it by you first. My friend has a house on the Hood Canal in Brinnon and she asked if I wanted to get away for a weekend and house sit for her and her dog. She's going into the hospital for a minor surgery procedure and doesn't want to kennel the dog. It's a beautiful place right across the highway from the canal and she owns part of the beach so we can dig for clams or simply pick them and oysters up at low tide. Interested?"

Was I interested? A weekend getaway with Anna in a secluded house with its own beach where I can gather clams and oysters? How quickly can I say yes? "I think I can work that into my busy schedule. When do we leave?" I listened for the next five minutes while she filled me in on the logistics of our meeting at the ferry dock, what we would need to take with us and what time we would need to leave. When I had all the information I needed, I paid for my breakfast, left a sufficient tip so I could get the same service the next time I came in and went outside to drive to the office.

There was nothing special in my mail or in my office phone messages when I got there. I was not surprised at either one since most of my work came by way of a few steady clients in the legal or insurance field or personal referrals. The personal referrals usually came in to see me in person to hire me to find a runaway teenager, or get evidence on a cheating spouse, or surveillance of an employee they suspected was stealing from their business. None of those showed up this morning, so after making two phone calls, and finally checking the secure messages on the computer that Bill Hart had installed in my office and finding nothing of interest from him, I went back to my place and packed a small bag.

I returned to my office where I had agreed to meet Anna. She parked her Jaguar in my normal parking spot, and we took my 4 Runner to the ferry. After loading, we went to the top deck where we ventured outside and stood on the rail. No matter the time of day or day of the year, if you stand on the rail of a ferry deck crossing the Puget Sound, it's going to get cold. Anna was wearing jeans, a blue sweater over a blouse that had a white collar that she had folded over the neck of the sweater and a leather jacket. I don't know if she was cold or if she just wanted to snuggle, but as soon as we stopped at the rail, she leaned against me as I stood behind her.

"Put your arms around me."

She didn't have to ask twice as I pulled her against me and leaned down so I could kiss her neck and smell the clean fragrance of her hair. That was one of the longest ferry rides of my life as I wished it across the sound so we could get to the cabin.

We spent the next three days in a lovely cabin on the Hood Canal. Just as Anna has said, it had its own beach. The first night we were there we had fresh steamed clams and oysters that we picked up on the beach. The house had a gas grill on the back deck which overlooked the canal, so I fired it up and roasted the oysters with some jalapeños and parmesan that I found in the kitchen. We topped it off with a bottle of wine and an incredible night of making love. I had heard rumors about the aphrodisiac effect of oysters all my life and never believed it, but maybe it was the oysters, the location, or more likely just Anna that made it a memorable night.

The next morning, we were awakened by the sound of a small herd of elk walking across the front yard on their way to wherever elk go in the daytime. I'm still amazed at the size of a bull elk seen close up. They're as big as a horse. We walked the dog, came back and I cooked breakfast, and Anna wanted to pick some blackberries she saw on the edge of the property.

The berries went into a cobbler she made to go with steaks I grilled that evening, prior to another bottle of wine and a night that made me regret the fact that finances kept her married.

*　　*　　*

Two days later I was back in my office when the phone rang. My cell phone was on my desk, so I reached for it. I realized when I touched it, that it was not that one that was buzzing but the secure phone that Bill Hart had provided me and that was in a desk drawer.

Reluctantly, I removed it. "Oh shit, what is it now?" I said as I pushed the green answer dot on the phone.

"Is that any way to speak to your boss?"

"You're only my boss if I'm working for you and so far, that is not the case."

"The operative words there are so far."

"I think we have a bad connection. You seem to be coming in broken and stupid," I said remembering an old Army phrase.

"Not nice…not nice at all. And here I had an easy favor to ask of you."

"The last time you asked me to do you an easy favor it almost got me killed. I don't forget things like that." If anyone who did not know us heard our conversations, they would either think we hated each other or we were crazy. We don't hate each other, our friendship goes back to Army days, but I'm not so sure about the crazy part. "What is it this time?"

"To be honest, this is a strange one, even for me and my operation. We got a message that filtered down or maybe up to me from the Dutch Embassy. Seems a professor from one of the Netherland's leading universities was found dead in a tulip field in your A.O," he said, using the Army term for area of operations.

I seemed to remember something about that from the news or somewhere, but I could not place it as he continued.

"Guy was some sort of whiz-bang expert on tulips, of all things. The first thing I thought of was, if he was found dead in the tulips that would save a lot of money on flowers for his funeral, but I got the impression they were serious, so I saved that comment for you."

I looked out my window and saw George shuffling down the sidewalk on the opposite side of the street. I knew once he got to where he was going and began his return trip, he's stop by for a cup of coffee. He glanced across the street to my office and when he saw me, he threw a half-hearted salute my way.

"So, you thought of me from the minute they said it happened in this area?"

"Not immediately, but when I found out who was behind the initial inquiry your name popped up first."

"Who made the request?" I asked knowing I would probably regret hearing the answer.

"It came from State by way of Agriculture, of all places." He hesitated so the magnitude of the request could sink in. "Can you imagine the State Department being concerned about a tulip farmer?"

I couldn't at the time, but all of that was about to change.

Chapter 13

It was two weeks before Bill gathered all the information from the various government agencies that were involved in the tulip expert's death and get them to me. I was amazed the day he sent them to my secure computer that he had placed in my office, because they came with somewhat of an apology from him. For him to apologize for anything was about as rare as seeing Haley's Comet.

The first page that was printed when I saw the email that said the information was in the computer started with: Don't let this go to your head, but I'm sorry it took so long to get this to you. That was as close as he ever got to apologizing for anything and it wasn't, as I read further, an apology for something he did or didn't do, it was for the other bureaucrats taking so long to respond to him.

I printed everything out and placed it on the corner of my desk. I planned to read it later when I was not otherwise occupied…like I was now. Sitting across from me was a very attractive woman with a steady flow of tears cascading down her previously meticulously made-up face. Next to her was a man, who like her, was well dressed and appeared to be approximately the same age as his companion. I did not know at the time if they were a couple or not.

"If you don't mind my asking, just how did you happen to decide I was the best person for this?" I asked and really wanted to know the answer. The lady, who identified herself as Cheryl Hadaway, called me three days previously and asked me if I could help her find her run-away daughter whom she thought was somewhere in Seattle. She was calling from Boise, Idaho and said her daughter had been missing for two weeks. I've had some success finding run-aways who think Seattle is the Mecca for music, drugs and living in a cardboard box underneath a freeway bridge. That's an image that is quickly dispelled the first time they have to dig through a dumpster behind a greasy spoon restaurant for a meal that someone else has partially eaten.

Cheryl spoke between sobs. "I...I have a friend in Seattle who knew the high school counselor who drowned, and you found out it was really murder. She said you did a great job and if anyone could find Anita, you could."

That immediately raised a bundle of red flags for me. My old SCUBA diving partner and friend Jeff had supposedly drowned, and I did not believe it from the day he died. After looking into it, I found out that he and his wife were part of a wife-swapping group and that he was dipping his wick into some of the senior girls at the high school who were past the age of consent. Lust and stupidity are one thing: statutory rape is a whole different box of Pandoras. I had to wonder if her friend was part of the alternative lifestyle side of the equation or had she been one of Jeff's high school love interests. Either way, I was not overly anxious to get involved...however, I do have a soft spot for any parent who has lost a child no matter the reason and a run-away can easily turn into a permanent loss.

"You're her mother, right?" I looked at her and then at him. "And you are?"

"A friend of the family," he replied.

"Okay, if...and I'm still in the 'if' stage, I agree to look for her, I will need some answers to some probably hard questions. The answers have to be honest, and I don't want to ask them twice or get them a piece at a time. Do we agree on that?" I was talking to her but looking at the friend of the family.

"Yes, of course. I'll tell you anything you need to know to find her." She opened her purse and pulled out several photos and handed them to me. Anita was a younger and even more attractive version of her mother. One photo was obviously from a high school yearbook. She wore a smile that said she was at peace with the world and had not a care, but the eyes told a different story. Even in the photo there was a depth to them unlike what is seen on a happy, well-adjusted teenager. The next photo was her at poolside with several of her female friends. All were dressed, if that is a good description of what little they wore, in string bikinis. Anita and one other girl were standing with their hands on their hips with their chest thrust forward emphasizing their blossoming bosoms.

"How old is she?"

"She'll be eighteen in two months---"

"So, I have to find her before she can make up her own mind if she wants to be found and returned or not."

"How could she not want to come home? We..." The friend stopped when he inadvertently interjected himself into the home-life conversation.

"Okay, let's talk about the 'we'. Are you her father, or still just a friend of the family?"

"I don't like your implications, Mister Maxwell."

I slid the photos back across the desk to Cheryl. "It's been a pleasure and I hope you find your daughter. Now if you will excuse me, I have other business to tend to.

Cheryl quickly put her hand on his. "Please, he didn't mean anything by that. It's just that we're all upset and tense right now. You've got to help us." She looked at him, indicating he was to offer some apology as well, which I did not expect, nor did I wait for.

"I need to know about her home life, and it sounds like that includes you." I hesitated. "I didn't get your name."

"Karl...with a 'K' Berry. Cheryl and I are...more than friends."

"Do you live in the same house with Cheryl and Anita? And if so, how does she feel about that?"

"Her father and I divorced when she was ten. I met Karl two years ago and...and we've been together since then. He moved into my...our house about four months ago."

I reached into a desk drawer and pulled out a contract. I rarely used a written document when I did work since it was usually for a lawyer, but I had one generate a contract once as a fee for serving divorce papers. I felt that it was going to be useful if I had to deal with Cheryl and Karl.

I handed the contract to Cheryl. "I'll need a minimum hire of a week." I pointed to a number on the page. "That's my normal daily fee...plus any expenses...fee in advance. I'll bill you for the expenses. At the end of the first week, if I have some solid leads, I'll let you know what I found and if you want me to continue to work for you, it's on a day-to-day basis billed weekly." I waited to see if she had any questions as she reached into her purse and pulled out a pen and signed the contract.

Karl was not a happy camper at that moment. I think he felt like he was left out of the decision process. "Are you sure this is what you want to do?" he asked Cheryl.

"If you mean finding Anita, what choice do I have?"

He shrugged and watched as she handed the contract back to me.

I pulled out a legal pad from a stack of papers on my desk. "I'll need some more information before I start. Most of it will be personal, but necessary."

Cheryl nodded.

"Was she happy at home?"

"She seemed…at least on the surface to be, but there was always something I could see in the background, maybe in her eyes that said she was putting on a front."

"Any boyfriends that may have left with her or enticed her to leave with him?"

"No. I can't think of anyone. She didn't date that much. She was somewhat of a…" She hesitated as she searched for a word. "A geek. She was a whiz on computers and always had great grades in math and science."

So far, this was not sounding like a typical runaway. I looked at Karl. "How did the two of you get along?"

"We didn't interact that much. I know she resented me. Especially when Cheryl told her I was moving in."

"Did she say anything prior to leaving that led you believe she was coming to Seattle?"

"The only thing outside of schools that she was interested in was the music that was coming from this area. Grunge?"

Ever since Kurt Cobain and others like Pearl Jam started the gunge movement in Seattle, it had been a drawing card for kids who wanted to be a part of it. A grunge loving geek would feel right at home hidden in Seattle.

"If she had a cell phone, I'll need the number and any address book or diary or anything like that she left behind." I stood up and extended my hand to Cheryl. "As soon as you get me those things, I'll start working on finding her. In the meantime, if you think of anything else that might help me, call or send me an email." After I shook with Cheryl, Karl put his hand in the small of her back and led her out of the office. I knew I was not going to like Karl with a K.

George must have been watching from across the street because as soon as Karl and Cheryl left, he opened my outer door and came in. "Colonel, you busy?"

"Come on in. I was just thinking about a cup. If you'll fly, I'll buy." I handed him a ten-dollar bill and he left to go across the street to a latte stand for two cups and a munchie if he was hungry. There was a fifty-fifty chance he'd come back with the coffee and a zero chance I'd get any change from the ten.

I pulled out the pages from Bill I had printed prior to Cheryl and Karl coming in and looked at them. The dead man was a professor at a university in Holland and was a world-renowned expert on the care and feeding of tulips. He had been working on a new variety that, according to the information I was reading, would be the biggest thing to hit the tulip industry since...what...fertilizer maybe? I didn't know enough about tulips to know what I didn't know.

The pages went on to say that he was on a sabbatical from the university and was here to study the industry in the Skagit Valley. According to a copy of an airline ticket receipt, he had been here a little over a month when he died.

It seems the university and by extension the State Department and Department of Agriculture wanted to make certain he had simply died and there had not been any foul play. Their interest seemed a little out of line, so I immediately suspected the good professor was not what he seemed or was not doing what everyone said.

To my amazement, George came back with two cups of coffee and something in a brown paper bag that he did not share with me. If there was any change, he did not share that either.

I pulled the lid from the cup and watched the steam rise. George had bought enough coffee for me that he knew how I liked it, so there was no need to slow play the sip. "What do you know about tulips, George?"

"Tulips? I know they's flowers. I got some in my yard. I got a job years ago working up north of here and they got more tulips growing up there than a dog's got fleas. You oughta take your lady friend up there and see them." George was very perceptive and knew I was seeing Anna. He didn't know her name or anything about her...at least I don't think he did, but he had seen her in the office several times and knew her gold Jaguar when she parked it nearby.

We drank in silence as we sometimes did when George drifted away in his mind to places most people have never seen, and will never see. After a few minutes, he stood and walked out of the office without saying another word. Such was the world George occupied.

Chapter 14

When I completed looking at the pages Bill had sent to me, I found that I also had a letter from the Embassy of the Netherlands to act as their agent in all matters involving the investigation of the death of the professor. That just added to my skepticism that I, and maybe Bill Hart as well, did not know all we needed to know about this situation. I made copies of all the pages, placed one set in my desk drawer and put another set in a folder I planned to carry with me when I made my first stop at the coroner's office. The last document in the stack that Bill sent me was a signed contract with a daily pay rate, an account for expenses and a bonus if I found "anything out of the ordinary." At that moment, I expected I would both earn and collect the bonus.

The Skagit County coroner's office is in Mt. Vernon near the corner of Continental Place and College Way. I found it somewhat ironic that it was last in line of three county government buildings and was next to the Parks and Recreation Department. I called ahead to make certain he was in, but I did not tell him what I wanted. I felt, under the circumstances, that I did not want to give anyone any more information than was necessary.

The drive up I-5 was relatively smooth and uneventful. I always get a charge when I see a sign for the turn off to the city of Cedro Woolley. I keep meaning to take the road one day and stop at the city hall and ask just how they came up with that name, but I always forget until it's too late. I passed the casino where I sometimes went to play poker but since they closed the poker room I had not been back. There are almost as many "poker rooms" in the Seattle area as there are latte stands but they play a variety of games they call poker, but none of them interest me.

It didn't take long to reach the coroner's office. I parked across the street and walked to the building. I have seen far too many dead people both while I was on active duty in the Army, and in civilian life, so I am not squeamish when it comes to visiting the coroner or going into a morgue. I draw the line on watching an autopsy, if possible. I've done it several times in the past and each time I hoped it would be the last. With any luck, if an autopsy was required on the professor, it had already been done.

Inside the building I was greeted by a young woman I assumed was an assistant since she was dressed in blue scrubs. I told her I was there to see the coroner and that I had not made an appointment but had called ahead to make certain he was in. That seemed to satisfy her need for me to have an appointment, so she pointed to a chair across the room from his desk. "Have a seat and I'll tell the coroner you're here. Did you tell him what you wanted when you spoke to him?"

"No. I just wanted to make certain I did not drive all the way up here for nothing."

I waited less than five minutes for Doctor Jacobs to come out of his office. He was dressed in a pair of grey pants, a light-yellow colored shirt and had a silk tie that was slipped down at the neck. He wore a standard medical lab coat and had his cell phone up to his ear as he extended his hand to me. He pulled the phone away and almost whispered, "It's a lady friend. You know how it is when they call." He spoke several times. Each one was to agree with something she said. He finished and turned his attention to me.

"You called?"

"I did," I said as I stood and shook his hand. "I'd like to speak to you about a recent death you handled." I nodded toward his office door hoping he would take the clue and walk back inside so we could talk in private.

"Must be the man we found in the tulip fields. He's the most interesting one I've had all month. Usually all I get are the old ones who die at home and an occasional suicide." He turned and opened his office door. "Haven't had an old-fashioned murder this year and only had one in the last two years. We have a quiet community up here. Not like a couple of miles north or south of us."

He was referring to Bellingham to the north and Seattle to the south. "I can imagine you like it that way, too," I added.

"Personally, I do, but professionally it's hard to justify even a part time coroner to the public come election time without some good reason." He had a large desk in the office and several mis-matched chairs sitting along the wall. He took one covered in green fabric and pointed to the others. I selected an off red color.

"What can I do for you"

I pulled out the paper from the Embassy and handed it to him. "I've been retained by the government to—"

"To what? Make sure I did a good job? Or the sheriff did his?" He leaned forward and handed the paper back to me.

"Let's not get off on the wrong foot to begin with. I'm not here to check up on anyone. Since he was a foreign national, they wanted to make certain that their requirements for an investigation were met as well as those for the county and city if appropriate." I didn't know what else to say, but that sounded like a good start, even to me as I said it.

He stood and went to his desk. "Here is a copy of my report. I made two in case I had to send one to

101

the Netherlands.   I   guess   since   you're   their representative, I can give it to you." He handed me a folder.

"Did you find anything unusual with his death? And what did you determine was the cause?"

"He died from blunt force trauma to the side of his head---"

"Murder?"

"I didn't say that, and I didn't speculate on that in the report, although I could have." He opened another folder and handed me several photos. "I'm certain of the cause of death, but I'm not certain of the way he died." He pointed to one of the photos. "As you can see, there is a very large stone near his head. He could have tripped and fallen on it in the dark."

"But?"

"But these tulip fields are very important to the farmers   and   the   people   up   here.   They   take exceptionally good care of them, and I think it's highly unusual to find a stone of that size just lying between rows of flowers."

I   held   the   photo   and   then   looked   at   several others. None of them had any indication of stones in the field. "What did the sheriff think?"

"The sheriff thinks it would be very bad for the area if a foreigner turned up dead in a tulip field. He accepted my opinion of blunt force trauma, possibly caused by a fall in the field."

"Somehow I get the feeling that you may not completely buy into your own theory."

"I'm a retired medical doctor. I sold my practice years ago. My wife passed away last year, and I've been the coroner up here for almost ten years. I'm very comfortable and very good in this position, and I have a lady friend who doesn't look at me as an old fart. I'm a doctor, not a detective. I leave all that to someone   with   a   badge...or   a   letter   from   the embassy."

I thanked him for his time and candor, took the folders with the autopsy report and the one with the photos and left his office after asking directions to the sheriff's office.

The reception I got at the sheriff's office was only slightly better than that at the coroners. After explaining who I was, who I represented and what I wanted to three different people, I finally was shown into the office of the detective who worked the case.

"What do you think you're gonna find that we didn't?" he asked as soon as I explained the who, what and why of my being in his office.

"Hopefully nothing, but that's not the point."

"And that point would be?"

"He was a foreign national and they have some requirements we don't when one of their citizens dies out of the country. They just want to make sure all the t's are crossed and the i's dotted." I was getting good at my bullshit explanation. He seemed to soften a little and we talked for another fifteen minutes. When I was satisfied that I had gotten all the information he had or would give me, and getting a copy of his report, I thanked him and asked where I could collect all the personal belongings the professor had on him when they found him.

He directed me to an office in the basement. As I looked for and finally found a set of steps leading down, I wondered if every police station in the world, military or civilian, had a basement they used as an evidence room. Every station I think I ever went to in the Army had just such a place. Once I was at the lowest level of the station, I saw a door that was marked as the Evidence Room. I knew when I opened the door, I would find an older, probably overweight police officer who was finishing out his career hidden in the basement.

I was shocked when I opened the door. The person behind the desk was a young, not beautiful, but good-looking female office who appeared to be in her mid-thirties. They say one cop can always spot another one and it must be true. "Not what you expected, was I?" she asked.

"I didn't think it was that obvious," I managed to stammer.

"That's okay, I see it on almost everyone who comes down here if they have ever been in an evidence room before." She stood and left the desk and came to the counter that separated her from visitors. "What can I do for you?"

I handed her a copy of the letter from the embassy. "I'm looking into the death of Professor Jacob Dirksen, and I'd like to retrieve all of the personal effects that you have."

"Not a problem. If I recall, he only had a few items on him." She left and went to a shelf where she pulled down a brown paper bag that looked like they got them at the same place his local super-market got theirs. "Here you go," she said as she placed the bag on the counter. "I'll need you to sign for it if you want to take the bag with you." She handed me a form and I signed, picked up the bag, found my way out and left the building and the city.

The drive back to my office was uneventful and I did not take the time to make the side trip north and inquire about the naming of Cedro Woolley.

I had hardly gotten back in the building when I heard my land line phone ring. I hurried inside, placed the bag I got from the evidence room on my desk, and got to the phone before the recording came on. "Maxwell here."

"Oh, good you're in. I called several times earlier today and left a message." I recognized the voice as that of Cheryl Hadaway, the mother of the missing teenager. "You said if I found anything she left that might tell where she was to give you a call and I found something."

I took a seat and pulled out a yellow legal pad and prepared to write down anything she told me that was of interest. "Okay, what did you find?"

"I found three letters from a boy I had never heard of, and the address is in Seattle. Do you want me to read them to you?"

"No, I'd rather you put them in the mail and send them to me. Don't touch them any more than necessary. My address is on my business card. The letters may be very helpful in finding her."

"I thought so. That's why I called you." There was a catch in her voice. "I know she didn't like it when Karl moved in, but I didn't think she'd run away because of it. If I had, I'd never have---"

"You can't blame yourself until we find her and know why she did what she did. It may have nothing to do with you or Karl."

"Do you really think so?"

This was not the time or the place to give an opinion, so I was about to end the call when I heard the unmistakable sound of her crying. I felt that she had more to tell me.

"Is everything all right?" I asked but I wasn't sure I wanted to know the answer.

"Yes..yes...I think maybe it is, but I'm not sure."

"Okay, take a deep breath and tell me what else you have." I never quite knew what taking a deep breath did, but everyone seemed to recommend doing it.

"I...I got a call from Anita."

"Is she okay?" I could picture her in an orange jump suit with a deputy standing behind her, saying "You have the right to make one phone call. Make it a good one."

"I think she is. She said she may want to come home."

I could tell by the way she said it, there were some conditions to her coming back and I was willing to bet they had to do with Karl with a K.

105

"Why did she say she may want to come home and not that she was ready to do it?"

"Her condition was that Karl not be there when she came back." Cheryl's voice was getting a little stronger now that she was talking and not crying.

I didn't want to get in the middle of a family feud, but that did not surprise me. "What did you say to that?"

"I didn't know what to say. It's not like Karl and I are engaged or even talking about getting married or making our situation permanent, but…"

"But she's asking you to make a choice between Karl and your daughter."

"That's right and I'm not sure what to do. What would you suggest?"

I couldn't answer fast enough. "Oh, no. You need a marriage or family counselor and not a private investigator. As a matter of fact, since you found her, or rather she found you, and I had nothing to do with it, I'm going to tear up our contract and you can find the help you're going to need to get through this."

There was a long pause on her end. "Mister Maxwell, are you married? Do you have children?"

Now she was hitting below the belt, but for some reason, I felt an obligation as a parent to respond. "I'm divorced but I have two daughters. One is married and the other is in college."

"What would you do if it was one of your daughters?" she managed to get out between the sobs that had re-started.

Anna and I had never really discussed my daughters and since she didn't have children, they did not enter into our relationship. "I don't think I'm the person to ask that question to. I've been incredibly fortunate with my daughters, even during the divorce. And we still maintain a good relationship, although neither of them live close to me. The best advice I can give you, and I hesitate to even say this, is to think with your head and not your heart."

"Right now, I'm not sure I can tell them apart."

I knew I was getting in over my head and although I felt sorry for her, there was nothing I could do to help at this point. "I know once you have time to think it over, you'll make the right decision," I said to the silence at the other end of the conversation.

Finally, she spoke to me. "I wish I shared your confidence in me, Mister Maxwell."

"Do this," I said as I looked at my watch noting that I had been on the phone with her for almost half an hour. "Make the best choice you can for all the people involved and give me a call in a month and let me know how it turned out. Can you do that?"

"I'll try."

"That's all anyone, yourself included, can ask of a person." We exchanged "good-bye's" and she ended the call. I sat at my desk for a minute then pulled out the calendar book I kept in my desk drawer and made a note for a call from her in a month. I closed the book and for the second time, I stood and got ready to leave the office.

If her daughter got the same impression of Karl that I did, I didn't want to speculate on when or if she would come home.

Chapter 15

My interest in a teenage runaway was second to my curiosity about what was in the brown paper bag sitting on my desk. I knew it may be too late, but I didn't want to touch anything that may have some impact on what happened to the professor, so before I opened it, I went into my bathroom and found a pair of latex gloves. I slipped them on and came back to open the bag.

The first thing I pulled out was his wallet. It was a triple fold with a driver's permit issued in Holland with his name on it. First good news is that he was using his own name. The wallet also contained an international driver's license in his name, several credit cards from banks back home and an identification card from his university. Altogether, nothing of special interest at the moment. He had a little over two hundred dollars in US currency, mostly small bills and less than a dollar in change. There were several business cards mixed in with the currency. Two were from operations in the Skagit Valley, one was from a local taxi company, and another from a real estate agency. When I turned the cards over, the one from the taxi company had a number written on the back in ink. Two keys were hanging from a key ring advertising a local Seattle bar. The detective told me he had a set of keys for a rental car on him and after processing the car, the rental company came and picked it up. I had no doubt that when his next credit card bill came in, he would have a charge on it for them having to drive all the way up north to pick it up. Fortunately, they'd get stiffed for the bill.

The best thing I found in the bag was his cell phone. It was a very nice and I assumed a very expensive model. I played with it a few minutes in an attempt to activate it, and finally decided that the battery was dead. Fortunately, it used the same power cord as the phone Bill Hart had provided to me, so I plugged it up and placed it on the edge of my desk. I'd have to leave it there for a couple of hours to get a full charge on it and then I'd have to see if it was locked or if I could get any information from it.

I placed the business cards and the credit cards on my printer and made copies of all of them. Then I made a second copy of the one business card with the phone number written on the back. I put everything back in the bag along with his wallet and money. The only thing I kept out was the key ring. Keys fit locks and locks mean doors and doors usually lead to something and that was the only something I had.

After sitting at my desk in the quiet for a minute trying to think of which direction I wanted to turn next: looking for a missing teenager or getting more deeply involved with Bill Hart in something that I instinctively felt was much more complicated than I knew now.

My mind was just about made up when I heard a phone ring. I have three phones in my office. I have my cell which buzzes and doesn't ring, my land line which still rings and another phone that Bill had installed when he first conned me into working for him. It was a secure phone and as such, had a very distinctive ring tone. Bill's morbid sense of humor took over when he had WHY DON'T WE GET DRUNK AND SCREW set as the ringtone. Fortunately, it had only gone off a couple of times when I had someone else in the office and had to explain it.

"I knew it was too good to last," I said as I answered the phone.

"No way to talk to an old friend who just wants to help," he said.

"The kind of help you give is sometimes like holding the basket for the executioner to drop the victim's head in."

"I don't think there will be any head chopping this time. Looks like this is a straight 'find out what happened or who done it and close the case'. Nothing could be easier."

"Let's talk about the who done it. Is somebody thinking it was not an accident?" I could see the waters getting muddier the more we talked.

"There's always the indication of foul play when a body is found in unusual places or circumstances, and this qualifies as both."

I took a deep breath as I knew he was right. "Okay, who and why do they think he didn't just get drunk, fall down, hit his head and die?" I knew the drunk part was my editorializing, since his blood alcohol content was consistent with having a drink or two for dinner several hours before he died.

"Don't kill the messenger. I'm not the one asking the questions or needing the answers. I just pass on what I'm told or asked to do."

"Unless Lannette, your latest love interest has suddenly convinced you to buy a little cottage with a white picket fence and a yard so she can start growing tulips, I'm going to call bullshit on that last comment," I said as I took a drink from a half-warm cup of coffee on my desk. "If this was a simple death of a foreign national, you'd be the last to have any interests in it, so why don't you tell me at least as much as you can, if not all that you know."

He took his time in answering since he knew I was right. "Okay, here's the deal...or at least as much as I know right now. On the surface the dead professor was just that. He was a professor at a university in the Netherlands and he's dead."

"Brilliant deduction," I took another drink and drained my coffee cup.

"Don't get testy. Remember, I'm on your side. Anyway, I'm going to go out on a limb and agree with you on this one. There's more to the good professor than we know right now, but I'm working on finding out what we are missing."

"Okay, that's a start." I knew if Bill dug deep enough or in high enough places, he'd find out what was going on. "You said State and Agriculture Departments were involved. Does that make any more sense to you than it does to me right now?"

"No, it doesn't, and I want to attack this from both ends. You run down all you can out there, and I'll do the same here in Washington. Together we're bound to get to the bottom on the who and the why."

I hated to agree, and I refused to do so and give him the satisfaction, but we had always worked well together, and I thought we could do it again. "I've got his personal belongings…at least what he had on him when he was taken to the coroner's office. Not much to go on, but I'll give it a shot." I didn't mention the two items I found of major interest. I wanted to call the number on the back of the taxi company's card and see if I could find out what the keys fit. "I think he was staying at one of the hotels downtown, so I'm going to see if he's still got a room that he paid for in advance and if not, see if they cleaned it out yet. If I find something, I'll let you know."

"Good idea. You work your magic out there and I'll do the same here. I'll get back to you in the next day or two or as soon as I have more intel." As was his normal custom, he ended the conversation without saying a "good-bye" or anything to indicate it was over. I knew that was a holdover from our Army days. If you initiated a call on a radio, you were the one who ended it. In the civilian world, it was to show who was in charge, as if to say, "I've decided this call is over and I'm going to end it."

I continued to sit after placing the secure cell phone back in my desk drawer. It was then that I suddenly realized for the first time since I opened my business, I had two and possibly three cases at the same time. I figured that my looking for Cheryl's missing teenager was now closed, but I wouldn't bet the farm on it. My insurance fraud case with Getz was something I needed to give some more attention to, and if past projects were any indication, Bill had just handed me the shitty end of the stick.

Although I was not entirely certain what I was looking for in either case, I had promised Getz that I would look into his situation, so I felt an obligation to pursue it first. I decided that my first stop would be to the attorney's office who formed the corporation. Maybe I could find out more about the principals than I had on the state website. I did a quick search on the computer and found a good address for the attorneys and decided I would pay them a visit. I didn't want to just show up, so I wrote their phone number on the edge of a piece of paper I had on my desk and after closing the computer gave them a call.

The woman who answered the phone had a slight accent that I recognized as German. After spending several years in Germany with the Army, I picked up enough German to hold a decent conversation. After securing an appointment for the next afternoon, I asked her if she was German and did it in what I thought was her native language. She surprised me by responding in German but quickly informed me she was from a small town in Holland where German and Dutch along with English was spoken by most of the residents. I noticed that she referred to her origin as being from Holland and not the Netherlands. That information may come in handy for me later.

It was almost five when I finished speaking to the lady whose name I found out was Gerda, and it was time for me to wrap it up and either go home and cook or find a place to have dinner. Unfortunately, each choice meant I would be dining alone. Anna was, I assumed, at home equally alone. I would call her later and if she did not answer, I would spin a hundred situations in my mind of why she didn't and where she might be.

I left the desk, took my coffee mug to the bathroom and washed it out. It was more of a courtesy than anything else, since it was almost black with built-up coffee stains. At least it matched the bottom of the glass pot sitting on my coffee maker. After a lifetime of Army coffee, the stains or the strength of the coffee didn't bother me.

Chapter 16

The war in Afghanistan was in full swing. I was a captain and the Company Commander of a Military Police company charged with securing the roadways for the multitude of convoys they coalition forces assembled and used to resupply their men and women in uniform.

As the Company Commander my name was on the blame line for everything that happened or didn't happen with my company. Unlike the movies and stories about how things were done in WWII, in the modern Army everything was counted, serial numbered, signed for and expected to be returned in good condition when the military member, no matter what service left the combat zone. I had platoon leaders in the form of lieutenants and senior sergeants who kept most of their men in line and accounted for their equipment, but occasionally, I wanted to see what they did once they left the security of our base of operations.

I'm not superstitious, but it was a Friday the thirteenth and I decided to accompany a platoon that was providing security and traffic control for an infantry column moving in Humvees. The terrain we passed through was better suited for mules and horses than wheeled or tracked vehicles. Roads were nothing more than rutted dirt tracks that had been used since before the Light Brigade made the same mistake the Russians and now, probably the United States was making. Steep mountain peaks that rivaled those of the Rockies back home blocked the horizon on either side of the road. Villages with houses made of mud bricks and little else crowded the sides of the road, making travel extremely difficult and even more dangerous as this is where most ambushes happen. If the convoy was ambushed on an open road there was at least a chance for the vehicles to pull off the track onto the open landscape and put up a fight. In the built-up areas we were at the mercy of villagers who may have accepted medical aide that morning and spent the afternoon behind a machine gun trying to kill the men and women who had helped them only hours earlier.

We had several vehicles ahead of the convoy to clear any local traffic that might impede the mission. Other military police vehicles were interspersed in the convoy for both security and additional firepower if needed. As we slowed for the second village we came to, we knew that they had been alerted to our approach. If the kids were not out begging for candy, cigarettes or anything else they could get, we knew we may be rolling into an ambush.

Three of the convoy's Humvees trailed behind two of my vehicles. They were allowed to pass unharmed through the village, but then all hell broke loose. The fourth and fifth vehicles were immediately hit with IED's. They were damaged sufficiently that they blocked the only road through the village. I knew instinctively, as did everyone else who had been in country longer than a week, that the last vehicles were next to go, thus blocking our exit to the rear and our escape to the front. We were in deep shit, and we knew it.

The streets emptied of civilian villagers who did not want to kill us, so any person we saw was a target. The M-60 machine gunner standing in the ring mount in my Humvee opened up as did others in front and behind us. I heard the infantry Company Commander on the radio as he called for helicopter gunships to suppress the fire so he could do a hard right to break contact and go cross country to get out of the kill zone.

Not wanting to wait, most of the men and the women in my company returned fire to the shooters who were using the ground level houses and some of the rooftops as shooting platforms. I jumped out and spotted one shooter in a doorway less than twenty yards away. He raised his AK-47 just as I fired my MP-3. I was faster than he, and I watched as his body jerked when the rounds tore through him. I didn't have time to dwell on the fact that I had just killed someone when another shooter stitched a line of holes in the door of the Humvee I had just exited. Before I could turn and engage him, I heard the clatter of expended brass bouncing off the roof of the vehicle as my gunner sent the shooter on the way to find his virgins. He smiled, gave me a thumbs up signal and trained the gun back the way we had come from.

I was looking up when I was enveloped in silence. I felt myself slipping into a dark hole. For a moment all was as black as the darkest night, then I experienced a light show not unlike a Fourth of July fireworks display. I saw gold and silver flashes mixed with deep reds and some other colors that I can't describe. I didn't think I was dead, but I would not have bet on it. I was on my knees beside the Humvee as my head slowly returned to my control. I shook it and touched my forehead with my right hand. Perhaps to check for holes or to make certain it was still in one piece. I felt the sticky moisture that even in my present condition, I recognized as blood and in all likelihood, it was mine. I saw my weapon on the ground beside me and when I reached for it with my left hand, I found that it did not work.

"Captain Max. You okay?" Someone was calling my name, but I couldn't answer. The sound of the person calling my name suddenly turned into a dull buzzing.

When I finally realized the buzzing was not his voice but was real, I found myself on the floor beside my bed. The blood I had imagined in my nightmare was the sweat pouring down my face, and the buzzing was my cell phone.

I was out of breath and my mouth felt like it was filled with cotton when I answered. It took three attempts before I could make a sound that even slightly resembled a word. "Hell...hell...hello?"

"Are you okay?" Anna asked.

"If I'm still alive, I think I am," I mumbled as I picked myself up from the floor and walked, cell phone in hand, to the kitchen.

"You don't sound so good. Are you sure you're okay?" The concern in her voice was evident.

My head was much clearer now and I put a container in my coffee maker and pulled the handle down to start making a cup of what was probably at that point, a life support system item. "Yeah. I'm alright. I just..." she didn't let me finish.

"Another nightmare?"

"This one wasn't a nightmare. It was a full-blown stallion, born and bred as a racehorse, purebred Arabian." I watched in anticipation for the coffee maker to produce. "One of the worst I've ever had." I looked at the clock on my microwave. I never changed it when the time changed so it was only accurate six months out of the year. I had to either add or subtract and hour when I looked at it. After I got it in full focus and did the math, I realized that it was nine-thirty in the morning. Normally, I would be either in the office or on the way by this time. The coffee was finally ready, and I quickly poured a cup.

"Okay," I managed to say between sips of the very hot coffee. "Let's start this conversation all over again."

"Good morning, my dear," she said.

"That's a great way to start my day," I responded as I took my coffee and headed back to my bedroom to get ready to go to the office.

"I'm coming to your side of the Sound today for an appointment. If I do it right, and you take me to dinner and maybe your place for an after-dinner drink or whatever, it'll be too late for me to catch the ferry and I'll be forced to spend the night with you."

"Forced?"

"Don't you want to exert your manliness on occasion?"

"Okay. I'll go by the hardware store today and get some rope, maybe some chains and a whip or two."

"Don't tease me." She laughed. "On second thought maybe I do want you to tease me...just a little."

"Your wish...as they say." I opened my closet and pulled out a fresh shirt and placed it on my still-unmade bed. One of my many lingering habits from a lifetime in the Army, was making my bed every morning. It was one of the, I later found out, many things my ex-wife did not like about me.

"I can call you later today and let you know what time I'll be free...well...maybe not free but certainly reasonable." She was in rare form for it to be this early in the day. "What's on your agenda today?"

She knew I had agreed to work with, or more accurately, for Getz, so I told her I was planning to go talk to the lawyer who formed the corporation.

"Do you think there is something amiss with the articles of incorporation?"

"No, it's just that I don't have any other ideas at the moment." I pulled a clean pair of pants from a hanger and placed them on the bed beside my shirt. Now all I needed was underwear and socks.

"Good luck. I hope you either find something or come up with some more ideas," she hesitated. "I'll let you go now if you're sure you're okay."

"I'm good. Unfortunately, I've had these in the past. It just takes massive doses of coffee and a shower to get my heartrate back to normal." We exchanged good-bye's and she hung up, freeing me to head for the shower.

One of the main things I like about my place is the shower. It's big enough for two and Anna and I share it almost every time she come here. The size makes it an anomaly for the rest of the place. It was either specially built during construction for a very large owner or someone who didn't like to shower alone. Whatever the reason, I enjoyed standing beneath the flat, overhead source of the spray.

After the shower, a quick shave and dressing in the clothes I had selected, I left and headed for my office. I stopped at a bakery on the main street and picked up a Danish which served as my breakfast. There was no time for the Tree Topper.

Since I didn't plan to spend much time in the office, I grabbed a spot on the street in front of my building. While getting out of my 4 Runner, I heard my name called from across the street. "Hey, Max. You got a minute?" Mayor Valentino was crossing the street and throwing up his hand in a "thank you...sorry" to all the cars that had to avoid hitting him. "I've been wanting to talk to you." He stood in front of my 4 Runner as if to keep me from getting back into the driver's seat and speeding away. "You been out of town a lot lately. If you don't stay in town more, I may get the idea you don't like our fair city." He laughed aloud at his joke.

After such an emotionally draining start, the day looked like it was going to be one of those rare days in the Seattle area where the sun shines, there is no rain, and the sky is a magnificent shade of blue. "I think I'll call this place home for a little while longer." I passed by him and went to the front door of my office and unlocked it. "I'd invite you in for a cup of coffee, but I have an early appointment and I won't have time to make any." I stepped inside and he followed me.

"I've already had so much this morning that my bladder feels like a fifty-five-gallon drum...but I didn't stop for coffee."

The thought that he was stopping for a cup never entered my mind. "So, what can I do for you?" I asked and immediately regretted it.

"You know the election is coming up in a month and since you turned down my suggestion that you run for city council, I thought maybe you'd put a couple of my signs in your window." He pointed to the large window overlooking the street. "I'd get lots of exposure," he hesitated and looked me in the eye. "And you and I both would benefit from it."

I didn't know how much he could do to hurt my business or my reputation, but the not-so-subtle veiled threat was there. "How 'bout if I support your campaign with a donation and my vote. I can't afford to play favorites with signs, and I know if I put one of yours in my window everyone else running is going to want one there as well."

"I guess you're right, so if you want to make that contribution while I'm here, I'll take it now."

Chapter 17

The law firm that handled the purchase of the now destroyed properties was in a small building in Ballard. It's a Seattle neighborhood famous for the Ballard Locks where people came to watch the salmon return from a lifetime in the Pacific Ocean to make their way to the many rivers and streams in Washington where they were hatched. The city, or maybe it was the state, constructed a series of glass enclosed observation areas that were underwater at the locks. During spawning time, there were almost as many tourists as there were salmon at the locks. The city's other claim to fame was the multitude of large, mostly crab fishing boats that spent any time here that they were not in Alaska braving terrible conditions to catch a million pounds of crabs.

I took Aurora Avenue and then cut off to surface streets to reach NW 65th Street. The building I was looking for was on a side street and sat between a fast-food taco stand and a strip mall that had seven places for a variety of businesses. Only four of the spaces were occupied. A beauty, nail and tanning salon anchored the north end. Next to it was an insurance agency. Two of the vacant stores were next to the agency. The only other place that appeared to be in business was a real estate office. The neighborhood was on the brink of either getting gentrified and having all the real estate prices match the rest of the Puget Sound or turning into an area where the homeless pitched tents and cardboard shacks on the sidewalk and were ignored by the city and any social service designed to assist them.

I parked on the street in front of the law office, got out and put enough change in the meter to give me an hour before a meter maid came by and gave me the opportunity to buy stock in the city.

When I entered, the office was adequate for a small firm doing a variety of legal matters and not specializing in any one area like the firms in the downtown Seattle area. Come in here looking for a divorce, a will, a lawsuit against a motorist or a slip-and-fall in the local supermarket and they had someone who handled it. Likely, that same person would take on any number of those cases. I halfway expected to see a flashing neon sign outside advertising Ambulance Chaser Law Firm.

I was greeted by an attractive African American woman who appeared to be in her mid-thirties. She was dressed in a very nice green dress and had a string of pearls around her neck. Her hair was cut short and framed her oval face. A brass plate on her desk indicated her name was Karen. "May I help you?" she asked after looking up and seeing me standing inside.

"Yes, I don't have and appointment, but I'd like to either speak to, or make an appointment with the attorney who completed the corporation documents for the Porel corporation. I called earlier and spoke to Gerda. Is she available?"

"And may I ask what your interest in that corporation is?" She smiled, but I knew she was more than a receptionist. She was also the firm's gatekeeper. No one got by her unless she knew why. Just knowing that made me think there was more to the corporation and perhaps the firm than I knew, but would have to find out.

I handed her my latest, computer-generated business card that indicated I was an Insurance Liaison. If she had never heard the term before, I felt like I could bullshit my way through my qualifications and reason for being there.

"That's an interesting occupation. I don't think I've ever met an Insurance Liaison before. Exactly what do you do...?" She looked at the card. "Mister Maxwell."

"I'd have to take you to lunch to have enough time to tell you what is expected of me and then I'm not sure either one of us would be any wiser." I gave her my best smile.

She handed the card back. "I'm afraid my lunch calendar is filled for the foreseeable future, Mister Maxwell, so give me the abbreviated version and I will know who to refer you to."

We were now in a game of one-upmanship and if I was going to get any information I had to win. "No offense, Karen, but unless the entire firm worked on the articles of incorporation, all you have to do is either see if the attorney of record is available now or give me a day and time to meet with him or her."

It was immediately obvious that very few people walked into this office and challenged Karen. If looks could kill, I knew I'd be dead on the floor. She took her time looking at a computer screen and then punched a number into the phone console on her desk. "I have a Mister Maxwell who is an Insurance Liaison here and he'd like to speak to you. You're free for the next twenty minutes if you want to see him now or I can have him make an appointment." She held the phone and listened, then, "Insurance Liaison. He's interested in the articles of incorporation for the Porel corporation." She listened again while the other person either told her to send me packing or pull the file and send me in. After placing the handset back on the console, she indicated a nearby door and informed me that I could go in, and Mister Weider would see me. As I stood up and passed by her desk, she said, almost under her breath but loud enough for me to get the message, "for twenty minutes."

123

Mister Weider was standing behind his desk when I entered. He was dressed in a brown suit that went out of style in the last century which may have been about the time he passed the bar exam. He had a mass of unruly white hair that looked like it had not been combed or cut in months, although he could have intentionally kept it that way to keep people off guard as to his other habits and professional competence.

He pointed to a chair that was covered in a blue flowered pattern. "Have a seat, Mister Maxwell. Karen said you were interested in the Porel corporation." He took his seat behind the desk. "May I ask your interest?"

"I just want to ask a few questions and clear up some concerns my employer has."

"And what are those concerns and what do I or my firm have to do with them?" One of the things every officer in the military if he, or now she, is destined to go into combat is that a good defense is most often a good offense. When you are surrounded the best course of action may be to attack. It did not take a genius to see Mister Weider was about to be in attack mode.

"Nothing earth-shattering, I assure you. It's just that he had two recent losses to residential fires for vacant properties owned by corporations." I waited to see if I got a response.

"And that affects me, how?"

I opened the briefcase I had beside me on the floor and pulled out a file folder. I kept the top of the briefcase open so he could not see that the folder I opened did not contain anything. "According to his records, you were the attorney of record for the two corporations who owned the properties." Before I could say anything else, he jumped on my comment.

"I represent quite a few corporations engaged in a lot of businesses. I don't inquire as to what that business is or how they conduct it unless I have an ongoing attorney-client relationship with them." He stood up from his chair. "And I resent the implication that I am a party to any improprieties with a client, so if that's all you came for, your time is up."

I continued to sit and looked at the empty folder in my briefcase. "My intent was not to insinuate that you had any part in the loss of the properties. I'm just attempting to make sure all the t's are crossed and the i's dotted." Now it was my turn to stand. "He did say you recommended a property manager for at least one of the corporations. Is that correct?"

The old man pulled himself to his full height and came at me. "It's time for you to leave, Mister Maxwell and I don't expect to see us doing any business in the future." He pointed to the door. I took the hint, closed my briefcase and moved in that direction.

As I put my hand on the door, I turned to face him. "You may not realize it, but you've been very helpful and perhaps our paths will cross again in the future." I'm sure if he'd been thirty years younger, a few inches taller and a few pounds lighter, he would have taken a swing at me as a parting gesture.

One of the great things about the Seattle area is there is a coffee shop within a hundred feet of where you are anyplace in the metro area. Name brand. Off brand. Chain. Mom and Pop. One of a kind or a drive through in a parking lot. The choices were endless. Find one, go inside, purchase a cup of something that took two minutes to order, and you could sit for hours and not be asked to leave or buy anything else. I found a small shop on the street not far from the law office. I pulled into a street side parking space and went inside. My order was simple. A large black coffee. No milk. No sugar or anything else. After having spent the major part of my life drinking Army coffee and then switching to the stuff I made, I could drink anything in a coffee cup. I found a small, round top table with two straight-back chairs and took a seat. I had the briefcase with me because I really did have some information in it that Getz had provided. I opened it and pulled out the name of the management company for the two properties. The company had an address in a part of Seattle known as White Center. It was not far from the coffee shop, so I decided after I finished my drink, I'd pay them a visit.

I found the address and rolled past it to make sure I had it right. My first impression was that if I had found it, and went inside, I'd need a tetanus shot before I got back in my car. It was located on the corner next to a shop that advertised phone cards in several different languages, several different brands of imported beer and a flashing sign that told passers-by the amount of the next lottery jackpot. The clientele coming and going looked like the ones who depended on the possibility of hitting the next jackpot just to bring their financial situation back up to broke. The ground outside the entrance was littered with discarded losing lottery tickets and pull-tabs. I missed having a weapon with me when I left the car and walked to the entrance for the Keller Property Management Company.

The inside of the building was not much better looking than the outside. There were not as many discarded lottery tickets on the floor, but they were replaced by several bottles and cans that had been used as ashtrays. I didn't bother looking for or expecting anyone to be sitting at a desk as a receptionist on the other side of the door when I pushed it open. When I got inside, I was immediately bombarded with the ear-shattering sounds of music that was a combination of heavy metal and country. If I had normal hearing, I would have blown an eardrum, but since I was already partially deaf, I couldn't imagine how loud the noise was to a normal person.

The room was dominated by a large, wood desk that was probably made of oak. It was light colored and at one time probably had a finish on it that was more than cigarette burns and coffee stains. The man seated behind it put down his magazine and looked up when I closed the door behind me.

"Yeah?" His professional greeting to a possible client left much to be desired.

"You do property management?"

He looked at me like I had just asked if he had ever been to the moon. "Wait a minute. Let me check my business cards and the sign on the door and the one on the building and see if that's what we do." I noticed the magazine he placed on the desk beside his lit cigarette featured several couples engaged in consenting activities that left nothing to the imagination.

"Maybe I was wrong, and this is a comedy club?"

"That's a good one." He picked up the cigarette and took a long drag from it and let the smoke escape through his nose. "I'll have to remember that." He put the cigarette out by dropping it into a nearby soda can. "Now that you've seen the dinner show, what is it that you need?"

I decided to change my approach. "Friend of mine said you handle some of his property."

"We got a lot of clients. Who's your friend?"

"It's a lawyer I used to draw up some paperwork on a couple of houses I want to cover with a corporation."

"You must have a lot of property to need a corporation."

"No. I just want to protect myself. I don't want some renter falling down and suing me for a hundred grand because he skinned his knee." I waited for a response.

"Yeah, renters can be a pain in the ass, that's for sure."

"And I need it if something happens to the property. You know. An earthquake or a fire or something."

He was paying me more attention now. "Can't be too careful these days."

"You're right. I got a couple of places I may need someone to manage."

"Well, you're in the right place. That's what we do. They new places or what?"

"I'd say they fall in the category of 'what.' Not some of the best places in the city but I used to make a buck or two renting them out." I took a deep breath. My years as a military police officer and the time I had spent in my own business gave me a good read on people. That combined with pure gut instinct, said I was on the right track. "Hell, I'd probably be better off if they just burned down."

He handed me his card. When I looked at it there was the name of the company and address and a single name for the person I assumed I was speaking with. It said his name was Jones and it made no distinction as to it being his first or last name. "We're a full-service management company. Let's talk."

I took his card, put it in my jacket pocket and moved a stack of newspapers from a chair and took a seat.

Chapter 18

"How many places you got and where are they located?" he asked while firing up another cigarette. He spoke again as he let the smoke flow from his mouth. "We kinda specialize in this side of town. We don't do a lot down in the middle of the city. No condo's or that sort of thing." He laughed. "You know what they say. The only thing white in White Center is the name of the neighborhood."

"That's why I picked this area. I can pick up three or four of the pieces I'm buying now for the price of one condo on Queen Ann."

"And the people who rent the properties we represent ain't exactly the upper crust of Seattle society." He took a long pull from the cigarette and held it in his lungs. As I watched and waited for him to exhale, I noticed he was smoking unfiltered cigarettes. I hadn't seen anyone doing that for years. He finally exhaled and opened a drawer on the right side of the desk.

"Here," he said as he slid a piece of paper across the desk to me. "This is our standard contract. Fill out one for each property and we'll be in business."

I pulled the sheet closer so I could read it. "I notice you conveniently forgot to mention what your fees are for managing and what I get for my money."

He laughed and placed his cigarette on top of another empty soda can. "You noticed, huh? We get the first month's rent and twenty percent of each month after that."

I slid the paper back across the desk to him. "That's a little steep. I think I can beat your price."

He just nodded. "Maybe so, but you can't beat our service. Like I said, we're a full-service company. If you have property in this neighborhood, you can't be too careful. People skip out on the rent, knock holes in the walls, steal everything that ain't locked down and half the stuff that is." He hesitated and looked at me. "And fire is something you really have to be aware of around here."

I didn't want to seem too anxious to find out about the fires, but I thought I was on good ground. "Yeah, I did some research on some of the stats in the neighborhood before I bought my last two houses. Fire does seem to be a real problem."

"It is if you don't have the right management company and the right insurance." He picked up what was left of the still-burning cigarette and dropped it through the opening in the top of the can.

I picked up the management agreement, folded it and put it in my pocket. "I think we'll be able to do some business. I'll get back with you in a day or two," I said as I left.

I checked my watch when I got outside and realized that I was leaving and heading back into the main part of Seattle just as the afternoon rush hour traffic would be hitting the streets. Seattle has always been rated as one of the worst cities to drive in by the people who rate such things, and I completely agree with them. Some even say that if Seattle had been the model city for Interstate highways, none would have been built after they finished the downtown portion of I-5. The only good part about my leaving his office when I did, was that the traffic going all the way across the city would keep me occupied until about the time I needed to be back at my place to meet Anna.

I took the Edmonds exit from I-5 and drove into town. I proceeded to my office and pulled into the

130

parking space that came with the building when I signed the lease. There was just the hint of a little drop in the temperature as I stepped from the 4 Runner and headed for my front door. I wanted to go in and check messages to see if I had anything new from Bill. I knew he was like a pit bull when he had a project. He'd sink his teeth into it and not let go until he was satisfied that he'd done all the damage possible.

I half expected to see George as I put my key in the lock and opened the door. The floor just inside was littered with several letters, a catalog of some sort and a few advertisements that my mail carrier had dropped through the mail slot. By opening the door, I pushed them aside so I could get it. One time the carrier dropped an unusually thick catalog through the slot and when I pushed the door open it became wedged beneath the door and it was a serious struggle to get it open.

Once I was inside, I locked the door behind me as I did not expect, nor did I want to see anyone else that day. I was ready to go home, take a shower and get ready to take Anna to dinner and whatever else the evening held for us. I thought to myself that with a give-a-shit attitude about my business, I'd probably be better off not having one. I pushed that thought aside and checked my computer to see if Bill had left a message or anything. When I first started working for him, or more specifically, when he conned me into doing it, he set up a secure communications network in my office. I had a computer and phone line that I was sure was a part of a larger network that was completely off the books in some government accounting office.

No lights were blinking and there was no indication of his having contacted me, so I turned around and headed home for my shower and my evening with Anna. The drive from the office to my place took less than ten minutes, so I knew I had plenty of time to get ready even though she did not mention a specific time.

I was giving my shoes a quick shine when I heard a car door slam outside on the street. I got up and looked out the window overlooking the row of parking spots in front of my place and saw a gold Jaguar sitting there. I watched Anna as she walked toward my front door. I didn't know where she had been or what she had been doing in Seattle all day, but she looked like she had just stepped from a dress shop and beauty salon. She wore a pair of dark blue pants and a white blouse. I couldn't tell from looking at it, but I knew instantly that it was made of silk. She once mentioned to me that if she could get away with it, she would only wear silk blouses with nothing underneath them as she liked the feel of the material on her bare skin. I immediately offered to let her do just that any time we were together. When she asked if that offer extended to when we were in public, I had to backpedal. Sharing her was not on my agenda.

I put my shoes on the floor and walked to the front door. I opened it and awaited her arrival. She stepped up on the short rise leading to the front door and reached her hand out. I took it in mine and held it as she entered. As soon as she was inside, I closed the door and took her in my arms. The kiss was long and serious and was returned in kind. When we broke the kiss, she lay her head on my shoulder and snuggled in while I continued to hold her.

"If that was an appetizer, I can't wait for the main course."

"Patience, my dear, patience," she whispered in my ear.

She pulled away and looked down at my feet where I was only wearing black socks. "Are you dressing or undressing starting with your shoes?"

"I'm completely flexible on that," I said as I stepped back a few inches. "I'll let you decide which it is.

"Put them on and take me to dinner and I may let you take them off later," she teased.

"Just my shoes?"

"Yours and mine and maybe…" She gave me a quick kiss on the tip of my nose, "And maybe some other excess items of clothing."

We took my 4 Runner, leaving her Jag still parked on the street. When I first met Anna and we became more than just friends, she was reluctant to have her car anyplace close to where I lived or my office, in case someone she knew saw it, and asked questions she did not want to answer. Since she and her husband now had a legal separation, she was less hesitant about being seen in public with me. We had recently gone to a jazz club in Seattle and during a break in the show, a couple she knew from Whidbey Island came by our table. It was just prior to her legal separation, so for all intent and practical purposes she was still married, and the other couple knew both her and her husband.

The woman, whom Anna introduced to me as Julia and her husband Charles, gave me as cold a look as I have ever had.

"Julia, this is Max. He's a private investigator who's doing some work for me." Julia's somewhat reluctant response to that was to extend her hand.

"A private investigator? I hope Anna is not in any kind of trouble." Her smile was colder than her handshake.

"If she was, you know I couldn't tell you about it. Client confidentialities, you know." Before she could ask any more questions, and I'm certain she had a million, Charles took her hand.

"Let's leave Anna and her…" he searched for a word to describe me, "Her investigator in private." He chuckled at his play on words. and led Julia to the bar.

Anna watched them disappear in the dark club. "I'll bet she's on her cell phone calling everyone she knows on the island before she gets a drink in hand."

"Will that be a problem?" I asked.

"Oh, I'm sure by the time she gets through telling it, we were having sex on the table at intermission." Anna gave a hearty laugh at the situation. "Even in the small town in Georgia where I grew up, we had the neighborhood gossip. She was better than a twenty-four-hour news station at keeping up with what was happening or what she thought was happening." She reached across the table and took my hand in hers. "I'm a big girl. I knew what I was doing when we became more than diving buddies and I have no regrets. Now, go get us a drink before the music starts again."

I replayed the day Anna and I met as I waited in line for our drinks. I needed a SCUBA diving partner and the owner of the local dive shop suggested Anna who was also looking for a partner for a local dive. We made the first dive with no problems except for my realizing just how attractive Anna was. One the second dive, she came back to my office to change and during the process she very deliberately and seductively dropped the towel she had draped around her. We made love in the upper part of my office, and I haven't been the same since.

I got our drinks: a gin and tonic for me and a champagne for Anna and as I was taking them back to our table, I saw Julia several tables over from ours and just as Anna had predicted, she had a cell phone glued to her ear.

Anna never mentioned Julia or the incident again, so I don't know what, if any fallout there was for her.

Fortunately, we didn't have to worry about being seen together in public anymore. For that reason, I chose a well-known restaurant on the waterfront in Everette, a community north of Edmonds. Several years ago, the US Navy moved a major operation to

134

the city and as a result, many businesses followed suit. At least three high-end restaurants now dotted the waterfront. Like most eating establishments in the area, except for fast-food hamburger and taco stands, the main fare of two of the three was seafood. The exception had an extensive menu or old-fashioned red meat in the form of steaks. I'm not much of a fish guy, so Anna frequently indulged me, and we ripped into a filet.

The restaurant had a small room for private parties, and it was filled with navy officers in dress uniforms. After watching for a minute, I determined it was a promotion party for one of the lieutenants who was about to become a lieutenant commander. I had several promotion parties and I even remember one or two of them.

Anna noticed a banner congratulating the officer. "Did you ever have a party like that?"

"Army promotion parties tend to get a little rowdy. I don't think I ever attended one where the general public could witness what went on. Mine were all in the officer's club where I was stationed."

"You? Rowdy?" She smiled and took a long drink from her flute of champagne.

"Hard to believe, I know but in my younger days after a few too many adult beverages I did let my hair down." Before I could tell her any more bullshit stories, our server brought two filets. After taking away our salads, he placed the meat on metal plates that had been heated and slid one in front of me.

"Sir, would you please cut into the filet and make certain it is prepared to your satisfaction."

I cut into it and assured him it was perfect. He placed another one in front of Anna and watched as she did the same. We ate in silence for the first ten minutes. Anna was the first to speak. "So, what are you working on now? We haven't heard from Bill Hart in a few weeks. Is he giving you time to practice your chosen profession?" She looked up. "Whatever that is."

"As a matter of fact, I do have an actual client and I'm doing some work for him." I hesitated a second too long before saying anything else.

"And Bill?"

I downed the remainder of my drink. "What do you know about tulips?" I asked.

"I know they're flowers, and they have an annual Tulip Festival up in the Skagit Valley, but I can't imagine either one of you having an interest in tulips, so why did you ask?"

"What makes you think that question has anything to do with either of us?"

She placed her fork on the side of her platter and stared at me. The first time she did that, I noticed her eyes had the softest shade of brown that turned to dark chocolate as she probed the depth of my mind.

"Guilty as charged, your honor. He's got something he wants me to check out in the death of a professor from the Netherlands who was found dead in one of the fields up north."

"Is that the paying client you mentioned?" She continued to probe.

"No, I do have a real client. He's hired me to investigate what may be an insurance scam. He owns an insurance agency and two of the properties he insured recently burned."

"Bad luck?"

"Maybe, but more likely a way to collect an insurance policy on a property that is in a bad neighborhood and would not return a profit if it was flipped and rented."

"Insurance fires are a way of life if you have rental or commercial property. There are management companies who specialize in having an arsonist on their call list."

"You're kidding." I said. I never had any rental or commercial property, so this was a new area for me.

"Think about it. If it's residential and it costs too much to repair it after a renter moves our and take everything with them to include the copper wiring in the walls, it's cheaper to burn it down and collect the insurance. For commercial, if a business is not making money and the owner can no longer afford to pay the rent and can't get out of the lease, they simply burn the place down." She took a drink and looked at me like she was surprised that I wasn't aware of this part of doing business.

"I think we need to discuss this is depth."

"Let's do it after we have dessert…at your place."

Chapter 19

The only dream I had that night was snuggled up next to me. After leaving the restaurant, we pulled into the parking lot next to the Edmonds waterfront. The lot serviced the several restaurants situated on the edge of the water and a couple of shops selling things geared to the tourist trade. There was a long pier reaching out into the water that was anchored by the walkway that ran along behind the businesses.

The lot was also where people parked to take advantage of a stroll along the waterfront or for those who did a dive into the underwater park the city maintained.

I got out and opened the door for Anna to step out into the now-chilly night air. Like all residents of the area, she always had a light jacket and a coat available to put on, depending on the time of day and the temperature. The night air called for a coat which I helped her slip into. Once she was dressed to ward off the night chill, I took her hand in mine and we walked along the edge of the waterfront.

We were on the high ground above the waterline. The city had constructed a seawall of large timbers like railroad ties that extended four or five feet above the rocky beach below us. The beach, if one stretched the meaning of the word, was rock strewn and did not resemble a sandy beach anyplace in the world that I had ever visited. It was low tide, and we took a set of steps cut into the seawall and walked along the beach

"Why Edmonds?" she asked as we watched the ferry pull slowly away from the dock.

"What do you mean?"

She looked at me. "You never told me why you settled in Edmonds. I know you spent some time here when you were in the Army, but it was never a real home, was it?"

That was a question I had asked myself on occasion and the best answer I ever came up with was that I really didn't have any other place in mind. My oldest daughter had been accepted at Gonzaga in Spokane, but she was living in a dorm, so it didn't matter where we lived. My youngest was in her sophomore year in high school and didn't want to start over at a new school, so we just planted the flag and bought a house in the little seaside town north of Seattle.

"It just seemed like the thing to do at the time. I really didn't think it would be my last move, but it seems it has turned out to be just that," I said as I reached down and picked up several stones.

"I'm glad, for many reasons, that you're here," Anna said as she leaned to the side and rested her head on my shoulder. "I hope you stay for a long time."

Every time she said something like that my head, and if I really admitted it, my heart, was filled with emotions that I hadn't felt in more years than I cared to remember. I slipped my arm around her and pulled her to me and just held her. "I don't think you have anything to worry about as far as my leaving. This is only the second state I have ever registered to vote in or held a state driver's license, so I don't want to take a driver's license test someplace else."

She broke away and stepped back. "Well, at least you're being practical about it." I saw her smile in the dim light that came from the streetlights that lined the waterfront.

I took one of the stones I had picked up and skimmed it across the smooth surface of the water. "Three skips. Not bad," she said as she watched the stone skip across the water then disappear. "Hand me one." I gave her a stone and she managed to get three skips from hers as well. "I used to do that on a farm pond my grandfather had in Georgia. The most I ever got was five."

Only one small stone remained in my hand, and I was about to sail it out across the Sound when I thought better. "Give me your hand," I reached out for Anna. "This may sound silly, but I want you to have this," I said as I placed the rock in her hand. "Let this be a reminder that what we have is stone cold, and rock solid."

After awaking the next morning, I slipped from the bed and went into the kitchen to prepare coffee for us. I don't know if it was the aroma of fresh coffee or the sounds I made as I banged around in my kitchen that awakened Anna, but I was reaching for two coffee mugs when I felt her arm wrap around me. I was only wearing boxer shorts, so when she leaned in close, I felt her bare skin against mine. "I'm only going to give you a year or two to stop doing that," I said as I pressed backward into her.

"I'll put that on my calendar, so I don't forget."

I pulled the mugs out of the cabinet, filled both and placed them on the table that served as both a place to eat and one to do all manners of other things like serve as a home office, a flat place to fix anything that I could repair and on occasion a poker table.

"Is there a dress code? If there is, I may not be allowed in," Anna remarked as she took a seat, still in the nude.

"Just be careful not to spill the coffee. It's hot and I'd hate it if you burned anything."

"If I did, would you kiss it and make it better?"

We finished the coffee without incident, but later I practiced kissing all the places she could have burned had she spilled hers.

"Will I see you tonight?" I asked as I opened the car door for her to get into her Jag.

"I think I need a night off. I've got some things I need to do, and I must be home to do them." She leaned up and gave me a kiss. "But you can call me and talk dirty over the phone if you want to." I heard her gentle laugh as she put the key into the ignition and started the car.

Reluctantly, I watched her drive away as I stood beside the street where she had parked. Once she was out of sight, I got in my 4 Runner and drove to my office. I wanted to talk to Getz and let him know what I had found out the previous day.

There was a light mist of rain falling. It was not enough to get a person wet, or to even require the windshield wipers on the car to be working a steady arch. I pulled the handle on the wipers and let them make one pass on the windshield as I got in and headed for the office. I only had to do it once again before I pulled into my parking space. They say Seattle sells more sunglasses and umbrellas than any other city in the country. People buy sunglasses on the rare days when they really need them, and then lose or break them prior to the next time. The same for umbrellas, except it's the tourists who buy them after coming to the city not realizing that it should have been the first thing they packed prior to the trip.

There were several pieces of mail on the floor beneath the mail slot in my door when I opened it. Generally, the only mail I got at the office was a few utility bills and an over-abundance of form letters inquiring about the extended warranty on my vehicle or wanting me to take out a policy to ensure that if the sewer line broke between my house and the street I would be covered. The mail I held in my hand all fell into that category, so I didn't even bother to open any of it as I tossed it into a trash can beneath my coffee maker.

I didn't plan to be in the office long, so I didn't fire up the machine as I usually did when I got to the office. After two cups with Anna earlier in the morning, I felt I had already exceeded my recommended daily allowance of caffeine, at least until I picked up a cup at a coffee shop sometime during the day ahead of me.

There were no lights blinking on my out-of-date answering machine or anything new on the secure computer that Bill Hart had provided me. The answering machine was a relic of times past and most of my messages came to my cell phone, but for reasons I'm not even sure of myself, I kept it sitting on my desk and attached to my land line.

After taking a seat at my desk, I dialed the number I had for Getz. He answered on the third ring.

"The Getz Agency. How may I assist you?"

This was the first time I had called him, and I didn't expect him to be that formal when he answered. "Max here. I've got some information I think you need to know. You want it over the phone, in writing or you want to do it eyeball-to-eyeball?" Over the time I had been in business, I found that some people prefer to have all my reports to them, no matter what I was working on, in writing. Some just wanted the highpoints over the phone and others wanted to talk it out in person.

"Let's meet for lunch at the same place we did the last time I came to your office. I really liked their clam chowder. One-thirty work for you?"

It was a little after ten, so I only had three hours to kill. "I'll meet you there." I wanted to have my vehicle there in case I wanted to leave before he did. Even though he technically, was my employer, I didn't want to spend any more time with him than was necessary.

"Sounds like a plan. I'll see you there," he said just as I heard the line make the distinctive sound of another call coming in. "Gotta run. Another call is waiting."

After I ended the call with him, I sat for a minute as I contemplated what to do to fill the three hours. I glanced up, looked outside my office through the glass door in the front, and saw that the light mist had transitioned to a light, but steady rain. I watched several cars pass in front of the office and thought, "what the hell," so I got up and placed coffee in the upper portion of my coffee maker and filled a pot with water to pour into it.

While I waited for the coffee to brew, I picked up a two-day old Seattle newspaper that had a crossword that I had not worked on. I folded the paper and placed it in the middle of my desk, pulled out a pen and looked at the first clue. It was a five-letter word meaning "garbage." The word trash worked very nicely, and I was moving on to the next clue when my cell phone played the ring tone song I had selected for Bill. As soon as I heard Jimmy Buffet, I forgot about the crossword puzzle.

"You didn't get wet coming to work this morning, did you?"

Sometimes I think Bill has my office wired for sound and had cameras hidden discreetly around the inside and outside on the street. "What are you talking about? It's a bright, sunshiny day here in the beautiful Pacific Northwest. As a matter of fact, I'm wearing shorts and a Hawaiian shirt and after I hang up on you, I'm going to the store to get some sunscreen."

"And I've got a really tall monument here in Washington that I can sell you."

I looked outside and a hard rain was now falling. "Now that we've gotten the bullshit out of the way, what's the occasion for this call?" I asked as I got up from my desk and poured myself yet another cup of freshly brewed coffee.

"We got a little more information on the dead tulip guy that I thought you might find interesting."

143

"The dead tulip guy? Don't you even know his name yet?" I asked as I took my first drink.

"Of course, I do, but right now he's just a man from the Netherlands who was found dead in a field of tulips. After we finish this conversation and you get to work, he'll have a name and a background."

I wondered if the information I had gotten from the coroner and the sheriff where he was found was incorrect. With Bill's first mention of the request for him and by extension, me, to investigate it came from both the State Department and the Department of Agriculture, it could be any number of things, none of them very good.

Chapter 20

"Seems our dead tulip guy is somewhat of a star when it comes to tulips in the Netherlands. He's one of the country's best and maybe one of the world's most prominent experts on the care and feeding of them." I heard a buzzing sound as another, probably even more secure phone came to life in Bill's office. "Hang on a minute. I've got to take this call." Without waiting for me to respond, he placed me on hold.

I continued to work on the crossword puzzle until I heard his voice on my phone again. "That was a very timely call. Just got more information on our guy."

"The dead tulip guy?" I couldn't resist.

"Now who's making light of the recently deceased?"

I folded the newspaper and set it aside. I wanted to get all the information Bill had since I was going to be doing something regarding the professor, but I still didn't know what. "Cut to the chase. Tell me what's so important about this man."

"As I was saying, he's probably the best expert in the world on tulips and the government doesn't want to lose him. According to the information I've gotten so far, there is a high-level government office whose sole purpose is the proliferation and protection of the tulips in the country. Seems they declared war over them once. But that's another box of Pandora's we don't need to open."

I could see the rain falling even harder than it was when I arrived and the sky was getting darker, so I knew it would be a day without sunshine...once again. "If we're not going to open that box, which one will we open?"

"Do you want to start with State or Agriculture?"

When he mentioned those two names, he was referring to the United States Department of Agriculture and Department of State and that meant the professor was not just your run of the mill dead guy in the tulips. "I can see where Agriculture might have an interest in him, but State? Don't you find that a little strange?"

"I did until I got the call a few minutes ago. It looks like the professor was on the verge of duplicating a color and type of tulip that hasn't been seen in several hundred years. For them, it like discovering the Holy Grail. They know it existed but then it disappeared, and the only thing left is some documentation and a few paintings."

"And State's involvement is?" I was even more curious now.

"They have some sort of tax on tulips exported and if this thing he's working on is real, they stand to make a bundle on it, but..."

I didn't let him finish. "If someone or some other country gets it, they make the money."

"Welcome to the world of agriculture, the likes of which neither of us ever knew existed."

I listened to Bill for almost an hour as he relayed what he had been told and the mission he had been given and was now passing down to me. By the time we ended the conversation, I had two pages of scribbled notes I took while I talked and listened to him. I did not mention the few items I had been given that were taken from the professor's pockets and turned over to the sheriff's department and then given to me. One of the things Bill and I tried to instill in our men when we were on active duty, was that a smart man is a quiet man. I hoped my being quiet was also a smart move since I was the one on the ground looking into the man's death. Half-way through the call we were both no longer referring to him as the dead guy in the tulips. We were using his name and title. He was now Professor Jacob Dirksen. He was just as dead and it was still under mysterious circumstances, but at least he now had a name.

"The last call I got from one of my contacts at State asked if we could get back to them in a week."

"A week?"

"That's what they wanted but that's not what they're going to get. I got them to extend the deadline for two weeks, so you have three weeks to find out all you can about him and why he was found dead in a field of tulips in Washington."

"Gee, thanks. Would they like me to come up with a formula for cold fusion while I'm at it?"

"No, but they did mention that the tulip that he was trying to replicate was called the Semper Augustus and it's special color of blue."

"And maybe that's why he was found in a field of blue tulips?"

"I don't think they have information at that level. They're biggest concern is that he was found in a tulip field in one of the largest tulip-growing areas outside the Netherlands. I think that alone will give you enough to start working on this one."

I hated to admit it, but I knew he was right. There was a definite connection there and all I had to do was find it and find out why it connected and do it in three weeks. "Okay, I've got a meeting in an hour, but as soon as I get out, I'll start doing some legwork. In the meantime, if you get any more calls from government agencies, hang up on them. I don't want anybody who is known only by initials to be involved as well." I had to smile since I knew most of Bills contacts and his assignments came from places like CIA, FBI, DNI, NSA and a few others that he probably didn't even know their initials.

"I'll try to keep it as clean and low-profile as I can, but with the level of interest, I can't make any promises to you.

*   *   *

I had an hour to kill, so I decided to drive down to the waterfront. The restaurant where I was to meet Getz was there and so was the dive shop I occasionally frequented. That was where I was first introduced to Anna. When an old friend was reported to be a drowning victim in the Edmonds Underwater Park, I didn't believe it. He and I had been dive buddies for some time, and I knew him to be a highly qualified and competent diver. I wanted to see where he was supposed to have drowned but I didn't have a dive partner that day. The best way to get dead as a SCUBA diver is to dive alone. I asked the owner of the dive shop to recommend someone, and he gave me Anna's number. We did a dive that day and one other one before we became more than dive buddies.

I had my own tanks and other necessary gear and was not really in the market for anything else, but with almost an hour to kill, the dive shop was as good a place as any to do it. The place was the hang-out for local divers heading for the San Juan Islands and tourists who want to dive the Water Park. The owner was showing a young couple a map of the park and telling them what to expect when they made the dive. The Park is a series of grids laid out almost like streets. Large pieces of concrete dot the area. It was on a piece of rebar where my friend was handcuffed and allowed to drown. His dive buddy was the first suspect, but he proved to be innocent, and the real killer was a local police officer.

I looked at the newest equipment and considered purchasing a new knife, but I held out and passed on buying it. After spending half the time in the shop, I drove the short distance to the restaurant to meet Getz.

One lingering habit from my military days is to never be late. I was brainwashed to believe it was better to be two hours early for a meeting than to be two minutes late. Getz seemed to like this restaurant better than either of the other three along the Edmonds waterfront. The last time we met here he mentioned that he and another client had tried one of the others and both agreed that this one was the best.

I parked and got out of my vehicle and walked to the entrance at ground level that served the second floor where the restaurant was located. They had a long series of walkways both with steps and a ramp for those who could not navigate steps and an elevator. Once a guest used the elevator they never took it again, unless it was absolutely necessary. The elevator's back door opened to a food storage area where fresh fish were cleaned and then moved upstairs by the same elevator. If the guest rode up with the lingering smell of fish, they either didn't go inside or they ordered a steak when they dined.

I took the steps and once I was inside the hostess, a woman who was dressed in a long black skirt and a white blouse, picked up two menus after asking me if I was alone. "I can seat you at one of our tables near the window if you'd like," she said as we weaved our way between tables enroute to the window seat she indicated.

At the table, I took a seat facing the door. There was no back wall, but I was positioned so that I could see anyone entering. As I pulled out the chair and she placed a menu on the table in front of my seat and another across from it, she asked if the other guest would be my wife. She wore a name tag indicating her name was Fran, which could have been real, or one she used at the restaurant. Fran was probably in her early forties and had held together quite nicely. When she placed the menus, she lay her left hand flat on the large folder to make sure I saw that she did not wear a wedding ring, in case I was interested. I felt flattered, as it was a clear indication that she was either trying to get a larger tip or she was showing some interest in my being more than a lunch-time acquaintance.

"No, unfortunately, it's a guy and not a very good looking one, if you ask me. I hardly think he meet your standards." I smiled as it said it.

"I do have high standards," she said as she gave me a wink and walked away. Things like this never happened to me before I met Anna.

A male waiter came and poured two glasses of water and asked if I wanted anything stronger to drink. I contemplated a double gin and tonic just so I could put up with Getz, but decided against it. As I thought about it, I wondered why I felt such hostilities against the man. He had never done anything bad or out of line with or to me and our relationship had been strictly professional in the past, and I didn't think this one would be anything else. I was on the verge of convincing myself to like him, when Fran approached the table with Getz in tow.

"I think your friend is a very good-looking man, contrary to what you said," she said and she stood beside the table while Getz took a seat.

"Am I missing something here?" he asked as he unfolded his napkin.

"Not really. I just told her I was waiting for someone, and he looked like he just escaped from a circus side show." Fran and I both laughed at his confusion.

"It wasn't that bad, I assure you." She gave him a very sexy smile. "If either of you gentlemen need anything, just let me know."

Getz held up his hand to catch the attention of our waiter. "What the hell was that all about? I don't know about you, but I'm going to have a drink with lunch. I've had a hell of a day, so far."

"Yes, sir, can I start you with a drink?" The waiter stood by the table.

"Scotch, water back for me," Getz said and then looked at me. "You gonna have one or do I have to drink alone?"

I decided one gin and tonic would get me through lunch, so I ordered one just to be on the safe side. After I gave my order to the waiter and he departed, I looked at Getz. "Rough day?"

"Like you wouldn't believe. One of my clients was in a car accident. Clearly his fault and we did not contest that, but the injured party wants a half million dollars for pain and suffering." The waiter placed the drinks on the table and waited for us to order. "Clam chowder and a Caesar salad for me."

"Sounds good. Give me the same." I waited for him to leave. "Was the person hurt enough to justify that kind of money?"

"Fuck, no. The biggest pain is the pain she's causing in my ass. She's got an ambulance chaser lawyer who has a reputation of taking claims to the day of trial and then settling on the courthouse steps on the way in." He took half of his drink in one long gulp. "I'm willing to pay and I will, but not that much and it's gonna cost her a ton to have this guy ride the case for at least a year." He finished his drink and motioned for the waiter to bring another. "I need some good news from you. What have you found out?"

Between his second drink, my first one and our chowder and salad, I explained my visit to the property management company his client used and what I found out at the lawyer's office.

"So, they're both using the same law firm and the same property management company? That alone is enough for me to hold up the claim on any others that use the same people." He pulled a piece of bread from the basket sitting in the middle of the table, buttered it and took a bite. "Anything else?"

"I have an idea after talking to the management company, but it may get a little complicated.

"I'm all ears."

Chapter 21

It took two refills of our coffee while Getz lingered over a piece of key lime pie for me to explain what I had found out and the plan that I had come up with. By the time I finished, he sat back and covered his mouth with his white cloth napkin to suppress a belch. "You really think that'll work?"

"Unless you've got a better idea, I think it's a least a place to start. If they take the bait you'll see if they are running a scam on you or if your fears were unfounded."

He fumbled around and pulled his wallet from his back pocket. "I'll put this on my card, since you'd charge me for expenses anyway." He slid a gold credit card from a compartment in his well-worn leather wallet and placed it on the edge of the table. The waiter who had been hovering in the background waiting for us to leave rushed to the table and grabbed it.

"I'll be right back with your check, sir," he said as he picked up the card.

"Just bring us the bill. I don't think you're going to try to stiff us by padding the charges." If Getz was hoping the waiter took his comment as joke, he was sorely disappointed.

By the time I left the restaurant, I realized I had almost blown a whole day and the only thing I had accomplished was a long lunch meeting with Getz and the opportunity to give him a plan of action that may or may not work. I couldn't think of anything else to do, so I drove the short distance to my office so I could do nothing there.

I saw George across the street standing in front of the Mexican restaurant when I pulled into my parking space. He saw me as well, so I expected him to allow me to get in the office and then I would see my front door open, and he'd come in. Once when he was in the office, Mayor Valentino came in as well. George said a quick hello and left the two of us alone.

"Why do you put up with someone like that? Everyone in town knows that he just roams around and stands outside some of the businesses until they let him do some work for them. It's more out of pity than a need for labor, I think."

It was at that time that I decided I liked George much better than the mayor.

As I had expected, George was only a minute or two behind me. Ever the cautious or perhaps the courteous one, he slowly entered and looked around to see if there was anyone else in the office prior to his coming completely inside. "Afternoon, Colonel. You alone?"

"Just you and me and a bunch of ghosts that we don't want to talk about, George. Come on in." I motioned for him to take his usual seat on my sofa. "You had your quota of coffee for the day, or can you use another cup?"

"I always got room for one more." He hesitated taking a seat knowing I would either offer a cup if I had some made or give him money to purchase two cups from a nearby latte stand.

I handed him a ten-dollar bill. "I'll buy. You fly," indicating if I paid he had to go get the coffee.

"Be right back."

Someday George will prove me wrong and after paying for the coffee, he's going to come back in the office and give me my change. I didn't expect it to happen in my lifetime and I was not disappointed when he returned and I realized the two cups of plain, middle of the road, nothing special coffee had just cost me five dollars a cup.

"I was down in Seattle yesterday and I seen your lady friend's car parked on Capital Hill." He hesitated as he took a drink and waited for a response from me.

"Yeah, I knew she was down there, but I wasn't sure what part of the city she was visiting." If he was waiting for a more serious response, I'm sure I disappointed him. "Were you working down there?"

"No. I went there to see an old Army buddy. He owns a laundry and dry-cleaning place." As he often did, George slipped away into his own thoughts for a moment. "He learned it in the Army at Fort Benning and worked there when he came back to Seattle after we was in the Nam. He was able to buy the place when the owner died, and his widow didn't want to run it no more. He calls me sometime when he needs some help. He's got a bunch of big ol' washing machines in the back of the building. If they all ain't working, he gets behind. That's when he calls me."

For almost the first time since I first met George, he spoke more than a few words and I learned something about his life.

"He's lucky to have a friend he can call on when he needs help."

George stood. "If we can't help a friend, we ain't much of a friend," he said as he turned and walked out.

I sat, just staring out the front window at the gathering evening for a few minutes after he left. A light fog was rolling in from the Sound and making its way across the city. When a weather system came in of the Sound, it seemed to follow the ferry into town then, after passing over the ferry dock, made its way up the main street to the center of town. The weather for the day could not make up its mind about being rainy or just cloudy and misty. It had changed several times during the day, and it now seemed to have

155

decided that a light, but steady drizzle mixed with the fog was the way to go.

With nothing else to do, I pulled out the items I had been given that were taken from the professor when the sheriff found the body. I placed them one-by-one on my desk and examined each to see if I could come up with anything I had missed the first time I examined them. The only things that caught my eye again was the key that fit something and the card for the taxi service with the phone number on the back. The number was a good place to start, so I punched the number in my cell phone and listened as it buzzed on the other end. It only took three rings for it to be answered, not by a person but by a recorded man's voice who called himself Patrick. I listened as Patrick explained he was not available at the minute but for me to leave my name and number and where I wanted to go and what time I needed to be there, and he'd get back to me as soon as he could.

The card was for a taxi service with a Seattle address. Since Patrick's name was on the card and his message offered to pick me up, I had to assume he was a driver and Professor Dirksen had used him. I thought for a minute and then dialed his number again. I told him I needed to be picked up at a coffee shop near the Pike Place Market. I gave him a time that was after the evening rush and that gave me time to grab some dinner if I was in the mood before I met him. I left my number and told him to call back and confirm when he got my message.

I was down to the bottom of the cup of coffee that George had bought for me and brought to the office when my cell phone buzzed. I had it lying on my desk and the vibration sounded like a sick woodpecker as it jiggled on the wooden furniture.

"Hello?"

"Hello, this is Patrick. You wanted a ride tonight?" The voice had a rough edge to it. Patrick sounded like he had a heavy smoking habit.

"Yes. I need to meet you at seven thirty. Can you do that?" I looked at my watch and saw I had less than two hours. It could take me that much time just to drive to the meeting and find a place to park.

"Not a problem. Where do you want to go?"

"I don't have the address right now, so I'll have to give it to you when you pick me up." I hesitated, then added. "I'll need you to wait for me, so it may take up to an hour. Do you have a rate for that?" Since I was spending Bill's or probably the Netherland's government money, I really didn't care as long as I could get some information from him.

"I can run the meter or make it a flat fifty dollars an hour. It's up to you."

"Let's go with the flat rate." I knew anything not on the meter would go directly in Patrick's pocket and he may be a little more inclined to share information on the professor if he had any.

"Great. Have you and I done business in the past?" There were some serious street noises in the background, so I knew he was on the road.

"No. A friend recommended you."

"I'll just pull up in front of the coffee shop and you can come out. I'll have to double park and they get a little testy about that around that time of night, so keep your eyes peeled for me. I'm never late. I'm sure your friend told you that, too."

"I'll see you there." I ended the call and placed my cell phone back on the desk. Once again, I found myself with time to kill and nothing to do, so I called Anna.

I picked up my cell phone and dialed her cell. If she was working from home, she may not want her housekeeper to know she was taking a break just to talk to me. Since meeting Anna, we had gone from SCUBA diving buddies to a relationship that I could not even give a name. We were together almost daily in one way or another. I was divorced and she was now legally separated. I knew she probably would

157

never be divorced as her husband had made it clear to her that since he had made a small fortune since they married and there was no pre-nuptial agreement, for financial reasons, he would never divorce her. Even prior to their separation, we had become serious lovers. If I was honest with myself, I'd admit to both her and me that I did love her, but under the circumstances, it didn't seem like something I needed to say.

When I called, she always answered with only one word.

"Hi."

That was all it took for me to feel like a teenager sometimes. "Say it again," I said.

"Say what?"

"What you say when you answer the phone."

"You mean hi?"

"Okay, now I'm going to roll over and smoke a cigarette," I teased.

"If you're in bed, just stay there and maybe I'll consider joining you."

If I hadn't already made an appointment to meet Patrick, I might have taken her up on the offer, if it was a real one. "As much as I'd like to see you tonight, I have a meeting downtown with a taxi driver who it appears Professor Dirksen used when he was in the city. I want to find out where he was staying and where the driver took him. I don't have much else to go on to start."

Anna had joined me on several missions that I got from Bill Hart, so she was aware of the basics of this one as well. "How do you know that's the driver he used?"

I held the card in my hand and turned it over and over. "He had a business card from the taxi company with a name written on the back on him when the sheriff went through his pockets. I got it when the evidence clerk gave me his personal belongings, so I called the number and it's a driver for the company."

158

Outside the rain was getting serious. I saw two people who were sharing a large umbrella as they ran from their car to the Mexican restaurant across the street from me. Just as they reached the entrance for the restaurant, a gust of wind caught the umbrella and flipped in inside out. While the man wrestled with it trying to get it back the right way so he could fold it, the woman hurried inside and watched from the open door in obvious amusement.

"Are you meeting him tonight?"

"At seven thirty near the Pike Place Market."

"Did you tell him you're not looking for anything except information? If you didn't, you may have to take a tour of the city on a rainy night."

"We agreed to pay a flat rate and keep it off the meter, so I don't think he'll mind driving."

"If it's not too late, call me when you get back."

"What do you consider too late?"

"This time tomorrow," she teased. "Just call."

I agreed, got up from my desk and left the office. I had a light jacket that was perfect for the rain and the accompanying chill of the evening. I put it on as I stood outside my door and checked the street prior to heading for my 4 Runner. I left my parking space and headed for the Interstate. It was a little after six, so most of the traffic in a normal city would be heading out of the downtown area as the workers made their way to the suburbs. Not so for Seattle. No matter what time of day or night, drivers expected to see slow and stopped traffic for no real reason. A flat tire with the car on the side of the road, will cause a mile-long backlog as everyone has to slow to take a look as if they had never seen a flat tire before. A fender-bender is a sure way to be an hour late for anything.

The drive to the Pike Place Market took all the allocated time I had planned. By the time I found a place to park in one of the relatively close-by parking lots and walked to the coffee shop, it was time to meet Patrick.

I was cutting it closer than I like for meeting him. The coffee shop was half-filled with people who were either trying to get out of the rain if they were tourists or locals getting their last caffein fix prior to heading home. The line was short so I waited my turn and ordered a regular coffee just so I'd have an excuse to take a seat near the window and wait for a taxi to roll up and double park.

The wait was less than five minutes. I dropped my half empty coffee cup in the trash on the way out and looked at my watch. Patrick was one minute early. 7

Chapter 22

It didn't take rocket surgery to figure out that the death of Professor Dirksen and the interest shown in it by two US cabinet agencies was more than just a tourist who happened to fall down one night in a tulip field and crack his skull enough to die. As soon as Bill called me and gave me the limited background on the situation it as if a large neon sign was flashing over the field saying: CAUTION! You may be about to get in over your head.

I had very little to go on, but I had been involved in enough serious investigations to know that the best way to start one is at the beginning with the information available. This one started in the tulip field and all the information I had was a business card with Patrick's name on it and a key that probably fit something, but I didn't have a clue what or where. I was counting on Patrick to fill in some of the blanks when I slipped though the rain and got into the rear seat of his taxi.

The warmth of the taxi felt good even though I was only in the rain for a few seconds. I settled into the relatively new four-door sedan and watched as Patrick turned his head to look at me. "Where to, boss?"

I got an immediate impression of the man from those few words. I could see he was dressed in a flannel shirt that was popular when I was a kid in elementary school and had regained its status with the residents of the Pacific Northwest, both male and female. It was supposed to give the wearer a rugged, maybe even that of a lumberjack or something equally woodsy, look and on Patrick it worked. His voice in person was as harsh as it was on the phone. There was the faint odor of cigarette smoke still lingering in the taxi that was probably the last puff taken before he had to get back in to answer a call for a pick-up. He placed his right arm on the top of the bench seat where he sat as he turned. I noticed he wore a watch on his right wrist and not on the left.

"Just get us out of the downtown area for right now." I said as I pointed to the front of the taxi.

"Can do." Patrick put the taxi in gear and pulled away from the curb amid the sound of at least two angry drivers honking their car horns. "You got any place in mind or do you just want to ride around a get a good look at the city?" Before I could answer, he continued. "If you're not from around here, this is sorta the typical weather for this time of year. We get a bad rap for having so much rain, but I read that Houston, Texas has more per year than we do."

It was obvious that Patrick knew his way around the city streets and did not care for those who were not as knowledgeable or did not give way to his driving as he sped through the city streets and headed for the Interstate. "I can take the next street and put us on the Interstate and we can go north or south or we can just keep on city streets." He turned to look over his shoulder as he spoke while we were stopped at a red light.

"How about if you find a place to park and let's talk about what I want do and see." I watched as he silently shrugged and pulled away from the light as it changed to green.

The streets were wet, and I could hear the traffic splashing through the occasional puddle of standing water. Patrick found an open space on a hill overlooking the city. If I had been a tourist, I could not have asked for a better view. Unfortunately, I was not, and the view was not what I was after.

"I got your number from a friend who said you drove him some while he was in the city."

"Always glad to get a positive recommendation."

"He said he had a great time while he was here and I wanted to go to some of the same places, so I thought you might remember where you took him."

A passing car hit a large puddle and splashed water over the driver's side and hood of the taxi. I saw Patrick give a slight flinch, but I wasn't sure if it was a startle reflex from the water or from my asking him to take me to some specific places. "I get a lot of riders, so I can't remember where I take somebody. Don't know if I'll be able to help you or not." He turned in the seat and faced me full on.

"My friend was from the Netherlands...Holland and had an accent. That may help you remember."

"German or something like that?"

"Yeah. That was him. He's a professor at a university and was here doing some research. You remember driving him?"

"Uh, maybe."

I immediately recognized his hesitation as a stall to see if I would pay for the information I was seeking. After pulling out my wallet and extracting a one-hundred-dollar bill, I held it up so he could see it. "Here, I said I'd pay fifty to keep the meter off. Let's call the other half as a fee for information." I handed him the bill.

"You a cop or something?" he asked as he took the hundred.

"No, but I do need to know about the professor."

"He in some kind of trouble? If he is, I haven't seen him in a long time."

"Actually, nobody has seen him. He's missing."

"Fuck you, mister. If you think I had anything to do with it you can go to hell and get-the-fuck out of my taxi. I pick up a fare and take them where they want to do. What they do when they get there is none of my business."

163

I held up my hand. "Take it easy. I'm just trying to get a feel for what he did while he was in Seattle, and you know more about that than anybody right now, so let's start again." I pulled out another hundred and held it where he could see it. "I need information and it's obvious I'm willing to pay for it if you're willing to earn it.

I could see the interest building in his eyes. He wanted the money, and at the same time, he was curious about why I was willing to pay him. Patrick nodded to the hundred I held in my hand. "Okay, what do you want to know?" He reached for the bill which I pulled back a few inches.

"Just so we both understand. I may already know more than you think I do, so don't fuck with me." I handed him the money. "We clear on that?"

*　*　*

It was almost midnight in Washington, D.C. and Bill Hart and Lannette, his current love interest, were about to go to bed. This was after a dinner at a restaurant in Old Town Alexandria and a bottle of wine with dinner and several drinks, as they sat on his large leather sofa getting each other in the mood for a no-holds-bared session in bed. Bill once told me there were three levels of sex for him. He could make love, could screw or he could fuck, and he much preferred the latter.

I knew from working with him, that any woman who held his interest for more than a few dates, and Lannette fit in that category, had to enjoy it as much as he. I don't think he was into giving or getting pain, but anything short of bringing blood or leaving a bruise seemed to be in his bag of tricks. Since she had been with him for several months, it was safe to assume that she enjoyed it as much as he.

The buzzing of a cell phone was the only thing that stopped a nearly nude Bill from leaving the sofa and taking a completely nude Lannette to his bed. It was not just any cell phone, but one that when its ring tone broke the silence or, as it did now, the mood, he was duty bound to answer it.

"Don't. Let it go just this once," Lannette could hardly talk as she whispered in his ear.

"If only," Bill said, as he reached for the phone he had placed on an end table beside the sofa when they first began scattering clothes all over the room. He picked it up and looked at the screen to see if he recognized the number. The green name on the screen indicated the call came from Iron Man. "Aw, shit. This may take a while," Bill said to Lannette, as he untangled himself from her arms and legs. Iron Man was his contact at the Department of State.

"Hart here."

"Are we secure?"

Bill looked at Lannette, knowing she could hear anything he said, but would be unable to hear Iron Man. "I'm alone. Go ahead."

Lannette had been around Bill enough to know when to leave him by himself, so she eased off the sofa, moved behind Bill and placed her nude body against his equally bare back to give him one last tease prior to her leaving the room.

Bill listened while Iron Man explained that they were now working with their counterparts in the Netherlands on the death of Professor Dirksen. The latest information he had received from them was that the did not believe the professor would be the kind of person who would be found dead in a tulip field. They did not accept the sheriff's determination of an accidental death and wanted to press the issue.

"So, what do you want me to do about it? I've already got a man looking into it." Bill padded over to his cabinet where he had a small bar. He pulled out two glasses and found a bottle of scotch. He continued to listen as he poured two glasses and then filled one half full of water for Lannette. Both of them drank scotch. Bill did his neat, and Lannette always had a water back.

He listened for another minute before asking. "Was he traveling officially or as a private citizen?"

"As far as I know it was private, but…"

"Yeah, but. When's the last time you got a call about a private citizen from another country who died while he was smelling a bunch of flowers?" Bill took a small sip of the scotch and let it lay on his tongue as he listened to Iron Man.

"Copy that, but it's in official channels and since the ball is in your court, I thought you'd want to know the level of interest."

"Okay, I'll pass it on to my man on the ground. He's probably my best so if there is anything more, he'll find it." He took another sip. "Do you have a suspense date to get back to them?"

"Yeah. Yesterday as usual. Just do the best you can and keep me posted. I know your team will get to the bottom of it, if anybody can."

"One more question and don't give me a bullshit answer. If this is so important, why are you passing the baton and not handling it with your own assets?"

"Good question, but I'll have to get back to you on that." Before Bill could call bullshit on his answer, the line went dead. Bill knew that there was much more to the professor's life and by extension, his death that he did not know, and he did not like to be in that position. He knew he'd have to come up with something to tell Max but that could wait till morning. Right now, he had more important things to take care of and she was in his bed. He picked up his glass, downed the remainder of the scotch and refilled the glass. With drinks for both of them, he headed for the bedroom.

Chapter 23

Patrick drove slowly through the University District where the streets were not a crowded, but the sidewalks were filled with clubgoers and college students either hiding beneath umbrellas or running and ducking the rain by stopping at any available doorway.   I reached up and tapped him on the shoulder. "Find a place to park near a coffee shop. We can go in and talk."

"There's one about a block from here. Now, all I gotta do is find a place to park," he said as he slowed and checked both sides of the street.   Two minutes later he cut the steering wheel hard to the left and made a u turn in the middle of the street. "Here's one and it's close to the coffee shop, too." Only two other motorists took offense to his driving skills. One blew his horn for an inordinate length of time. The other just lowered his window, stuck his arm out in the rain and silently flipped Patrick off. "Some parts of the city, I wouldn't have done that for a million dollars. I couldda got shot down there." He pulled into the space and stopped the engine. "I got an umbrella in the trunk but we're probably better off just making a dash for the place." He pointed several doors down from where we were parked.

"Good idea. You go first. I'll follow." I didn't want to take a chance on Patrick suddenly deciding he'd done enough to earn the money I gave him and have him leave me in the rain and him haul ass in the taxi.

Patrick's door opened into traffic so he had to wait a minute for a light to hold the cars behind us before he could get out. Once he was out, to his credit he came around to the passenger's side to open mine. I heard the soft sound of the doors being locked by a remote key fob as he closed my door after I exited.

We fast walked down the street and went into a coffee shop that was half filled with each table holding at least two people who from their ages looked like college students. I walked up to the counter to order. The barista was an attractive young woman who had long, coal black hair that had it not been swirled into a bun probably would have hung straight down her back. She had the dark, almond shaped eyes of someone of Asian ethnicity. She asked for my order is un-accented English so I had to assume she was not a recent immigrant but may have been born in Seattle. I ordered a black coffee and turned to Patrick to see what he wanted. Before I could ask him, she spoke to him.

"Oh, hello Patrick. I didn't see you come in. You want your regular?" She spoke to him while she filled a large paper cup with my coffee.

"Yeah. You know me. If it ain't broke, don't fix it. I don't have to waste time ordering, so I keep getting the same thing each time I come in here." Patrick spoke to her and avoided looking at me, even though I was holding out my credit card to pay for our drinks. I realized it was a show of force on his part to let me know I was in his territory.

The woman handed him a large paper cup and before she put a lid on it, I could see a level of foam floating like an angry thundercloud on the top of whatever he was drinking. I handed her the card. "I'm getting both of ours."

She took the card with hardly a glance at me and rang up the total. I added a nice tip when I signed it and handed the slip back to her. I pointed to a table in the back of the room. "Over there," I said to Patrick. My goal when we first came in was to get to a place where we could talk without being disturbed.

168

Now I had to add being overheard since this appeared to be a regular stop for my driver. I didn't know who else besides the woman behind the counter knew him, but I didn't want to find out in the middle of a conversation.

"Her name's Kate, at least that's what she goes by here. I think she has an Asian name that's different, but she doesn't use it. We've been friends since I started coming in here off and on about a year ago." He took the lid from his drink and tasted it. "You like Asian women?"

I was learning more about Patrick as the minutes passed. Not only was he a driver for the dead tulip guy, but he may be a source of women for fares who are so inclined. That was some information I would file away for future use, if needed.

"Is that one of the services you can provide your fares?"

"Don't get me wrong. I'm not a pimp, but I know the clubs where a man might get lucky if he was so inclined." He took another drink. "You never did tell me who you are and what you want from me. The meter in the cab ain't running, but the one in my head is and that two bills ain't gonna last all night."

I leaned across the table and got in his face. "Remember when I said, 'don't fuck with me?' Keep that in mind while we're sitting here. I want to know about my friend from Holland. Where did you take him?" I remembered the key that I got from his personal items that I did not know where to use it. "And I want to know where you picked him up."

Patrick sat quietly and sipped on his drink. Two tables over from where we sat, was another table where two couples sat. There were two females and two males, all of whom had large college textbooks open in front of them. It looked like a normal study group with the two women doing all the studying and the men preferring to study the women. I saw one of the women slap the hand of the man sitting beside

169

her. I couldn't tell where the hand had been or what it had been doing, but she was clearly not happy with it.

"You sure you're not a cop?" Patrick asked when he finally decided to talk to me again.

"Why? Are you doing something that's against the law? If so, I couldn't give a rat's ass less. I'm not a cop, but you can pretend I am if it makes answering my questions any easier for you."

"I got nothing against cops, and I don't mind talking to them 'cause I ain't doing nothing that I need to worry about."

I heard the solid sound of flesh against flesh as the man at the other table got his hand slapped again. Whatever he was trying to do wasn't working or he was going about it all wrong. "Okay," I said to Patrick. "Let's start at square one. Unless my friend had you on the payroll like I do right now, there is a record of where you picked him up and took him at your dispatch office, but..." I leaned forward and lowered my voice. "I'll bet he made you the same offer I did and most of his trips were off the meter."

Patrick made a useless effort to stifle a small smile.

"So, if that's the case, your dispatcher didn't know you were working off the meter and the company was losing money...kinda like they're doing right now. You see where I'm going with this? I don't want you to lose your job just because you like to make a little money on the side, but..."

"Okay...okay. Like I said, I get a lot of tourists and some of them don't speak English, so you've got to give me something else to go on, so I know who we're talking about."

"Fair enough." I had his international driver's license, so I pulled it out and slid it across the table to Patrick. "Now do you remember?" Patrick's facial expression gave him away as soon as he looked at the photo, but he tried to suppress it.

After taking the license and looking at it for a minute, he finally spoke. "Yeah, he does look a little familiar, but like I said, I get a lot of passengers who speak German."

"You're not doing yourself any favors, Patrick," I said as I took the license from him. "Remember when I told you not to fuck with me? Well, I think you may have temporarily forgotten but I know you're not going to do it again." I spoke to him in a very low, serious but non-threatening manner. My daughters once accused me of having the ability to yell without raising my voice and I think Patrick may have just experienced that as well. "I never said he spoke German. You're the one who did, so I must assume that not only do you remember him but that you and he spent some time together."

Patrick looked down at the nearly empty cup of whatever he was drinking and picked it up. He swirled the remainder of the drink around in the bottom of the cup while he made up his mind to talk to me or try to get out of what may, in his estimation, was becoming a serious matter. After a minute of silence on both our parts, he finally spoke. "Let's just say for instance that I do remember your friend…if he is a friend, but no matter what he is, what next? Where do you fit into the picture and what is your interest?"

Outside the rain was now falling in sheets as it does in Seattle. It transitioned from a mist that morning to a gently, but steady rain, and by mid-afternoon to the downpour that was falling outside. The harder the rain fell, the fewer people ventured out in it. The four people who were supposedly studying a table over from us were gathering up their books and laptops and packing them away in a variety of canvas or leather bags. Once everything was cleared from the table and packed away, they went to the door and after talking a long look at the outside weather, made a dash into the rain, and disappeared.

"You asked some really good questions, Patrick and as soon as I answer them, you and I will become partners of sorts."

"But I may not..."

I held up my hand to stop him. "We don't always get what we want, my friend and I assure you that you will not be in any danger, physically, mentally or especially for you, financially because of our partnership." I knew I had his attention, whether it was curiosity or a measure of fear, so I pressed the issue. "How much do you make in a day driving...assuming you do it all on the meter?" I leaned closer. "You can add any time off the meter you drive for cash, tips and any other ways you get paid. Give me a total." I sat back so he could think about how much he wanted to inflate the figure.

Patrick removed his coffee cup from the brown paper napkin he had sat it on and pulled out a pen. I watched as he made an elaborate effort to put a variety of numbers on the paper. He mumbled to himself as he wrote. Once he was satisfied with the number, he turned the napkin so I could see it. "Most of my fares are either around town or from a hotel to the airport. Downtown it's a flat rate plus extra for additional passengers or suitcases. Runs to the airport are on the meter. I figure in a day, I'll make about three hundred around town and another hundred going to the airport and fifty in tips, so that comes to five bills a day." He placed the pen beside the napkin and for a fleeting moment I felt like I was in an auto showroom and the salesman had just come back from talking to his sales manager and this was the deal they had approved.

Like any good customer, it was time to negotiate. "I know you're not driving your own car, so let's take away about a hundred a day for the lease fee." I marked the number down a hundred dollars. "How about gas? If you make that many trips you have to buy a lot so, let's say another fifty a day for fuel. That brings us down to three-fifty." I looked at him. "Does that sound more realistic?"

"I…I guess when you figure it that way, it's about right."

"Good. So, here's what we're going to do. You pick me up tomorrow morning at the same place you picked me up tonight. I'm going to pay you to take me everyplace you took my friend. I'm going to be a nice guy and pay you four hundred dollars a day in cash. I don't care how you account for it with the company, but we're going to start with one day and if I need more, you're going to drive another day."

"Okay, but you still haven't told me who you are and why you want to know all this stuff about the professor."

"Let's just say you and I both have a vested interest in where you took him and what he did while he was here." I stood up and nodded to the door. "We're gonna get wet, but it's time to get back on the road."

Patrick drove me back to the hotel and before I left the taxi I leaned forward and looked at the number on the meter and the placard with his name and license number on it. "Don't be late," I said as I pulled out my cell and took a picture of the information, before I exited and watched his taxi leave the hotel entrance and splash through the wet Seattle night.

Chapter 24

I keep my cell phone on a nightstand beside my bed so that when I wake up in the middle of the night, I can have something to do. I check messages, the national and local news, weather and if I can't get back to sleep, I'll play a game of solitaire or poker. It's also useful if I need to set an alarm for any reason, which rarely happens. The one thing it rarely does is wake me up with a call, that's why it took a moment for the sound to register with me. Occasionally, Anna would call late at night, but she usually slept in, so I knew there was only one other logical reason for it to ring.

I had a special ring tone for Bill Hart, and I didn't have to look at the caller identification as soon as I heard WHY DON'T WE GET DRUNK AND SCREW. "This better be good. If we're not at war or you're not in jail, there's no reason to call at this hour." I looked at a small clock on my dresser and saw that it was a quarter to five in the morning for me and three hours later for him on the east coast.

"I figured you'd be awake if you were alone and if you had company, I thought waking you up would give you a chance for some exercise prior to heading to work."

"I'm alone and I was asleep, so make it quick in case I can start over." I sat on the edge of the bed and ran my hand through my hair.

"Just so you know this is in response to a call I got last night about midnight while I was otherwise engaged. Nothing like a midnight call from the State

174

Department to break the mood. Once the flame has been dowsed there's no getting it back."

"But that's not why you called, is it? You really don't want to discuss your love life, or lack thereof at this hour of the day." I got up and walked to the kitchen while holding the phone to my ear. I knew more sleep was out of the question, so I filled a container with water and prepared to make a pot of coffee.

"Thanks to that call, I didn't have a sex life last night." I could hear the frustration in his voice. Since meeting and taking up semi-permanent housekeep with Lannette, he has mellowed some, but there will always be an edge to him that time and romance will never erase. I think it comes with the turf after spending a lifetime in uniform and I'm afraid I may have the same affliction.

The water sizzled as it hit the hot burner and dripped through the coffee filter on its way to the pot ready to receive the dark brew. I think I mumbled something to Bill about waiting until I could get a mug and pour myself a cup. One of my personal crazies is I hate to do anything in the morning until I have brushed my teeth. That even included kissing Anna when we awaken in the same bad. I don't like to eat or drink until I've cleared out whatever accumulates during the night. I think it's because I have a terrible habit of snoring and probably sleep with my mouth open, thus drying it out and possibly inviting all sorts of germs and other things that go bump in the night into it.

I made an exception as I took a seat at my kitchen table. "Okay, I've got my heart started and taken my first breath for the day, so tell me why you called."

"I called you because I got a call last night about our mystery dead guy in the tulips, except now he's not just a dead guy in a field of tulips, he's a dead and possibly murdered college professor who the Dutch government is most interested in. So much so, that they have contacted our State Department and asked for assistance in finding out what happened."

"We pretty much knew that already, didn't we?" I asked as I took a drink of coffee.

"We did, but we got it a piece at time, and we didn't realize how far up the political chain his death would take us."

I could see that I was going to be much more deeply involved in this than either of us first thought. With the cell phone on speaker, so I could continue to listen to Bill, I stood from the table and went to my room to find what I was going to wear since I knew as soon as I ended the call, I would be on Bill's payroll.

"I'm working on one good lead out here, but if you or your contacts at State have anything that I don't, I need to know about it right away." The selection of a shirt to wear was the biggest wardrobe decision I had to make as I normally got several day's wear out of pants prior to changing them.

"About the only thing I have coming is some notes on his work on that special tulip he was developing. You probably won't understand them any more than I expect to be able to do, but I'll send copies in case you run across anything or anybody who may have an interest in them." He hesitated, then added. "I've gotta run. Another call coming in. Get your ass in gear and find out something so we can close this action out." As usual, he ended without saying anything to indicate the call was over.

I set the half-full coffee mug on the counter in the bathroom and prepared to shower, shave, take care of my teeth and face another day of uncertainty.

The weather had cleared from the night prior as I drove to the hotel where I was to meet Patrick. I figured my chances of his showing up were about seventy-thirty in my favor. He didn't strike me as the kind of guy who would pass up a chance to make a nice day's pay with no expenses, but if he knew or did

176

something relating to the professor's disappearance, he was subject to go to ground and I'd never see him again.

The table where I sat in the hotel's coffee shop had an unobstructed view of the street and the passenger loading drive in front. I got to the table twenty minutes prior to the time I had scheduled to meet Patrick. While I watched and waited for him, I saw the hotel's guests come down to the coffee shop for meetings they had arranged with local business contacts. It was obvious who was the client when the guest stood and greeted the newcomer at the table. Even though I could not hear most of the conversations, I knew each arrival was offered breakfast or at least a cup of coffee. Several offers of coffee resulted in one person being served a stainless-steel pot of hot water, a cup, a selection of teas and either cream and sugar or honey and lemon. The few women who were guests and met a male client were extremely business-like in their mannerism as I'm sure they didn't want to appear to be anything but professional.

Patrick was three minutes late when he pulled up in front of the hotel. He was sent to a spot near the end of the driveway by the bellman who was directing the traffic flow as taxis came and went. Drivers were not allowed to leave their taxi to come inside and look for passengers, so I placed several dollar bills on the table to pay for my coffee and went outside to meet him.

He must have been looking in his rear-view mirror, because as soon as I got outside, he left the driver's seat, came around the taxi and opened the door for me. "If we're going to be together today, you might want to give me a name. I'd like to have something to call you." I ignored him as I climbed into the back seat.

As soon as we pulled away from the hotel and onto one of Seattle's busiest downtown streets, I leaned forward. "You can call me Ben." It was a name I used once when I was working undercover in Europe with Bill. He decided I would be Ben and he'd be Frank. He thought it clever that we'd be Benjamin and Franklin in Paris, a place where the old man lived and, if history is to be believed, worked his way through many of the ladies of the night. While the colonists were fighting for their lives, he was having the time of his.

"Okay, Ben. Where to this morning?"

"Let's go back to that coffee shop we were in last night and we'll come up with an itinerary." We pulled out from the hotel and merged with the morning drive time traffic heading into the city. Seattle has a very good public transportation system that covers the entire area, but you'd never know it by the cars on the roads in the morning and afternoon. The Washington state ferry system is synchronized with the various cities and transportation hubs so commuters from outlying areas on some of the islands around the metro area can get to and from work. With the ferries running on a set schedule, it made for a lack of overtime or late work for those who depended on them. Miss the last ferry and you'd wind up in a hotel room or sleeping on a bench some place.

Patrick weaved his way through the traffic and probably for the first time with a customer in the back, took the shortest route to the desired destination. With the meter off and his working for cash, there was no advantage to taking the long way just to build up time and miles. This time he found a parking spot directly in front of the coffee shop. It was a lucky thing as it was the only vacancy in the entire block.

Inside, we stood at the counter behind several other customers, some of whom appeared to be college students, and a few were dressed in suits and other business attire. The Asian barista from last night was not on duty and had been replaced by a man who was so large that I wondered how he fit

178

behind the counter. "Can I help you?" he asked as he looked past me to the attractive woman in line behind Patrick.

"Dark roast coffee for me, and whatever he wants," I said as I stepped aside for Patrick to give his order.

"I'll have a venti caramel soy latte, extra hot, no foam. Double cup it and no sleeve." Patrick said as if he ordered this every day and the barista quickly made notes on the cup as he spoke. It took a few minutes for them to orchestrate his order and less than a minute to fill a cup with mine. We took the cups to the same table we occupied the night before and once again, there were several tables already filled with students poring over laptops and open books.

I watched as Patrick peeled the lid off the cup in his hand and took a cautious sip of whatever-the-hell he was drinking. "How do you remember all of that just so you can get a cup of coffee? Do you do it every time you come in a place like this?"

"Lady friend had me sample one like this that she was drinking, and I liked it, so I've been ordering them ever since." He took a drink. "You should try it sometime. Order something besides black coffee. Live a little."

"I'm afraid if I drank one of those I'd die of a sugar coma or clogged arteries, in the middle of the store. I'll stick with this," I held up my cup. I drank a little and then placed the cup on the table. "Here's what we're going to do today. You're going to take me every place you took him. I don't care if it was on the meter or off. If he went there, we're going back today. Understand?"

Patrick took a minute to think of his response. "Under normal conditions, I'd tell a man like you to fuck off and leave me alone, but there's something about you that says that might not be the smartest thing I ever did." After he got no response or reaction from me, he continued. "I took your friend...if he really

179

was your friend and I'm not convinced of that, to several places in the city...but..." He stopped.

"But what?"

"But most of them were at night."

"Clubs?" Although I knew very little about the man, a tulip expert did not seem like the typical Seattle club goer. "What kind of clubs?" Seattle had a vibrant jazz community, and I knew from my time in Europe that they liked American jazz.

"How well do you know your friend?" Patrick did the air quote thing with his hands when he referred to him as my friend.

I knew he was about to tell me something out of the ordinary, so I wanted him to continue. "Remember, I told you I already know more than you think I do, so tell me everything you know about him and his club habits." I waited for an answer.

"His tastes ran a little outside the norm for most cities I think, but not here in the DPRS where anybody, anything and everything is accepted."

His reference to the DPRS was the Democratic People's Republic of Seattle, a name given to the city by those who may not share the liberal views propagated by the city government. "Keep talking."

"I don't know if you've spent much time in the city or know much about it, but there are some underground clubs and other places that cater to a specific audience."

"Meaning?"

"Your friend was into some kinky shit."

Chapter 25

Byron Getz left his office and went to see a friend who claimed he was in the real estate business. He and Getz had done business for years and he had never indicated he had a real estate license to buy and sell the mostly low rent houses and apartments he owned. If any of his tenants were asked, they would probably describe him as a slum lord. For Getz's purposes, he was exactly when he was looking for. The man had the money and the foresight to put together his initial property purchases beginning at least ten years ago before prices went astronomical in the area. Most of his properties were teardowns at best, but they stayed occupied. He owned two motels on Aurora that were used by ladies of negotiable affections and a few long term renters who paid their rent using Social Security or veteran's benefits checks prior to spending the remainder on adult beverages or non-prescription pharmaceuticals. As long as they paid the rent, didn't burn the place down and only required an occasional visit by the Seattle police department, he left well-enough alone.

He kept an office in a small house in the Greenwood section not far from the Seattle Zoo. It was the nicest property he owned and served as his residence and office. Getz found street side parking a few houses down from where he was headed. There was no sign on the door indicating the resident ran a lucrative business from the unassuming looking home that sat on a slight rise above the city street. He knocked on the door and waited for a response from inside. Since he had called ahead, he did not have to wait long for it to be opened.

Ed Sewell was in his mid-fifties and had the build of a middle weight prize fighter. He kept himself in shape by running several miles a day on the path around the lake. He and Byron had been to lunch or dinner several times and each time, Byron was amazed at the amount of food he consumed. When he asked about it, Ed told him he either worked it off in the daytime running, or at night making love.

"Hey, come on in," Ed stood back and opened the door for Byron. "I just made a fresh pot of coffee if you want some," he said as he closed the door after taking a quick look up and down the street as if he was expecting someone else.

"I'm good, but thanks." Getz had been there enough to know that the front room that had probably been the living room when the house was occupied by the previous owners, was now his office. He went to a chair next to the desk that dominated the room and watched as Ed opened a small refrigerator and pulled out a power drink.

"I keep coffee for anyone who drops by, but I don't drink the stuff." He pulled the tab on the top of the drink and took a sip. "What can I do for you? I know I'm up to date on my insurance premiums."

"No, you're good on that. I've just got something else. I have a problem and I think maybe you can help me."

"You know I will, if I can. What is it?"

"I need three houses I can burn down."

*   *   *

I didn't know as much about Professor Dirksen as I had told Patrick. I had no idea what he meant when he said the professor was into some kinky shit. I decide the best way to find out was to just let Patrick tell me. "And just how did you find out about this side

182

of him? Did he tell you or are you just a great judge of people?"

"I missed the boat on him at first. Kinda like I did with you, and I'm still not satisfied that you're not a cop of some sort." I didn't respond, so he kept talking. "The first night I picked him up at the hotel, he just wanted to ride around and look at the city. If you're not from here, and it's a clear night, Seattle is one of the most beautiful cities anywhere." We were still seated, and I watched as the nearest table with the college students closed their laptops, books and left. Except for a man at a table closer to the entrance who was alone and spent his time checking his phone while he drank what looked like a tall glass of iced tea, we were the only people in the place.

"Where did you take him?"

"We just cruised the city. I took him to the Pike Place Market, Pioneer Square...you know. All the tourist places."

"But that's not what he wanted, was it?" I was fishing and I hoped Patrick took the bait.

"It was the first night. When I took him back to his hotel, I knew he was going to be in town for a few days, so I gave him my card and phone number and told him if he wanted to see anything else...maybe things not listed in the tourist's brochures, to give me a call. I do that with all the big tippers, so I didn't think a lot about it until the called me the next afternoon."

"What did he want?"

"He didn't say right away, like maybe he was afraid to, or once I found out what he wanted, maybe he was ashamed to."

"Afraid or ashamed? What did he want to do?"

"He asked about some of the underground clubs I mentioned. When I finally found out what he wanted, it was drag clubs."

"Drag? As in drag queens?"

"Exactly. That's what he wanted to see, so I took him to one that's a little off the beaten path."

"Where you get a fee for everyone you bring?"

"Hey, I'm out to make a living just like every other stiff out there. If I make a little on the side, it don't hurt nobody."

Except the professor, I thought without saying it aloud. It may have had an impact on his death which now was looking more like murder than an accident. "Did you take him in or just let the doorman know it was you who brought him?"

"He wanted me to follow him in. He said if he liked it, I could keep the meter running and wait for him and if he didn't like it…"

"You had another place to take him"

"Yeah, but I took him to the top of the line first, and he liked it, so I waited for him. I dozed off and he had to wake me up when he came out."

"What time was that?"

"A little after one am. By the time we got back to his hotel he had a seventy-five-dollar tab. He gave me a hundred and called it a night. I got a call the next day about noon saying he wanted me to pick him up again that night and we did it all over again."

"Same club?"

"To start with. He was only in there about an hour when he came out with a woman…maybe…it was hard to tell on his arm. He wanted to go to another club, but she was all over him in the back seat. I could see it all in my rearview mirror, so before I could get to the other club, he changed his mind, and I took him back to his hotel."

"And the woman too?"

"No, he kicked her out on Broadway…of course with the woman and I ain't so sure she actually was a she. I've had some of them in my cab in the past and if you don't know, you can't tell, but it didn't seem to make a lot of difference to him. They went at it like two rabbits in heat in the back."

I had to take a minute to let this sink in. This was not what I expected to hear from Patrick about the professor.   I'm not sure what I expected but this wasn't it. "Did he call you to take his friend home?"

"No, the next time I heard from him was about the same time the next day saying he wanted me to drive him again that night. This time he was very specific with where he wanted me to take him."

"And where would that be?"

Patrick pushed back from the table and crossed his arms over his chest in a classic move of hostilities and protection.

* * *

"Are you out of your fucking mind?" Ed almost sprayed a mouthful of his power drink when Getz said he wanted to burn down three of his houses. "You running some kind of insurance scam…against your own company?" He stood and walked to where Getz was sitting and stood in front of him. "If you are, I'm not sure I want to be a part of it," he hesitated and then smiled, "unless it pays good, and we can't get caught. They don't like arsonist very much in this part of the country."

Getz held up his hand to stop Ed from getting closer and to keep him from incriminating himself in case he was, or had been, involved in arson scams in the past. "Hang on a minute. I don't want to really burn them down I just want someone to think I want them torched for the insurance."

Ed backed off and looked long and hard at Getz. "I think I'm getting it. You want to run a scam on somebody who's running a scam. On you? Is it one of your clients?" He went back to his seat behind the desk. "Tell me what you want."

For the next thirty minutes, Getz explained to Ed what he and I had come up with as a plan to see if the insurance fires were legit or not. It was going to require a leap of faith from a friend to a friend or an iron-clad set of court documents in case they didn't trust each other as much as they thought. Friendship was one thing, but business was business and sometimes they did not match.

"Did you come up with this all by yourself? I never saw you as the devious kind and this falls dead in that category." Ed opened his second power drink and dropped the tab in the trash can next to his desk.

"Not all my idea, but I'm the one who uncovered the possibilities that some of my insured were running an insurance scam on me." He relaxed since he knew Ed was now interested in helping him. "I've got a PI that I work with on occasion, and he's the one who came up with the idea. I have to give him credit for that."

"Sounds like a good guy to know. I may want to talk to him about a couple of my renters who may be running drugs from a house our near SeaTac."

The area around the Seattle/Tacoma or SeaTac airport was notorious for drugs and prostitution. It had been a favorite location for the famous or notorious Green River Killer to pick up the prostitutes he later murdered over a span of many years.

"Some of my renters may never make the society pages but I try to keep crime to a minimum and drugs are like a flashing red light that says come raid this house and see what you can find. I don't need that kind of publicity. I know I don't have the best reputation in town, but I want to keep what little I have."

"Let's take it one at a time. Help me out and I'll give you all of his contact information and you can have him help you." Getz smiled, knowing he and Ed were about to make a deal. "How do you want to do this? A handshake, or do you want some paper on it?"

Chapter 26

The more I spoke to Patrick the deeper the story of the good, but lately dead, professor got. Every tourist and especially every military personnel who ever spent time in Europe knew of Amsterdam's reputation as a place to buy and use drugs without worrying about arrest and they also knew of and quite possibly visited the famous red-light district if for nothing more than to say they had been there and to make sure it really did exist. Because it did, I was under the immediate impression that Professor Dirksen was either a customer there or came to Seattle to see if he could find the same thing here...whatever the "it" was that he was seeking.

"Where did you take him after that?"

"I don't know why, but I'm going to trust you when you say you're not a cop. I didn't do anything that's against the law, but some cops might not see it that way. I can't afford to lose my job. This is all I have, so if you're really a cop, do the decent thing and be honest with me, just like you want me to be honest with you."

"Last time we're going to have this discussion." I pulled back my jacket to show I was not armed, nor did I have a badge attached to my belt in the same fashion as some detectives and undercover officers have. "I am not a cop of any sort. I don't have a badge and I couldn't arrest you, even if I wanted to."

Patrick thought for a minute then got up and walked back to the counter where he ordered another round. He got regular coffee for me and the custom concoction for himself. When they were prepared, and the barista handed the cups to him, he brought them back to the table, and took a seat."

"Do you have a name for the man? He never told me, and I never asked."

"His name was Jacob Dirksen."

"Was Jacob Dirksen, as in he's changed it, or he's no longer Jacob or anything else?"

"Let's just talk about where you took him. We'll worry about who or what he is later." I knew at some point I was either going to be forced to tell him Dirksen was dead, or he'd figure it out on his own, but that would have to wait. Right now, I wanted to re-trace his movements in the city, and Patrick was the only way to do that.

One of the barista's gave me a dirty look when Patrick came back to the table as if we were occupying a space where better customers sat and tipped for services rendered. I took the hint and got up from the table and went to the counter. "I'll have a refill on my coffee if you do that sort of thing, if not fix me another one." I placed a ten-dollar bill in the square plastic tip container. "This should buy us a little more time at the table," I said, as he handed me my coffee. The man, who wore a name tag indicating he was the manager, just nodded his head and went to assist another customer.

"You've got the first two days covered. Where did you take him the next night?" I asked as I pulled the lid from my paper cup.

"Like I said, there are some places in town that don't make the tourist brochures or the Chamber of Commerce places to visit list. Ask any cabbie and if he's been driving for more than a week, he knows where they are."

"And you've been driving for years, I suppose?"

"Two and change. I lost my job at one of the car dealerships on Aurora. I looked for a while and a friend who was driving let me ride with him for a week or so to see what it was like and since I knew the city, I thought 'what the hell' and I've been driving ever since. I'll never get rich, but I won't have to live in a cardboard box under a freeway bridge, either."

After that, I had the feeling that Patrick would be honest with me, and I'd be able to get as much information on Dirksen as he left behind in the city. "So, where did you take him?"

"There are a couple of places around that cater to some really strange kinks." He took a drink and thought for a second. "Although, I guess what's kinky to one person is normal for somebody else."

"What kind of places are we talking about?"

"Places where you can get your ass beat while hanging from the ceiling wearing a rubber suit with a tennis ball in your mouth." He looked over the rim of his cup as he drank to check my reaction.

"You took him to an S and M club?"

"No, but you asked what kind of places were available."

"Let's get this straight. I'm not asking for me. I don't give a rat's ass about why you took him someplace, I just want to know where it was and when you did it."

Patrick nodded his head indicating he understood. "The place he wanted to go is a house that has a specialty. If you're looking for a specific type of date, you can get anything you want. You place your order and it's custom made just for you."

He could tell from my silence that I did not completely understand.

"You want a six-foot tall redhead with blue painted toenails dressed like a high school cheerleader, it'll be waiting for you. You like that but want to change for a black chick with blonde hair who you can take to the opera, just place your order."

"They have that many escorts?"

He looked at me and gave a small smile. "Now I know you're not a cop. We're not talking about your average run-of-the mill escort, these ladies are not all ladies, that's why you can custom order whatever you want."

It finally hit me. "Transvestites?"

Chapter 27

Getz sat in his office, reading a contract he and Ed had agreed upon. For a reduction in his insurance premiums, that amounted to half of the profit Getz made on them, Ed would temporarily give his insurance agent a document saying he had permission to pretend to burn down three houses. When he finished reading it, he placed it in a folder and sat back in his chair and looked at Ed.

Ed sat in a very nice, leather chair with chrome legs and arms. It was a match for the remainder of the furniture in Getz's office. When he decided to go out on his own, Getz put a lot of emphasis and money into renting a nice office and furnishing it. His desk was solid mahogany and had taken four men to carry it into the office. He had a two-room suite, and for the first year, the outer office was vacant, and he used a secretarial service to answer his phones so callers would think he had a real person working for him. Whenever someone inquired about the woman who answered his phone, she was always at lunch or had the day off. He finally got to the point where business was good enough to hire someone for the office. All his files and other necessary documents associated with his clients were kept in that office and his assistant controlled the access to them. The contract he had with Ed was different, and he did not want anyone else to know about it.

After signing two copies, he placed one in a folder and gave it to Ed. The other copy, he placed in a similar folder and tucked it into a lower drawer in his desk.

"My investigator will return to the property management company and tell them he wants them to manage his property, which is yours. In the process, he's going to tell them he is behind on the mortgage, taxes and city required repairs and he'd be happy if they just caught fire and he could collect the insurance."

"And you have the fire policy, right?" Ed asked.

"I do, and it goes deeper than that. They managed some other properties that burned, and I'm convinced the fires were arson. If I can get them to agree to burn your places, I can sue for the return of the pay out and they'll go to jail. As I see it, we all get what we want."

"How are you gonna prove they're going to burn the properties? That sounds like where it could all turn to shit."

"We catch 'em in the act. I'll set it up for a specific time and have the right people there to catch them in the act and stop them." Getz stood up from his desk and came around to where Ed was seated. "Want a cup of coffee? I've got some in the waiting room."

"Only if you got something stronger to put in it. I'm beginning to think I need a drink of something stronger than coffee."

Getz came back into the office carrying two large mugs of coffee. He placed them both on the corner of this desk and then went behind it to his chair. When he sat down, he reached down to the bottom drawer in his desk, opened it and pulled out a bottle of brandy.

"Brandy okay? I keep it here for when I feel a cold coming on," he said with a smile.

"I feel more than a cold, so be generous when you pour," Ed nodded to his cup. "I don't know who this guy is that you're trusting with my properties, but if he's not as good as you think he is, you're gonna be out for the cost of my places. You know that, don't you?"

Getz handed the mug to Ed and raised his in a mock toast which was returned. "If I didn't trust him and think it would work, we wouldn't be having this conversation."

"I just hope you know what you're getting us into."

"Me too."

*   *   *

Patrick and I left the coffee shop and he drove us to a residential area not far from Capitol Hill. The houses were close together and were interspersed with condos. Like many other areas of the city when it became popular, the desire to live here went up, along with the price of housing. What had been a stately home built in the 1980's and sold for a price an average family could afford, was now home to a Microsoft millionaire, a Boeing executive or someone in the music or artistic community who paid more for it than the original owner's entire family would make in a lifetime. We stopped when Patrick double-parked in front of a two-story brick next to a building filled with five-hundred-thousand-dollar condos.

He pointed across the street. "See that house over there? Looks like any other house on the street, but if you went in, you'd think you were in another world."

"You've been in it?" I asked as I looked and agreed that it was a very unassuming place.

"No, but I've taken enough people to it to know what's there. It's called Delila's Dungeon. Almost every driver and probably as many cops know what, and where it is."

I leaned forward to get a better look. "You get paid to bring people here and keep them in business and the cops get paid not to run them out of business?" I sat back and Patrick made a half turn in the seat to face me.

"Everybody gets a little piece of the action." He smiled as he realized what he'd said. "No pun intended."

"What has this place got to do with my guy? Did you bring him here?"

"Yeah, this was one of the places he liked to visit. He brought one of his lady friends here with him once but after that he seemed to settle down with only one companion."

The information Patrick was providing me on the professor was giving me a completely different picture than what I had originally imagined a college professor who was an expert on the care and feeding of tulips was all about. "I think we need to go over his schedule day-by-day and hour-by-hour while he was here and with you."

We were still double-parked and for the first time, it seemed to annoy another driver. A car pulled up close behind the taxi and gave a long blast on the horn. Patrick ignored the car and the sound as he looked at me. "Your guy is dead, ain't he?"

Before I could respond, he put the taxi in gear and roared away from the irate driver behind us.

Patrick spoke as he weaved his way between and around the city's traffic. "If you're not a cop and you're this interested in him, just who or what are you?" We stopped at a red light and Patrick adjusted his rear-view mirror so he could see me as he awaited my answer.

"I've been hired to find out a much as possible about him and what he did while he was in the city..."

"Because whoever hired you don't think his death was natural or an accident?" He gave his attention to the street and not me, but he continued to talk. "You're either some kind of insurance investigator or a private dick." He nodded his head to himself as if he was agreeing with his assessment. "Either way, it don't matter to me, 'cause all I know about the man is what he and I talked about and the places I took him."

"And what did you talk about?"

"Like I said, he was into some kinky shit, and he wanted me to help him find places to scratch his itch. The place we stopped at was just one of a few places I took him." He looked sideways and up into the rearview mirror. "I'll bet you want me to take you to some of the others, don't you?"

I had a feeling I knew what was coming and I wasn't surprised.

"You know, I been thinking about our little arrangement. I agreed to drive you around for the money you offered but I didn't realize I was going to have to give you a play-by-play of where I took the professor and what he did when he was there. Driving's one thing. Guided tours are another. You see where I'm going with this?"

"You want more money." It was more of a statement than a question on my part.

"Don't you think it's fair? I mean, after all, look at all the leg work I'm saving you by you not having to try to find all this on your own." He held up his hand to emphasize the point. "And I don't think you'd be able to 'cause I'll bet I'm the only one he trusted to take him to the places he wanted to go."

I hated to admit it, but Patrick had a point. He was the only link I had to what the professor did or where he went when he was in Seattle, so since I was on somebody's else's payroll, I decided to pay him. "I'll add another two hundred a day to what I'm paying you and you and I will be like Siamese Twins until I want to separate." I waited for a response and when I got none I asked, "Do you have a family?"

"Why? You want to hire them too?"

"No. I just want to know if you have a home life that may interfere with what I need you to do."

"I'm divorced. Got one kid. He's in the Army stationed at Fort Benning, down in Georgia

195

someplace. I hardly ever hear from him. Only reason I know he's in the Army is because he just finished Ranger School. He wants me to come to his graduation." Patrick paused for a moment as he thought about the request. "I guess it's the least I can do. He and I haven't had a great father and son relationship since the divorce. Once he graduates, he's getting some kind of security clearance and they contacted me to see if I was a communist."

"Are you?" I had to ask.

"Going or a communist?"

"Both."

"I'm probably the only driver in the city who's not a communist or some other kind of whacko. This is Seattle, you know." He laughed at the irony of his remark. "But I am going, so I'll be gone for about a week. You think you can get along without me for a while?"

I was thinking about his being gone and what I'd do in the meantime, so I didn't notice exactly where we were until Patrick pulled to the curb, put the taxi in park and then turned in the seat to face me. "I think this is the place where his steady lady lives...or works. I brought both of them here one time and then picked her up a couple of times for him."

We were parked in front of a multi-storied apartment building. It was built in a horseshoe style with the opening facing the street. I could see a central courtyard in the middle. There was a small swimming pool surrounded by white metal furniture. Several round tables had large, folded umbrellas protruding from the center. I didn't think a swimming pool and the opportunity sit outside and get a tan was a great selling point for an apartment in Seattle, but I suppose some people take the sun where they can find it.

"Do you know which apartment is hers?"

"See. This is where you start to get a payoff for that extra money you're paying. You'd have to go to the manager and give him some bullshit story or knock on every door until you found the right apartment, or just ask your now reasonably paid driver."

"I'm waiting."

"I heard her tell him to have something delivered to apartment 368. Satisfied?"

"I will be after I knock on the door," I said as I pulled on the handle and opened the rear door of the taxi. "Wait here."

Chapter 28

"You didn't have to kill him." The man sat in his office surrounded by over seventy-five years of family history in the tulip business. Outside the window of his office on the second floor of the massive building that served as a combination of corporate offices, warehouse and research facility, he could see over three hundred acres of tulips in full bloom. The fields were divided into sections of no more than fifty acres where a particular color or type of tulip was grown, nurtured, and then had its bulb harvested for export to the international tulip market. To say the operation was large was an understatement. Started by the first Verhoeven two years after the end of World War Two, and German occupation of the Netherlands in 1947. It had begun as a modest family farm just outside Amsterdam growing vegetables for their own consumption and survival. The idea of planting a few tulips was made to add a little color and civility to the war-ravaged country.

Soon the garden produced enough vegetables that the family was able to sell some to supplement their modest income. Along with the vegetables, some of the occupation military personnel, in particular the Americans, wanted to purchase tulip and other bulbs to send home to wives and mothers. It wasn't long before the old man realized he could make more money selling tulip bulbs than vegetables, and the Verhoeven Tulip Company was formed in early 1950.

Since then, it had grown to be one of the two largest exporters of bulb in the country. Like their competition, they were constantly testing and experimenting to find a new color, a hardier strain, or another variety of the money-making tubers.

The fifth-generation owner of the business had been a student of Professor Dirksen and had remained friends with him over the years. It was during a conversation one night at an Amsterdam cabaret that Dirksen, who had too many drinks and probably let his guard down for a fleeting second, told his former student of his work and the success he was having in replicating the illusive Simper Augustus tulip. From that night on, Andre Verhoeven had a single goal in mind, and that was to be the first and only grower, not only in the Netherlands but in the entire world, who had the long-lost bulb. When he found out Dirksen was going to the United States, he knew that he would attempt to sell the bulb to a grower there, and he was determined that it would not happen.

"It was an accident," Andre heard his contact on the phone tell him.

"No...no...people die in traffic accidents, or they fall and hit their head in the kitchen. They don't accidently die in a tulip field."

There was a long silence on the phone while Andre waited for a response. "It...it wasn't actually an accident...well, it was, but not like it was reported."

"You're making no sense to me at all. I want to know what happened and if you lie to me, I will come to your house and burn it down with you in it." Andre was standing and waving his hands to emphasize his displeasure. Although the person on the other end of the call could not see him, there was no misunderstanding his meaning just from his tone of voice. "I can't talk to you any more right now. I'll call you back and you better answer." He slammed the phone down so hard it knocked a small vase containing a single blue tulip from his desk.

It was only a little after noon in the Skagit Valley, but after talking with, or more accurately, listening to Andre Verhoeven, Frank Richardson needed a drink, or something stronger to calm his nerves. He kept a bottle of very expensive scotch in a cabinet in his office. He kept it to share with some of his company's best customers. When he needed something stronger than he could get from a bottle, he had a special place in his desk drawer where he kept a supply of the white powder that helped him calm down. Calm down was what he needed, and he needed it immediately.

He pushed a button on the phone system sitting on the edge of his desk and waited for his executive secretary to answer. "Yes, sir. You need me?"

"No. I'm not feeling well, so I think I'm going to take a short nap. Don't disturb me until I notify you I'm awake." This was not unusual for him. He often made the same request when he had a guest in his office. The guest was always one of the sex workers he had come to him from Seattle. The large, white leather sofa occupying almost the entire wall opposite his desk in the office was his playground and play he did.

A phone call from Andre several weeks earlier had been the thing that put everything in motion. Andre knew Dirksen was in the area and would probably call on Frank at some point. His instructions to Frank were explicit: get the formula or any notes Dirksen has on the Semper and get them quickly. How he did it was of no concern to Andre, for the end would more than justify the means.

It took almost a month for Dirksen to finally arrive at Frank's office. In addition to talking about the Semper, Frank went out of his way to cultivate a personal and well as a professional relationship with him. They went to lunch several times and once met in Seattle where they visited several bars and nightclubs. One featured a drag show and when the performers came off stage and mixed with the crowd,

Frank noticed that Dirksen was quickly at ease with a busty red-haired queen sitting on his lap.

When Dirksen came to talk to him about the tulip, they talked for an hour and then Frank suggested they go to lunch. They went to a popular upscale waterfront café not far from the fields. As soon as they were seated both men reacted to the two very attractive women standing in the doorway. They were looking around and seemed to either be waiting for a table or looking for someone. Frank was the first to comment on them.

"See the leggy blonde on the right? She can do things to you, and for you, that you never thought possible." His smile to her was returned as she looked across the room. "Why don't we see if they want to join us?" Without waiting for Dirksen to answer, he stood and went to the entrance. After exchanging a few words, the two women followed him to the table where Dirksen sat.

"Ladies, this is Professor Jacob Dirksen from Amsterdam. He is one of the world's most eminent authorities on tulips." He turned to Dirksen. "Let me introduce Dianna and Venus."

"I'm Dianna," the blonde extended her hand to Dirksen.

Jacob stood and accepted the extended dainty hands offered to him by the new guests at their table. "A professor, really?" Dianna held his hand in hers as she spoke. "I don't think I've ever met a real professor." Her smile was having the desired effect on Dirksen. "Do you tell your students about the birds and the bees along with telling them about tulips?"

Lunch lasted for almost two hours, and they went through two rounds of drinks and a bottle of wine prior to leaving. Outside the afternoon sunlight, Frank took several deep breaths as he tried to clear his head enough to drive back to his office. Venus held onto Frank's arm as he shaded his eyes from the sun with his hand. "Who ordered such a sunny afternoon? I was hoping for rain or at least cloudy." He gave Venus a kiss on the cheek. "You know there's only two things to do on a rainy afternoon. One of them is to take a nap and the other isn't."

"I'm not at all sleepy. Are you?" Venus whispered loud enough for all to hear.

"It sounds like you may have a busy afternoon, Venus," Dianna said. "If you're going to be busy, how am I going to get back to Seattle?" She spoke to Venus, but she was looking at Dirksen.

"I think I may be of assistance if you require a ride. I have a rental at Frank's office." He looked at Frank. "I think we may have completed any conversations we required for today, so if you will take us back to the office, I'll secure my car."

Frank put his hand squarely on the left cheek of the well-rounded ass Venus had beneath a very tight pair of designer jeans. "You talked me into it. Let's go."

When they arrived at Frank's office he and Dirksen stood by the car while the women looked at a display of the variety of tulips that the company produced. "Something you need to know before you get too involved with Dianna. She's...well she's probably different from the women you're used to dating back in Amsterdam. Just be careful." He motioned for Venus to join him as he opened an outside door to his office and did not take her through the reception area where his secretary would see them.

By the time Dirksen and Dianna got back to Seattle, she had serviced his immediate needs and was prepared to do more once they were out of the confines of the car.

*   *   *

With Patrick out of town, I wanted to contact Getz and see where we were with the proposal I made to

202

him. The last time we spoke, he said things were moving rapidly along and we agreed to meet in my office as soon as I had a free day.

I had been spending almost all my time with Patrick running around the city looking for places and people Dirksen contacted or visited while he was in Seattle, so I felt I had been ignoring Anna. I called her just to hear her voice again.

"Well, hello stranger," she said when she answered.

"Guilty as charged, your honor, but I'm ready to serve any sentence you have in mind to atone for my crime."

"I think thirty lashes or dinner and dancing would do it."

Anna and I had discussed my lack of anything that remotely resembled an ability, or even a desire, to dance several times in the past. "I think I'll opt for the thirty lashes, if you don't mind."

"Oh, no. The accused doesn't get to pick the punishment. I was told about a new club in Seattle that has good food and an even better dance floor with live music four nights a week."

"Can I pick the three nights we go there?" I was serious.

"Not a chance. I'll come to your place tomorrow and we can check it out. If I like it, we can do all four nights."

The best part of what she said was that if we were going to go all four nights, it meant she planned to spend every night with me. That was enough to make me want to see if Arthur Murray was still in business so I could sign up for dancing lessons. When she came over and I had something to do that did not involve her and Bill Hart that put us in harm's way or in a situation where we could get killed, she usually went into Seattle and either visited friends or spent the day shopping. With the meeting scheduled with

Getz the next day, I didn't know how my days would be spent for a while.

"You drive a hard bargain, but I'll accept your terms," I said.

"Good. I'll catch the first ferry tomorrow morning and you can buy me lunch."

I hesitated but I had to assume that Getz and I would talk either over or through lunch, so I had to tell her that we could not have lunch together.

"No problem. I'll drive so I have my car and I can meet you for coffee or something and then let you take care of business."

"Define something," I said.

She did and I almost called Getz to cancel, but I had already made a commitment and I tried to stick to it when I made one. We agreed on the coffee meeting, and she ended the call. As soon as the line went dead, I called Getz.

"I'm glad you called. I worked out a deal with one of my clients, so let's meet and I'll tell you all about it."

The drive to my office earlier in the morning had been on one of the most pleasant days I had seen in Edmonds in a long time. The sky was a deep blue, with no clouds in sight. The snow-capped peaks of the Olympic Mountains across the Puget Sound looked like a series of freshly dipped vanilla ice cream cones. The rugged mountains forming the cones for the scoops always looked like they were posing a personal challenge to climb to anyone who saw them. I knew the rock-strewn areas throughout the area that the locals referred to as beaches would be packed with people taking advantage of the unusual weather. Sunglass sales would go through the roof as the few people who had them, probably couldn't find them and tourists didn't expect sunshine, so they had to buy them.

We agreed to meet in my office, but he said he wanted to have lunch at the same place where we had dined in the past when we met. I spent the time in my office doing mostly busy work. I sent out a couple of invoices for work that I had done and that had not been paid. When I finished that, I took my coffee pot off the burner and into the bathroom where I used a soap pad that was also a piece of fine steel-wool and attempted to cut the hard black, burned on coffee caked on the bottom of the pot. When I cut through the first several layers, I decided it if hadn't killed me by now, what was left was probably safe, so I filled it with water and fired up a pot of fresh coffee.

I finished up what I was doing in the office, had two cups of coffee and answered a phone call from a man who was certain his wife was trying to poison him by putting something in his beer. I convinced him if he was serious, he needed to contact the police and not a private investigator. His excuse for contacting me was that his wife was a deputy sheriff in the next county from Seattle. We discussed possible options and he finally decided the best way to proceed was to contact the state police. I agreed and he hung up.

I was thumbing through a magazine I found beneath my mail slot one morning. It dealt with food and wine and was a sample to entice me to subscribe, when Getz opened the street-side door and came in. My office door was open, so I waved him back to my office.

"You musta' been busy for the last week since I haven't heard from you," he said as he came in and took a seat on my sofa.

"Believe it or not, I do on occasion have a real client."

"I'm crushed that you don't look at me as a real client." He placed the briefcase he was carrying on his lap and snapped the locks open. "I got some papers in here I think you'll find interesting." He pulled out a folder and placed it on my desk and waited for me to open it and look at the contents.

After quickly scanning the pages, I realized he had a deal with a property owner to allow him, and by extension me, to set the property up to be burned. "Do you think this will work?"

"If it don't and they are not what I think or they actually are, and they burn the places down before we can stop them, I'm going to have to re-think my association with you." He pulled another folder from the briefcase and handed it to me. "This is an agreement between you and me...just so there's no misunderstanding about what we're doing."

I took it and before I could open it, he stood. "No need to read it now. Let's go get some lunch and I'll tell you what's in it."

We left the office and to my surprise the weather had not changed from the way it had been earlier. If anything, it had gotten better. We could see the Puget Sound was sprinkled with boats, both power and sail. When we got to the waterfront, the pier was dotted with men, women and a few kids holding fishing rods or pulling ropes tied to crab pots up from the depths, or lowering them after checking their contents.

"You a fisherman?" Getz asked as we pulled into the parking lot for the restaurant.

"Not in far too many years. I used to do it with my dad and my brother when we were growing up. After I went into the Army it seemed I didn't have time to do any of the things I really liked to do."

"I know what you mean. I used to play golf until I moved to this area. Not too many good golfing days out here."

We left the car and went inside where we had to wait for a table. Unlike the last time, we arrived at the height of the lunch hour. After a few minutes, an attractive woman of about thirty picked two menus from her podium and asked us to follow her. She was dressed in a long black skirt that fit snuggly on her very attractive body. She wore a light pink blouse that was stretched across her breasts almost as much as the skirt was stretched on her rear. I noticed the shade of pink lipstick was the same as what was worn by a girl I had a case of the screaming scorchies for when I was in junior high. Every time I saw that color, I immediately flashed back to a Valentine Day party at her house where we made out like neither of us had done in the past. I decide that night that this was the person I wanted to spend the rest of life with. We dated a few times and then made it official and declared we were going steady. That lasted until almost Christmas of that year when we went to a friend's Christmas party, and she was introduced to a guy who transferred in from a school in Florida. Like the old song, two dances later he stole my true love away. After I cleared my head from thinking of her, I saw several of the men turn and watch the hostess as she slipped between tables on the way to seat us at ours.

"Have you gentlemen dined here in the past?" she asked as she placed a menu in front of us.

"Several times in the past, but I've never seen you before." Getz was more interested in the hostess than the menu.

"I've only been here a few weeks." Her smile was one that said Getz was not the first one to hit on her.

"Well, you've just made this my favorite place to have lunch," Getz said as he returned the smile.

After she left the table, he watched as she worked her smile on two other men who came in. "Did you see a ring on her finger?" he asked as he picked up the menu.

"Does that matter? The way you were lusting after her indicated you'd like to take her to the back room, ring or not."

"If I remember correctly, you're not married either, so tell me you didn't get a quick flash of her in your bed."

As much as I hated to admit it, old habits were hard to break, and after flashing back to my high school days because of her lipstick, the thought did do a hundred-yard dash across my mind.

We didn't need the menu to decide what we wanted so when another, much younger woman came to the table, we ordered, and she left.

"Now that you've got your hormones in check for a few minutes, tell me what you've got me into," I said as I picked up my napkin, shook it out and put it in my lap.

"Okay, here's the deal. You tell them you've got three properties in different parts of the city and they're all losing money. Low rent. Non-payment. People moving out in the middle of the night and stealing everything to include the light bulbs. You got taxes and the city building inspector on your ass for repairs and upgrades. All eating you up. Casually, like maybe you're joking that if you could find somebody, you'd pay well to have them torched."

He waited for my reaction. When I nodded in understanding, he continued.

"If they bite, and I think they will, you'll arrange for them to be torched...with any luck you can get them to do it right away, so we don't have to wait. When you have the information, I'll arrange for an undercover operation at the house to catch them in the act. The law can deal with them for their part, and I'll take care of my end of it."

"What about me? I'm the one who's on the hook for setting it up. They'll try to shift some of the blame to me."

"It's all in the contract. You're working for me, and the actual owner has given his permission to use his properties as bait." He stopped talking when our food arrived. After taking a quick taste of his clam chowder, he buttered a piece of warm sourdough bread and took a bite. He chewed for a minute, then using his butter knife like a pointer, "I ran all of this through a lawyer friend, and he said we're all in the clear and fully protected.

My military police background said this may be the epitome of Murphy's Basic Law that says Whatever can go wrong will, and at the most inopportune time. "I'd like to see his opinion in writing."

"I do that, I gotta pay him. He told me that for two scotch and waters."

"Consider it a part of my contract." I left it hanging as I began to eat.

We finished lunch, Getz tried to get the phone number from the hostess, and she just laughed and told him she did not know him well enough but if he came back and she got to know him better, she'd consider it. I knew he'd consider that a challenge and that I'd be getting lunch invitations from him until he either got her number or she told him to go to Hell.

Back in my office, we decided I'd contact the management company the next day and see if we could put things in motion. I wanted to wrap this up during the week that Patrick was out of town, and I was not working on the death of the professor.

Chapter 29

I pulled the Keller Management Company card from my desk drawer and punched in the number on my cell phone. When it was answered I asked for Jones.

Without acknowledging his name, he responded. "Who is this?"

"A future client for your services."

"Oh, well in that case, yeah, this is Jones. Now who are you?" The man was all business.

I just realized I had not given him my name, so I had to come up with something. "This is Peter Miller. I came by to see you a few weeks ago and I think I'm ready to hire your services." I used the name Bill Hart had me use one time.

"We do a lot of things, so why don't you come in and we can talk eyeball-to-eyeball. I don't like doing business over the phone with people I don't know."

"Sounds like a good idea. I can be there first thing tomorrow morning. Nine work for you?"

"What did you say your name was? And when did we talk?"

I went over our past meeting and conversation, and he seemed okay with it, so we agreed to meet the next morning at nine.

With nothing to do for the remainder of the afternoon, I took my Toyota to the dealership and got an oil change. After that, I did the unusual, at least for me, I went to the large shopping center off the Interstate and just wandered around for an hour or so. I had a cup of coffee at the coffee shop and picked up a six pack of brownies on my way out. When I got back to my place, I fixed a drink and settled down with a biography of Stonewall Jackson I had been wanting to read for several weeks. I was on the second chapter when I got a phone call from one of my daughters. It's not unusual for her to call, but I am always on alert for the first minute until she tells me everything is okay. She'll occasionally mention her mother and my ex-wife just to let me know she's still around. Both the girls were hurt when we divorced but they were old enough to understand that even though we were no longer the family they had known all their lives, they still had a mother and a father. We talked for almost an hour. She caught me up with her life and then asked me about mine. She knew I was not sitting home alone every night, this being the exception, but she did not know all the details about Anna and me. She remembered Bill Hart from when we were in Germany and knew I occasionally did work for him, so I told her about my working on the professor who was found dead in the tulip field. I did not go into details, told her just enough so she would know I was keeping occupied and earning some additional money since her mother was getting half of my Army retirement as a reward for putting up with me and the Army for over ten years.

We ended the conversation and after dozing off twice trying to read, I went to bed.

*   *   *

The White Center section of Seattle is a transitional neighborhood. It's in the process of transitioning from bad to worse. From scary to dangerous. I took a chance and parked on the street in front of Keller Management a few minutes before nine. Several young men watched as I parked, and I hoped they heard the solid click as I activated the locks on my doors with the key remote. If they were interested in anything more than welcoming me to the neighborhood and wanted to relieve me of my vehicle, the lock was a minor inconvenience. It was a chance I was willing to take. I figured if my 4 Runner was not there when I returned, I'd add it to my expense report and get Getz to pay for it.

I pushed the door open to the Keller Management Company and went inside. The man I knew only as Jones was walking back to his desk with a cup of coffee in one hand and the largest cinnamon roll I had ever seen in the other. An unfiltered cigarette dangled from his mouth. He squinted his eyes as the smoke rose in his face as he spoke to me. "I got another one of these back there," he rocked his head to the rear to indicate there was another cinnamon bun. "It'll go good if you want a cup of coffee."

"I'll pass," I said as he walked by me and took a seat behind his desk.

"I remember you now. You're having some income problems with income properties that ain't producing income. Right?"

"That's why I'm here. I have the suspicion that you may be able to help me out with that problem." I waited to see his reaction.

He took his time, placed the thick paper plate with the cinnamon bun on his desk, took a drink from his coffee and took another long drag from his cigarette. "You need a management company?"

We were staring each other eye-to-eye to see who blinked first. I held his stare. "I need to eliminate my income problems."

He took almost a minute to respond. "I may be able to help...but it'll cost you."

"If anything were to happen to any of my properties, I'm covered. I've got good insurance. I'll probably have some left over after I pay off my mortgages to spread some around to anyone who helped me."

One of the things Bill Hart did for me when I first started working with him again, was to provide me with a fully believable false identification. I knew Jones would check me out at some point if he was the link to the arsonist, so I was prepared to give him any information on Peter Miller that he wanted. I had called Bill the day before and told him what I was doing and asked that my name show up on some property records in Seattle.

"I'm gonna need a day to two to check out your properties, you know, just to see if they're something we can help you with." He slid a yellow legal pad across the desk. "Give me all your contact information and the location of the places you need help with, and maybe I'll call you tomorrow." He had a fork on his desk which he used to immediately attach the cinnamon bun.

"Don't fuck around with this. I've got some insurance and tax payments due that I'm behind on. I need some relief, and I need it now." I tried to sound both desperate and convincing at the same time.

He chewed the mouthful of cinnamon bun, licked the white sugar frosting off the fork and looked at me. "I think we'll be able to help you." He placed the fork on the now-empty plate and pulled out a cigarette which he slowly lit. "This ain't a charity operation, you know. We need to talk about... let's call it management assistant fees."

I knew then that I had him hooked and this was an operation just like Getz thought. "I...I can't pay much up front...for obvious reasons, but once I'm out of the rental business, I'm sure I can meet your fees." I waited to see if he took the bait.

"Let's say for instance that one of your less than upstanding renters was smoking in bed and set the whole house on fire. A total loss, but he made it out alive. You have insurance to cover just such a tragedy?"

"As long as nobody is hurt, he could burn the entire neighborhood down. I wouldn't care."

He took a long drag from the cigarette and held it. When he finally let it out, he spoke through the smoke. "I'm not interested in the rest of the neighborhood. We're just talking about your property. It's insured?"

I nodded in the affirmative.

"And the policy is up to date?"

"Paid up until a month from now when I have to renew. The same time the taxes and repairs are due."

"Bring me a copy of the insurance policy and we'll see what we can do."

Getz had suggested that I have a copy of a policy he fabricated on the properties and had provided me one. I reached into my jacket pocket and pulled it out.

"Here, I thought you'd want to see it." I handed it to him.

He took the policy and as the cigarette dangled from his lips, he read it. Once he finished, he stood and pointed at me. "Stay here. I need to make a few calls. I'll have an answer in a few minutes." With that he opened a door in the back of the office and disappeared. Even with my limited hearing, I could make out some of the conversation he was obviously having on the phone in the next room. After about five minutes, he returned.

"Okay, here's how it's going to go down. Next Thursday you will have a massive leak in your water line leading to the house. Everyone will be notified that to repair it, they must leave for at least two days. It's up to you to make sure they're all gone. If anybody decides they can live on bottled water and not take a bath for two days, it's on you." He looked at me. "You understand what I'm saying?"

"I do, and I'll make sure everyone is gone. Then what?"

"We have a management team that will go out and check out the place. Sometimes they do some

214

really shitty electrical work and once or twice we had a place burn down after they inspected it." He snuffed out the cigarette he had been smoking and immediately tapped another one out of the pack.

"And just how much is this inspection going to cost me?"

He looked at the insurance policy. "You've got that shit hole insured for one point two million. You and I both know it's not worth that much and there's no way in Hell that you're gonna try to rebuild it, so when the smoke settles." He smiled. "On the off chance that our electrician fucks up again, you walk with a bundle. I think a full-service inspection is worth two hundred thousand."

Before I could respond, I heard the screeching of tires and the unmistakable sound of metal against metal as two or more vehicles crashed on the street outside. He barely looked up at the sound. I had the thought that he might be in the car crash business as well.

"I think that might be something I can work with."

"Thought you might like it. I need ten thousand in cash in two days. I'll have a contract drawn up for management services which you'll sign and then you never come here again. I don't care how deep in the shit you are with the other properties; this is the only one we will manage for you." He smiled. "And don't think our contracts," he did the air-quote with his hands when he said it, "are unenforceable. We have our own collection department and believe me, when we send them out to collect...they collect."

He sat in silence for a minute until I took the hint that he and I had finished our business until I brought the cash back, so I stood and, without saying good-bye or shaking hands, I left.

The police were just clearing the street from the accident I heard while I was in the office. A fire pumper was hosing down the street where one of the cars gas tanks had ruptured and spilled gasoline at the site. Several bystanders, either witnesses or rubber-neckers stood around watching as a wrecker hooked up one of the cars and pulled it aboard a flatbed on the back of the wrecker.

After I got around the accident, I pulled out my cell phone and called Getz. I had the phone synced with my sound system. If I was in the vehicle and got a call, it came up on a screen in the dash. The same went for outgoing calls. It was all hands-free as Seattle had some strange regulations regarding talking and texting while driving. It was enforced in conjunction with other traffic offenses and sometimes an overzealous patrol officer would see someone on the phone and pull them over.

I didn't want to have a conversation in which the officer asked me where I had been or where I was going. "Yes, officer I'm on the phone arranging for an arsonist to burn down a property for two hundred thousand dollars and I'm on the way to pick up ten thousand in cash as a down payment."

Getz answered on the second ring. I explained my conversation and what was planned. I saved the part about needing ten thousand dollars in cash until last. "You need what?" he yelled. "Why the Hell did you agree to that without checking with me first?"

"I don't think calling you and trying to explain I need ten grand to make sure my property gets burned to the ground is a conversation I wanted to have in his office."

I pulled onto I-5 and headed north just as another police cruiser passed me. "I'm on the Interstate and I'll be in my office in thirty minutes or so. I'll give you a call from there and tell you everything. I don't want to go into details on a cell phone."

"Yeah, I guess you're right. That'll give me a few minutes to figure out where I'm going to come up with the cash."

Chapter 30

Seattle traffic was supposed to get a break when the light rail network was put in. Most residents of the metro area still seemed to prefer to drive and complain about the traffic and I was one of them. I hardly ever needed to go to a place that the light rail was more convenient or speedier than using my own transportation. Even looking for a parking place, on the rare occasions when I had to find one in the downtown area, was easier than being at the mercy of a schedule.

I arrived at my office less than an hour after leaving Keller Management. I knew I was in the middle of what could be a long-drawn-out court battle where people would be sued and some would probably go to jail, but as much as I hated to admit it, my old military police background said it was okay to get them off the streets.

I parked and walked from the lot to the entrance of my office. I had just touched the door, when I heard my name called from across the street. I turned and saw the mayor waving at me from in front of the Mexican restaurant. "Hey, Max. Hold up. I want to talk to you." As the mayor, he was used to people automatically responding in the positive to anything he said, so he crossed against the traffic and came to my door.

I had already turned my back and was inserting a key in the door when he came up beside me. "Been a while since you and I spoke, Max." He was running for re-election and for the first time he had a serious opponent. He had been so secure in his last election that he hardly got out of his office or the accounting firm he owned to campaign. This time it was different.

He put his hand on my shoulder and walked into the office with me. I hate to have people I don't know or don't like touch me, so it was all I could do not to rip his hand from my shoulder and beat him over the head with it. Instead, I shrugged my shoulder and shook it off.

"Election time is coming up and I need all the help I can get. I'd like to put one of my posters in your window." He pointed to the large glass window overlooking the street. Prior to my renting the space it had been a mom-and-pop drug store. They used the window to advertise sales and specials during the holidays. I used it to look outside and see if it was raining or if my friend George was close by and looking for conversation or a cup of coffee. The mayor and I had the same conversation previously and I didn't want a poster then and I was even more convinced that I didn't want it now. Some things had come out in the local paper indicating he had not been completely honest in helping some of his clients with their taxes. The allegations were such that if proven, the client would get the shitty end of the stick and not Mayor Valentino.

"It's like I said the last time you asked me. I can't afford to play favorites when it comes to political candidates, and beside who cares who I support?"

Ever the politician, he gave me his best smile. "I think you'd be surprised at how popular you are here in town." He gave me a sleazy wink of his eye. "I know you're more popular with some of the not-so-local residents than others, but I'm only concerned about the ones who live in the city."

I took a second to get my blood pressure back down as I knew immediately that he was referring to

Anna. "Let me see if I can say this in a way that leaves no chance of your misunderstanding. I want you to get the fuck out of my office and don't ever come back in here again, and if you ever take the approach that you just did, you have no idea of the shit storm you will face." I realized I was talking through clenched teeth and with a stiff jaw.

"You can't talk to me like that. I can..."

I cut him off. "What part of get the fuck out didn't you understand? And you're in my office, not yours, so I can say pretty much anything I want." I pointed to the door, and he took the hint.

"I think you may regret this," he said as he walked out.

Unfortunately, he had a point, as his brother was the owner of the building, thus he was my landlord. I had a three-year lease with two years remaining, so unless he came up with some violation of the lease on my part, I was good for a while before I had to start looking for a new office. I was still steaming when I realized I was talking to myself as I prepared the coffee pot. The water was sizzling as it dripped through the burner when I heard my land line phone ring. I hesitated and thought about ignoring the phone and waiting for the pot to fill so I could get a cup when I realized it was probably Getz.

"Hello," I said in what I realized was a not very business-like tone.

"Damn, did you stop off and have a meal of razor blades for lunch? You keep answering the phone like that, and I'll be the only person who'll hire you."

"Not a good time for jokes. I just threw the mayor out of my office." I was watching the pot as it filled. When the last drip of water fell into the pot, I picked up my mug and walked to the pot where I poured my mug full.

"Probably not good if you want to do business with the city," he said.

"Even worse. His brother is my landlord. I'm sure he'll be looking for a way to put me on the street with no notice." I took a drink and let the hot coffee burn on its way down. "But that's not why you called."

"No. I can get the money and based on what you said, I think they'll probably try to burn the place on Saturday night. If we get all the people out and they want two days, that'll put it to Saturday. I imagine they'll want to do it at night, so I'm setting things up."

"I probably need to know the details so when I get arrested, I can mention your name and we can change places in jail."

"Not to worry. I've got enough local fire officials involved that we're in the clear."

I looked out the large window where Valentino wanted a sign and noticed him standing across the street talking to a lady who owned a dress shop several doors down from my office. She was holding two paper cups of something she had purchased from the latte stand in front of the real estate office. I wondered if she ever sent George over there for coffee for her and her staff and if she did, did she ever get any change.

"What time are you bringing the money here tomorrow? I'd like to get it done and over with as early as possible."

"I can be there by ten. That okay?"

We agreed and I ended the call. I looked at my watch and realized that it was almost happy hour. I hate to drink alone, so my first inclination was to call Anna but after the comment from the mayor I hesitated to ask her to come to me for a drink since I knew it would almost invariably lead to our spending the night together with her easily recognized Jaguar either parked in front of my place or in a spot here at the office.

She was now legally separated from her husband, so there were no consequences to her being here and spending the night with me, but politicians are basically snakes and I didn't want Valentino crawling from beneath a rock and attacking Anna. Instead of calling her, I opened my computer and checked the poker room at one of the local Indian casinos. I saw they were having a Texas hold'em tournament with a two hundred dollar buy in, so I decided to drive to the casino, have dinner, play and possibly win something in the tournament and then call Anna when I got home.

My favorite casino had recently stopped playing poker and closed the poker room, so I had to drive south toward Tacoma to find a game. I drove against the traffic as I went south until I got to Seattle and then I had to join the herd leaving town all the way to the airport. I got to the casino an hour before the tournament started so I had time to enjoy a nice steak dinner. Most of my meals were eaten at some type of restaurant, either fast food or a sit down. My schedule when I could keep it, or remember it, was to only eat two meals a day. If I ate lunch, it was usually a salad or a small sandwich. Dinner, when I didn't thaw something, was the big meal of the day. The exception was when I stopped by the Tree Topper for breakfast. If I made the stop, I didn't need, and usually didn't want anything else to eat until dinner. The place was old, not the cleanest place in the city, filled with people who generally ignored the no smoking ban and had a waitress who knew everyone who came in by order if not by name. By the time I could get to a booth, she had a mug of coffee and the remains of the daily paper for me. She knew I liked to do the crossword puzzle, so she'd gather up whatever part of a paper was left behind by a previous diner and hand it to me. I got the impression I was the only person at breakfast at the Tree Topper who did the crossword. She never brought me a paper with it filled in.

After dinner, I went to the poker room and bought in for the tournament. I like tournaments better than cash games as you can only lose the buy-in amount, although some tournaments allow the players to buy in multiple times. The casino was small if it or any other like establishment were to be compared to the one on the strip in Las Vegas. It had all the same games but in smaller numbers. The patrons ran the same social strata as the larger casinos. People in suits and ties with a trophy wife or eye candy on their arms yelled at the dice as they tossed them on the craps table. A winning roll got them a kiss or a squeeze on the arm from their companion. Men and women who looked like they were spending their rent and grocery money sat and watched the light show in front of them on the slot machine's screen. Stacks of chips were raked from the felt as the player's number failed to capture the ball on the roulette wheel. As I made my way across the casino floor to the poker room, I heard a yell as a player hit a jackpot on a slot machine. I was tempted to go to the source and see if the person took the money and ran, or was it re-invested in hopes of a bigger win?

The one constant, at almost every casino I had ever been in, was the cocktail waitresses. No discrimination in their hiring practices, here. This was a female only job and males need not apply and for good reason. Many of the women had to pay to work at the casino. Since they made so much in tips, it was worth it. It was the same for dealers. Once I had a blackjack dealer come to me for assistance in a custody case. She was afraid the judge would be put off by her job and award custody of her daughter to the soon-to-be ex-husband. She wanted me to follow him and document his excessive gambling habits. I watched him for two months during football and basketball season as he went to the games and to some of the local bookies and lost a bundle. This was in addition to the losses at the casino where the wife worked. All the dealers knew him and tried to get him to cut back but like compulsive gamblers anyplace in the world, he was convinced the next roll of the dice or spin of the wheel would be the one to solve all his problems. It never was, and never will be. The judge agreed that his gambling addiction far outweighed the negative aspects of the mother's employment and she got full custody.

I played until almost two in the morning when the tournament finally ended. I came in second and won a little over nine hundred dollars. That was enough to finance my next trip to a poker tournament when I decided to enter one. Two hours later, I was slipping into my bed, knowing I'd only get my normal three to five hours of sleep.

My phone's buzzing woke me a little after nine. I was surprised when I picked it up and looked at the clock. I had been asleep and did not wake to go to the bathroom for over five hours. That was almost a record for me.

"Hello?" My voice was still in sleep mode and was about two octaves lower than it would be in an hour.

"Max, it's Getz. You sound like I woke you."

"No. I had to get up to answer the phone," I said using an age-old joke. I swung my legs off the bed and stood. After stretching and scratching, I asked what he wanted.

"Got the money for you. How about we meet for lunch?" He laughed. "I want to take another shot at that new hostess we met the other day."

I was walking to the kitchen to pour myself a cup of coffee. I had the pot set on a timer, so it was hot and waiting for me. "I guess if she can stand it, so can I." My favorite mug was still in the sink, where I had placed it the last time I used it. After rinsing it out, I filled it and headed back to the bedroom.

"Only difference is that I'm not handing her ten grand in cash to play with, although it might be worth at least some of that if she would."

I let that comment dangle as I took a seat on the edge of the bed. "I'm about an hour away from the office. How about if we meet there at eleven?"

"Good idea and I'm bringing someone with me. He's my client who owns the properties were using. I thought you might want to meet him since you're setting his place up to be burned down."

As soon as we finished talking, I stripped off my boxers and headed for the shower. After a shave and brushing my teeth, I pulled out a fresh shirt and pants and put them on. When I retired and during the period I was still married, my wardrobe consisted of "wash and wrinkle" clothes. They were thrown in the washer, dried and hung in the closet ready for me to wear. Now I tend to buy clothes that I can take to the laundry since I don't have a washer and dryer and I refuse to sit at a laundromat and wait for them to wash and dry.

I skipped breakfast and headed straight to the office. The weather had turned to what most people think of about Seattle. It was dark, dreary and a light mist was falling. It was not the best weather, but it reminded me of the first time Anna and I had spent a weekend at a Bed and Breakfast in the San Juan Islands. She made all the arrangements and I met her there. This was prior to her separation, and we were still looking over our shoulder when we were together. It was a little farm with one main house and three small outbuildings that had been converted to bedrooms. Each one had a small wood-burning fireplace and its own bathroom, but meals were in the main house.

I arrived late in the afternoon, and she was already there. The island was fogged in and a mist heavier than the one falling as I entered my office was coming down. Anna had a small fire going and was sitting in a chair in front of the fire. Her legs were folded beneath her, and she wore a yellow silk gown. It was the sexiest thing I had ever seen. I don't

224

remember how long it took for us to be entwined in each other in the massive bed that took up most of the space in the room. We missed dinner and had some wine and cheese that she brought with her to regain our strength about midnight. I'm not sure either of us slept that night.

Chapter 31

I arrived at the office a few minutes until eleven. When I opened the door, there were several pieces of mail beneath the slot in the door inside the office, where the postman dropped them. I bent down and picked them up noticing that only one seemed interesting. I had a "to whom it may concern" form letter informing me that the sewer lines running from the street to my house were my responsibility and for a yearly fee this company would keep them clear. Since I didn't own the place where I lived, sewer lines were of no concern to me until they backed up. Another one was a political ad for Valentino's opposition and an advertisement for a local supermarket that seemed to be having a sale on everything in the store. The only thing that interested me was an envelope with the return address of a Seattle attorney whom I had done some work for in the past. I opened it hoping it would be another job offer. Before I could read it, I sensed someone behind me.

I turned and Getz and another man I did not recognize were standing on the sidewalk in front of my office. "Good timing," Getz said as he stood aside and motioned for the other man to enter. "This is Ed Sewell. He's the one who owns the properties." Ed grunted as he entered the office.

They followed me through the outer room and into my office. "I'll make some coffee if you want to wait for it," I offered, as Ed looked around the office as if he were about to make me an offer to purchase it, or he was a city official ready to condemn it.

"No, I think we can wait till we get to the restaurant." Getz took a seat on my sofa. Ed was still standing and inspecting my office.

"How about you, Ed? You want to wait?"

"I'm good." He focused on me. "Byron says you're a pretty good PI. That true?"

"If you ask me, I'd say I'm the best in the city, but I may be a little prejudiced."

"Yeah, I guess you might be." He pointed to the blank wall behind my desk. "I don't see no license or pictures or nothing hanging on the wall. You are legit, right?"

"I can show you a copy of my license if you like," I said as I opened the drawer on my desk where I kept the folder with my license, a copy of my carry permit and other assorted papers needed for my business.

"Naw, that's not necessary. I was just curious why you don't have it on the wall."

"I guess I never got around to putting it up, but now that you mention it, I think I'll do it first thing tomorrow."

"Now that we got that straightened out, let's go see if that hostess is still there."

I don't know if it was that she remembered us, especially Getz, or if she was just being a very competent hostess, but she greeted us with a blinding smile. "I don't know how you did it, but you're even more attractive this time than the last time we were here." Getz was circling for the kill.

"I'll bet you say that to every woman you meet," she said as she placed her hand on his arm and led us to a table.

"Only the ones I rate a nine or higher," he said as he stood beside the chair she offered.

"I guess I'll have to work a little harder to become a ten," she said as she pulled out another chair for me.

Getz was still standing. "At least tell me your name, so I'll know who to ask for when I come back."

"You don't have to ask for me by name. Anytime you come for lunch, I'll be here." She gave him another smile and left to seat another group.

"Son of a bitch. She's good, and I think I'm in love." Getz watched as she took another group to a table and seated them.

"You're just in heat," Ed said, and I had to agree with his assessment of our companion. "Don't let her job fool you. That lady's got class. She may be doing this because she needs the money or because she's bored at home, but somewhere inside that body and brain is a real lady that's out of your league."

"Your words cut me deeply," Getz grabbed his heart as he took his seat. "But you're right about the class thing. You can see it in the way she handles herself."

A waiter came and took our drink order. I got coffee. Getz got a bloody Mary and Ed asked for a scotch and soda. It didn't seem to be too early for either of them to hit the hard stuff.

Ed looked out the wall of windows facing the dock and the Puget Sound. "I think I came here once before. I was looking at some property in the city." Our drinks came and he ignored the waiter as they were placed on the table. "Wish to hell I had bought it. Prices have been skyrocketing since then." He turned and noticed the young man still standing awaiting our order.

"What's good today? Any specials?"

"Yes sir, we do," he said and then recited several fish dishes and a Caesar salad with either chicken or salmon.

Ed selected the steamed clams from the recited menu while Getz and I stuck with the Caesar and a bowl of clam chowder. I got chicken on my salad and Getz got salmon. We were half-way through our lunch when we heard the unmistakable sound of the

228

ferry horn announcing its departure. "You live around one of the ferry docks and you get used to the sound. Me, I live so far from the water, I have to drive to see it." Ed stopped eating and watched the ferry pull away from the dock. "Soon as I finish eating, we can get down to business." He shifted his focus back to the bowl of steamed clams.

Getz and I finished our meals and sat watching Ed fish a clam out of the bowl, spear the clam with his seafood fork, drag it through the broth and then put it in his mouth. Once he thought the bowl was empty, he took a spoon and dipped it in the juice to make sure there were no escapees resting on the bottom. He dipped the remaining bread in the juice until he was out of bread. I was afraid he was going to ask for another basket of sourdough, since there was broth remaining. He didn't ask for another basket of bread, but he did raise his hand to get the waiter's attention. When the waiter came to the table, he ordered another scotch, his third.

"Damn, that was good." I wasn't sure if he was referring to the clams or the scotch, but I kept my opinion to myself as he took the drink from the waiter. "Okay, now I feel like talking."

For the next hour we went over all the details of what Getz wanted, what Ed was willing to let him do and what my part in the operation was and would be.

By the time we finished, the early dining crowd was just coming in. Most of the establishments in the area had an "early bird" menu for the geriatric crowd who ate early, went to bed early and got up early. Like some animals and birds, they tended to arrive in packs. The group we saw was three men and a like number of women. I got the impression that there were two couples and two whom the others wished to be couples since a round of introductions were made to the single man and woman. Every time I saw a group of them, I wondered how long it would be before I justified my joining in the early crowd.

Ed looked at me. "Byron said you were a cop in the Army. That right?"

"I was a military police officer and worked most of my career in the intelligence field." I nodded.

"Then I imagine you've put this together like a military operation?"

"That was a part of my planning."

"Good. I was in the Army during Viet Nam. I recognize an Army operation when I see it." He laughed. "Although the last one I saw got my ass shot, but it got me out of the brush and into a hospital in the States. Had a two-star pin my Purple Heart on me when I was in the hospital...you ever get shot?"

"I did. In Iraq."

"It's not like in the movies, is it? Hurts like a bitch no matter how bad it is, don't it?"

I couldn't get him away from talking about his Army days for a few minutes, but suddenly it was like a light switch had been flipped. "But that's not why we're here. We can tell war stories after all of this is over. Tell me what you have in mind."

I told them in general terms what I thought would work and they agreed I was on the right track.

We agreed that I would go back to Keller and tell them which property I wanted them to "manage" and how long it would take to get everyone out of the building. Ed had a four-unit apartment unit with one vacancy which meant we'd only have to move three families. Even though the plan was to stop the arsonist prior to his or her putting the place in flames, we didn't want to take a chance on anything happening to the people who lived there. Ed didn't seem to be overly concerned if our timing was off and he lost the property to an arsonist.

"I contacted my underwriter and told them what we were planning," Getz said. "They weren't overly excited about it, but the prospects of getting money back sealed the deal. I had to agree to have one of their arson investigators with us the night it's going

230

down." He still had about half a good swallow left in his drink which he drank. "I'm going to talk to a friend who's a lieutenant with the Seattle FD and let him know what's going on in case things go south and we need a pumper in a hurry." He looked at Ed and then at me. "What are we missing or what have we overlooked that will bite us in the ass?"

"You know what they say, no plan survives first contact with the enemy."

"I guess you have to go back into the enemy's camp and convince them you're legit and tell them to burn my place down." Without waiting for a response, Ed stood, dropped his napkin on the table and motioned for us to follow him. "Let's get out of Dodge."

One the way out, Getz made it a point to walk by the hostess stand and speak to her. I saw the same toothpaste ad quality smile as she spoke to Getz and then took his hand in hers in what I thought was a friendly handshake. I noticed Getz had a bit of a spring in his step as we left.

When we got into his car, I found out the reason. In addition to shaking his hand, the hostess had slipped a business card from the restaurant into his hand. On the back of the card, written in a delicate hand, was a name and phone number.

Chapter 32

Bill Hart wouldn't admit it, even to himself, but he was sure he was in love. He met Lannette almost a year earlier when he sent Max to New Orleans to find the illegitimate daughter of the man who ultimately became the president of the United States. The President, a former senator from Louisiana, had gotten his mixed-race girlfriend pregnant when he was a law student in New Orleans. The son of a prominent, and very white family, it was decided to pay the woman to have an abortion and the matter was forgotten. The problem was that she did not abort, and a daughter was born. When Senator "Poker John" Herbert became the frontrunner for this party's nomination, there was a full-court press from both political parties to find the woman and see if she knew who her father was, and what she would do with the information.

Max found the daughter and her mother, and in the process Bill was introduced to Lannette whose cousin was a sheriff in Louisiana and who had to help Max and Anna escape the clutches of a team of hit men sent to kill the daughter to keep her from being exposed.

Bill and Lannette dated for several months and then she moved into his condo in Old Town Alexandria, Virginia. A divorcee, Bill had never contemplated a serious committed relationship, but all of that ended with Lannette.

Like most of the people in the area, Lannette also worked for the government, so she and Bill rode to work together every morning. The trip home was a different matter as there was no guarantee that Bill would come home, sometimes for a day or more as his position sometimes required long hours that lasted for days.

Bill pulled his car to the curb where he always stopped to let Lannette out. He leaned across the seat to give her a kiss. "I'll pick you up tonight…with any luck. I don't have anything hanging fire that should keep me in the office."

"One can always hope," she said as she returned the kiss and reached for the handle to open the door. "Call me if you can sometime today."

Bill always sat in the same spot and watched as she walked toward the entrance to her building. He couldn't explain it, even if he tried, but he felt more for her than he ever had for anyone else. Perhaps even his ex-wife when they were first in love.

Thirty minutes later he had left the District and was back in Alexandria where he had an office. Unlike most the people who worked in the area, he had his own dedicated parking space. He left the car, took the elevator from the parking lot to the floor where his office was located. Once inside the office complex he stopped by the communal coffee pot, filled a mug, passed on sugar and cream and went to his office.

As soon as he sat down, Gerald Warren, his deputy, stuck his head inside Bill's office door. "Morning, boss. You have a visitor waiting."

Bill could tell from Gerald's tone of voice and demeanor; this was not a routine visitor. "What can you tell me about him?"

"All I know is I got a call from State about ten minutes before he got here." He nodded toward the rear of the waiting room. "I stashed him out there so I could warn you."

"Is he with State?"

"I don't think so. He didn't show me any ID when he came in. He's got a little bit of an accent. German, I think." Gerald took a drink from the cup of coffee he held in his hand. "That's about all I can tell you."

"Thanks. Send him in and wait three minutes and come in with a message." This was a scenario they had used many times in the past. At the three-minute mark, Bill would know if he wanted to spend more time with a person. If he did, he'd tell Gerald he'd take care of the message and if not, he'd tell the visitor he had to take it and the meeting would be over.

A few minutes later, Gerald walked back into Bill's office. There was a tall, grey-haired man beside him. The man appeared to be in his mid-fifties, but the years had been very kind to him. He was a man that you see in print ads and television commercials posing as the dapper older gentleman who may be a politician or a captain of industry.

"This is Mister Peter Van der Beck." He handed Bill a business card.

The card had Van der Beck's name and the seal of the government of the Netherlands and an address. Bill knew immediately why the man was in his office.

"Please have a seat," Bill indicated his sofa. "Can I get you a cup of coffee?"

"No, thanks. I just had a delightful cup of cappuccino at a little café just around the corner from your office." The man took his seat and placed his hand on the arm of the sofa. He looked around the office. "Lovely place you have here, and I especially like your view of your capital city."

"Yes, I'm quite fortunate to have this office," Bill picked up the mug of coffee sitting on his desk and took a drink. He and his visitor knew why he was here, but neither wanted to be the first to broach the subject.

Finally, Van der Beck cleared his throat. "I suppose you are aware of my government's interest in any of our citizens who die while abroad." He

234

looked at Hart for an indication of anything. "And especially those who die under...shall we say...less than clearly defined circumstances."

"Like your professor?"

"Exactly." He hesitated. "Perhaps I shall have that cup of coffee you offered."

Bill pushed a button on his phone, spoke into it and they sat in silence until a tray with two cups, a silver carafe of coffee and small containers of sugar and cream were brought in and placed on a sideboard. "Please. Help yourself," Bill said as he rose from his desk and went to the tray.

After both had a fresh cup of coffee in hand, Van der Beck continued. "I understand that you have assigned one of your associates to further investigate the circumstances of the death of Professor Dirksen."

"That's correct. I received the request from both our State Department and that of the Department of Agriculture." Bill looked at Van der Beck. "That's a strange combination of departmental interest, don't you think?"

"Perhaps under different circumstances, it would be, but I can explain why we are so interested in his passing." Van der Beck took a drink before he continued. "Have you ever heard of the Simper Augustus?"

"I know the US Marine motto is Simper Fideles and the Coast Guard is similar."

"I'm familiar with both, but the Simper I'm referring to is a type of tulip that may have never truly existed and if it did, it has been lost for centuries."

Bill placed his coffee on his desk. "Now you've really got me confused. It if never existed, how can it be lost? I'm not much on flowers, but I can't see the connection."

Van der Beck laughed. "I fully understand. As you may be aware, my country is very proud of our history and its tie to the tulip. Several hundred years ago, a new strain of tulip was developed, due we

235

think, to a virus that infected a portion of that year's crop. It was said to be the most beautiful flower ever produced. No bulb of that particular strain exists and the only proof we have of its existence is some written reports and a few paintings. If the paintings, even after some three hundred years, do it justice, it truly was a magnificent species."

"The Simper Augustus?"

"Correct...and we have reason to believe that Professor Dirksen may have duplicated the formula for the virus that created the original. If that is the case, it would be worth a small fortune to the tulip industry."

"And worth killing for to the get the formula?"

*   *   *

I went to Keller the next day and made the necessary arrangements for them to carry out their end of the operation. Getz had given me the cash when we returned to my office from lunch. The serial numbers were all recorded and, although it was a calculated risk and equal to betting on a ninety-nine to one long shot at the Kentucky Derby, the hope was that the money would be either recovered or traceable. I'm sure Getz had a back up plan to recover the money from the underwriters who covered his clients in case he lost it.

The man I knew only as Jones took the packet of money and placed it on his desk. "I need some kind of a receipt for the cash and a contract for upcoming services," I said as I reached out and pulled the packet of money back.

"You don't trust me?"

"Trust is a two-way street. I trust you with the money and when the dust, or smoke clears, you trust me to pay to a hell of a lot more. See how that works?

He gave me a squint-eyed stare as he fired up another cigarette. I continued to hold the cash as he pulled a contract from his desk and filled in several blanks. According to the contract, I was hiring Keller Management with an upfront fee of ten thousand dollars to do a complete inspection and evaluation of my property and if they found it acceptable, we would enter into an agreement for the first month's rent and a percent of each month during the life of the contract. On the surface it looked like a legitimate contract between a management company and an owner who didn't have a clue what he was signing. The upfront and monthly fees were outrageous and nobody in his or her right mind would agree to them.

"How soon can you get the renters out? I want to get this done as soon as possible." Jones looked at my signature on the contract, signed another copy and made a duplicate on a printer that looked to be twenty years old. When it spit out the copy, he handed it to me.

"I'll need a couple of days, so I think Saturday will be a good day for your people to drop by."

He pulled a can of a power drink from a small apartment-size refrigerator behind his desk. "Give me a number to call you on. I'll call at noon on Saturday. If everything is in place on your end, say you want me to deliver a peperoni pizza. Nothing else. The next time we talk, I'll contact you." He pulled the tab and took a long pull. "And don't think that just because you and I don't meet for lunch once a week that I'm not keeping track of you and your property." He tried to look menacing as he spoke, but he failed.

I called Getz when I got back to the office and told him everything was set for Saturday night, so he and Ed had four days to get the renters out. I had done my part, so I left the details of who would be there and what they planned to do when the bad guys showed up and how long they planned to let them go before they stepped in and put a stop to it was not something

I needed to know. When I finished talking to him, I pushed the red button on my cell and placed it on my desk. I sat for a minute as I ran the mental tapes on what I had done and what was going to happen through my head. I was looking for anything that could get me arrested or something that could cost me my license, but I didn't come up with anything.

The mood was broken when I looked up at the sound of the door leading from the street into my office opening. It was George and I realized I had not seen him in several days which was most unusual for him.

"Come on in, George. Have a seat." He passed through the main room and came into my office and took a seat on the sofa. "Where have you been hiding?"

"Ain't been hiding, Colonel. I was down to the VA hospital."

"Are you okay?" I knew George was Viet Nam veteran with combat experience and was drawing a disability, but he never shared what it was for, and I never asked.

"I am now, but I thought I might not be on this side of the dirt much longer for a while."

I waited for him to explain further, but he just sat quietly. "I'll bet you could use a fresh cup of coffee. You feel like going across the street and picking up two cups and something to eat if you're hungry?"

"Oh, they patched me up almost good as new." He stood and I knew it was time for me to give him the money to buy the coffee. I also knew that whatever bill I gave him would never produce any change. "Here, this should cover it," I said as I handed him a twenty.

Fifteen minutes later he was back with two cups of coffee and a sweet roll of some sort for him, and no change from my twenty. "I woke up last week and couldn't hardly get out of bed. Felt like somebody done stuck a knife in my back. Went to my knees when I finally got up from the bed and I knowed something bad was wrong." He stopped and took a bite of the sweet roll and washed it down with several pulls from his coffee cup. "I wanted to walk down to the bus stop but ain't no way I could have made it, so I called the VA and they tole me to get an am'blance cause it sounded like I had one of them kidney stones, 'cept this felt like a kidney brick."

"Did they get it out?" I had never had one, but I knew several people who did, and they all agreed that it was a very painful experience.

"Yes sir. They shot some kind of x-ray, or something and smashed it into little pieces."

I didn't ask but I knew he had to piss it out and that had to hurt as well. "I'm glad you're okay. I can't afford to lose my coffee drinking buddy."

"Ain't going nowhere. Not for a long time, Colonel. I still got things to do." With that, he finished his coffee and the sweet roll, put the cup, and the paper from the roll in my trash can and left without a word.

I had two more days before Patrick would be back in town, so I did what every red-blooded American man would do. I called Anna and convinced her to spend the night with me. I felt bad because we seldom did things like a normal couple would do prior to spending the night together. We occasionally went to dinner, and we were a little freer with the places we went since she was legally separated. After I called her and made arrangements to pick her up at the Mukilteo ferry terminal, I checked the movie schedule in the newspaper. We had never been to a movie together and it was long overdue.

The parking lot for the ferry was filled with cars, trucks and a few campers. It was close to time when many people who worked on this side of the Sound got off and took the ferry back to their home on Whidbey Island. I found a place to park in the lot beside the old lighthouse. It was a tourist destination in its own right as there was the lighthouse keeper's cottage alongside the lighthouse. I'd never been in either of them, but I made a point to do it the next time I came to meet Anna.

She had her maid drop her off at the terminal on the other side of the Sound and walked onto the ferry. I watched it slowly ply its way across the dark waters and as soon as it docked, I left my vehicle and walked down to meet her when she got off.

"Welcome to my side of the world," I said as I took her in my arms and gave her a kiss.

"That sounds like a song title," she said after returning the kiss.

"I'll work on it." I took her hand and we walked to where I was parked. She had a small overnight bag slung over her shoulder which she placed in the back seat after I opened the door for her.

"I think we may want to discuss my leaving some of my things at your place, so I don't have to keep bringing them back and forth. What do you think?" she asked just prior to sliding into the passenger's seat.

That was something I had never given any thought, so it came as a bit of a surprise that she would be the one to raise the issue. "I think that's probably a good idea." I got into my side of the vehicle and put the key in the ignition. "That means you can spend more time with me."

"I may not spend more time than I do now, but it'll make it more convenient when I do." She took my hand in hers. "And we can be more spontaneous."

That was the best-selling point for me.

The sun was setting behind us as I drove up the hill and away from the ferry terminal. When we got to Aurora, I crossed over and did not turn right toward Edmonds and my place. I glanced to the right and saw a slight reaction from Anna, but she didn't say anything, so I did.

"I was thinking while I waited for the ferry that we don't seem to do many things that a normal couple would do."

"Do you think we're a normal couple?" she quickly asked, catching me by surprise.

"Hell of a good question, but I think we need to do the best we can under the circumstances." I was trying to concentrate on the traffic and Anna at the same time.

"And?"

"And I thought we'd catch an early dinner and then take in a movie. We've never done that before."

"Dinner and a movie." She smiled. "Sounds like a real date. Something I haven't done in far too many years." She leaned over and kissed me on my right cheek. "I like the way you think...can we sit in the back row and make out?"

We stopped at a steakhouse and had dinner. I knew Anna had a small gym in her house and she used it daily so she was not afraid to have a real meal. We decided to split a filet and baked potato. We had an individual salad, and she had a rum and coke while I had my usual gin and tonic. The movie was showing at one of the screens at the multi-plex near the shopping mall. When I went to the booth to purchase the tickets, I realized I had not told her the movie I had in mind and determined if she was even interested in seeing it.

I walked back to her and held out the tickets. "I guess I should have checked with you to see if you wanted to see this one."

"This is dinner and a movie date night, remember. You get to be in charge with all the details...until we get home. Then it's my turn."

"I really don't mind if we skip the movie and go home now."

"Not on your life. We're going to see a movie together tonight."

The movie was over close to eleven. We were back at my place by midnight, and I think we finally gave up and got some sleep as the sun was coming up. I lay with her in my arms as I watched the sun chase the darkness away. Every time I held her like that, I realized how lucky I was and how it could all disappear like a cloud before a windstorm, and there was nothing I could do about it. Any change in our relationship was completely up to Anna.

After a late morning wake-up and joint shower with a quick return to the bed, we went into Edmonds and had breakfast. She informed me just after we showered that she needed to get back home, so I took her back to the ferry terminal and watched as she boarded and waited until the ferry pulled away from the dock.

I went back to my office and checked mail and messages. I had a light blinking on my land line phone indicating I had three messages. I used the land line for business but most of the people I knew called me on my cell, so I assumed the message was from someone wanting to talk PI business or it was a caller selling something.

I pushed the green button and listened to the first message which was, as I assumed, someone wanting to sell me an ad in a calendar supporting something or someone. I didn't listen long enough to see the who or the what. The second was a hang-up, so I didn't have to do anything except wait for the third caller. "Hello. This is Patrick. If I've got the right number, you'll know who this is. I'm back in town a day early, so if you know who this is, give me a call."

That was from Patrick, my driver, who was filling me in on what the now-deceased professor was doing and who he was seeing. I had given a lot of thought to what he had said the first night about taking the professor to a club featuring drag queens and then to the escort services specializing in...what? This is where I was having some difficulty.

When I was stationed in Germany, we had a Soldier who worked part time in a drag club. He was, by all indications a good Soldier. He never gave his commander any problems and he was supposed to be dating a beautiful German woman. He finished his tour of duty and left the Army. On the other side of the coin, I had one Soldier in my unit who was trying to get the Army to pay for his sex change surgery. The Army refused and when his time was up, he began living with a man who we were told was paying for his re-assignment surgery. I saw them together once at a gasthause and had the former Soldier not come up and introduced himself, I would never have known it was the same person. His hair was shoulder length, perfectly styled, and he had on make-up that my wife (at the time) said was professionally applied. The most noticeable thing was the well-formed cleavage he had on display. No doubt they were surgery implants, but they looked natural, and he knew it. His companion was obviously amused as he watched the former Soldier and his former commanding officer exchange strained pleasantries. I knew the background of the person in front of me but several men, to include Soldiers, did not, and they were very interested in what they perceived as the well-endowed lady.

I preferred to know that any woman I have a relationship with is, and always had been a female. If the professor did not share my qualifications, it should not have been any of my business, but it appeared it may have led to his death and that made it mine.

I called Patrick and we agreed to meet and get back on the professor's trail later that night.

Chapter 33

There are two parking spaces on the street in front of my office which are usually filled with locals who come to the city to sit at one of the outdoor cafés or visit one of the boutiques that now fill every storefront as soon as someone moves out. I was looking out the front window in my office waiting room when I saw a car pull into one of the spaces. For some reason, I continued to watch as the driver got out and came across the front of the car, stepped up on the sidewalk and walked to the door to my office.

Five minutes later I was sitting across from a man who identified himself as Mister Van der Beck. He didn't use a title, but after handing me his business card with only a name and the seal of the Dutch government on it, I knew he was either a low-level diplomat or a high-level law enforcement official. My first guess was law enforcement.

"I understand you are investigating the death of Professor Jacob Dirksen on behalf of the US and Dutch governments."

"I am working for a government agency. Our government," I added.

"Ah, yes, and that request came by way of my government, so we are essentially on the same side with a vested interest in the good professor's death."

The way he tap-danced around the subject solidified my opinion that he was law enforcement. "That may be the case. If so, what can I do for you?"

"I'm glad you asked, General Maxwell. I should think it may be in our best interest to share any information we may have."

As soon as he referred to me as General Maxwell, I knew I was dealing with someone who had deep ties in the US government. I retired as a Lieutenant Colonel and because of one of the missions Bill Hart put me on, I got a promotion to Brigadier General from the Vice President of the United States. Along with the promotion came the promise that if I ever divulged any details of the mission, I would be brought back to active duty, court martialed and promptly shot. I never used the rank and very few people knew of the promotion.

For the next hour, we exchanged information on the professor, his work in tulip research, what he may or may not have discovered and speculated on why he was in the largest tulip growing area in the world outside his native country. The bottom line we both agreed on was simple. Like most things it came down to money.

"May I ask you a rather delicate question, General Maxwell?"

"You may, but only if you will call me Max and forget that I have that military rank."

"Certainly. After professor Dirksen was found in one of your tulip fields, several agencies began to look into his background to determine if there was any reason for his being found as he was."

I looked over Van der Beck's shoulder and saw George walking down the street. He stopped across from the office and looked my way. I don't know if he could see that I had someone sitting across from me or not, but he stared for a minute, and then continued on his way. It was the first time I had seen him stop as if he planned to come in and then not do so. He stepped out into the crosswalk that connected the four corners of the main street. The crosswalks made a square surrounding the fountain in the middle of the city. It was a combination round-about and four-way stop but most of the locals couldn't seem to decide which it was as they approached it and pedestrians took their lives in their hands when they tried to cross the street. George made it successfully across to the other side.

I stopped looking out the window and gave my attention back to my guest. "And what did those investigations determine?"

"When I spoke to your friend, General...or rather Mister Hart, he indicated that you and he had been military police investigators and worked in the intelligence field when you were in uniform."

"That's correct, and I'm sure that had a great deal to do with his asking me to look into the professor's death." We now seemed to be playing a game of 'I know something that you don't know.'

"One of the more interesting aspects of his life was his almost regular visits to one of the more famous red-light districts in Amsterdam." He looked at me for a reaction and when he got none, he continued. "It seems that the good professor had a particular interest in frequenting an establishment that had a very specific clientele." He pulled a silver case from the inside pocket of his suit coat, opened it and reached for a cigarette. "I'm sorry, I should have asked. Do you mind if I smoke? I purchased some American cigarettes, and they are much better than what we can get in my country."

I had no particular policy for or against smoking in my office, but I didn't have an ashtray, so I slid an empty paper cup toward him. "If you smoke, you'll have to use this as an ashtray. I don't think I even own one anymore."

He took the hint and closed the case without taking the cigarette out. "As I was saying, Professor Dirksen had a particular interest in what the more politically correct in society refer to as transgender. Are you familiar with the term?"

246

His use of the term opened an entire box of Pandoras for me. It explained more of where Patrick had been taking Dirksen and why. "I am and I think you and I need to meet someone who may be able to shed a lot of light on the professor and his activities here in Seattle." As we stood, I thought that Patrick may be a link in helping me, and now us, in finding out why Dirksen was found dead in a field of blue tulips.

*   *   *

Frank Richardson was seated at his desk working on some marketing reports based on the crops now growing in the field that had held his real cash crop of tulips earlier in the year. Once the tulip season was over, he and most of the other growers in the area turned to other crops. A ride through the thousands of acres between the Interstate and the city of Le Conner resembled a trip through the corn belt of Iowa. Corn, green and lush, grew as well in the soil as the tulips. His first crop of corn was on its way to market, and he had the sales report in hand. It looked like a banner year for both corn and tulips.

He was pulled from his thought process when his phone rang. The call came through directly to him and did not go through the phone system that was monitored by one of the workers in the front office. Few people had his private number. His gut instinct told him he knew who was on the other end and why.

"Richardson, here." He waited for the caller to identify himself.

"Are you aware that the government has sent an investigator to your area to look into the death of Dirksen?" Before Frank could respond, the caller continued in a much more forceful voice. "And do you know what that means? If he finds the girl, and she says anything more than what you paid her for..." His voice trailed off.

"Wait a minute. I did exactly as you said. I told you what happened was an accident and if I have to speak to anyone else, that's my story and I'm sticking with it."

"Anyone else?" the caller yelled. "Who have you spoken to already? You have not told me anything about that."

Frank stood from behind his desk. Although the air conditioning was running in his office, beads of sweat were forming on his forehead. "I told you the sheriff came by when I reported finding the body and he took my statement. I told him I had no idea who the man was or how he got into the field. I'm sure he believed me. We don't have any way of securing the fields at night, so they are open for anyone who wants to roam through them. We get a lot of teenagers, and the sheriff knows it, so his being here was not a big deal."

"Except for the fact that not many of the teenagers are found dead in your fields."

Richardson was clearly in a pre-panic mode. "Look, I did exactly what you told me to do. I found the girl and had her bring him up here. All I wanted to do was intimidate him to get the formula for the Simper Augustus virus. You conveniently forgot to mention that in addition to being a professor, he also had some serious training in martial arts. If he hadn't slipped when he was trying to land some kind of kick, I'd be the one they found in the field."

"What about the girl? What did she see?"

Richardson was pacing around the office as he talked. Before he could answer, his secretary came in with a message. "Frank, there's someone outside who wants to talk to you. He gave me his card." She handed Frank a card with the name Van der Beck on it. He took it and waved her away and out of the office.

"Oh, shit...oh shit," he said into the phone.

"What is it? What's going on? Frank...Frank...talk to me." The voice on the other end of the line was attempting to find out what was happening.

"Oh, shit," he said again as he put the phone back to his ear. "There's a man outside from the Netherlands and I don't think he's here to sell me tulip bulbs." He looked at the card. "All his card says is his name and it's got the seal of the Dutch government on it. What am I supposed to do?"

There was silence from his caller for a minute. "First," the voice advised, "first you don't panic. Get yourself together and talk to the man. Tell him exactly what you have been telling the local law enforcement officials. So long as the two stories remain the same, everything will be all right." Frank was nodding in agreement as he listened. "Trust me."

Van der Beck and I sat in a small area that served as a waiting room and outer office for the person who managed the operation where Dirksen was found. Van der Beck gave his card to the woman who greeted us when we arrived, and she took it in to her boss. We were waiting for either her or him to let us into the office. We heard the buzzing sound from her phone and watched as she pushed a button to silence it. "You can go in now." She stood and motioned us to the door.

Without waiting for her to open it, I pushed it and it opened into the office I had been in the first time I came to find out about the professor's death. Frank Richardson stepped forward to greet us.

"Sorry to keep you waiting but..." he cleared his throat and reached for a large drink container with the name of a local convenience store on it. After taking a drink, he invited us in. "Sorry about that. I must be catching something. My throat's been dry all morning." He pointed to a large green leather sofa against one wall. "Have a seat. Can I get you something to drink?"

It appeared it was almost an afterthought as he extended his hand, first to me and then to Van der Beck and we shook. After watching us take a seat, he returned to his desk and his office chair. "What can I do for you gentlemen today?" His voice cracked once when he spoke indicating, at least to me, that he was either going through puberty again, or he was extremely nervous. I put that in my mental file for future reference.

"As you can imagine if you looked at my business card, I am interested in the tragic death of one of my fellow countrymen, Professor Jacob Dirksen." Van der Beck hesitated and watched for a reaction from Richardson. It was an old interrogation technique that I had used many times in the past. Begin the investigation with an open-ended statement that many people took as a question.

"I don't know what else I can tell you." He looked at me. "I gave you all I knew the first time you were here."

"Yes, but I wasn't here with him, so if you will be so kind as to tell me what you know about the professor." Van der Beck was as smooth as silk.

Richardson took another long drink prior to speaking again. He cleared his throat and I noticed Van der Beck make an almost imperceptible nod of his head indicating he noticed the nervous gesture.

"We found his body early one morning as we were checking the fields. We do that as a routine during the Tulip Festival on a daily basis."

"Do you always check for bodies?" Van der Beck leaned forward when he asked the question.

"No...I mean I never found a body before. We look for trash. That sort of thing."

"You said 'we' found the body. You didn't mention anyone else with you when we spoke earlier," I said.

"That was just an expression...I was alone when I found the body."

"I see." Van der Beck pulled out a small note pad and took his time making an entry. "And did you check the fields…for… trash the previous day?"

"I don't' think I did…but I don't do it every day."

"So, what induced you to do it the day you found Professor Dirksen?" Before Frank had time to answer that question, he was hit with another. "And had you been visited by Professor Dirksen prior to your discovering his body?"

"No, I mean yes, he did come by, and we talked about our operation…but he left, and I didn't see him again."

"I'm sure you know he is…or was…one of the foremost authorities on tulips. World renowned." Van der Beck stood and walked to a window overlooking the fields. "He was working on a new strain of tulip." He turned back to look at Richardson. "Did he mention that to you?"

Richardson looked at his watch. "I hate to rush you gentlemen, but I have a very important phone call I have to make, so if you have no further questions, I'm afraid I'm going to have to cut this meeting short." He stood as a clear indication that we were no longer welcome in his office.

Chapter 34

Van der Beck wanted to see the area around the tulip fields, so we went into the local community of La Conner. It could be any small sea-side village almost any place in the world. It had one main street that ran along the waterfront. Businesses, mostly restaurants and small cafés were situated next to the water. The other side of the street contained the gift shops and the other tourist oriented businesses. All of this took up the three blocks of the city proper. At the end of the street was a large parking lot where some cars were parked and where others used it as a place to turn around and head back in the direction from which they came.

We made it half-way to the parking lot when Van der Beck spotted a place that advertised locally caught seafood along with steaks. "We Dutch derive much of our livelihood from the sea. That includes much of what we consume." He pointed to the sign. "A good steak is a rarity, even in Amsterdam. We have cows but most of them are milk producers. We don't have many we can sacrifice to turn them into steaks, so if you don't mind, I'd like to stop there."

I found a street-side parking slot and pulled into it. We were on the side next to the water, and only a few doors down from where we planned to eat. There was sufficient vacant space between the businesses that the city had numerous small areas where people could sit and watch the boats as they moved in and out of town or enjoy a meal outdoors. As we walked by the open spaces, Van der Beck seemed to be taking a mental movie of the city and all it had to offer. I almost thought he was considering moving here.

We stood at the entrance to the restaurant he selected and waited to be seated. During the short walk, we made small talk about anything but tulips and dead professors.

As soon as we were seated, he ordered a craft beer the waiter suggested. It was from one of the many small brewers that have populated the area over the last twenty years. I stuck with a glass of iced tea. True to his earlier desires, Van der Beck ordered a twelve-ounce sirloin complete with baked potato and salad. "I hope you don't mind my making a fool of myself," he said as the waiter took his menu.

"Nothing foolish about a good steak. I'd join you but I try to eat a light lunch and save my big meal for dinner."

"To share with your wife?" he asked as he took the first cautious drink from his beer.

"Divorced." I pulled a pack of sugar from a container in the middle of the table and dumped the crystals in my glass. "How about you?" I asked as I stirred my tea.

"I have a wife of over twenty years. She is a medical doctor in Amsterdam. Her specialty is treating kidney transplant patients." Evidently, he liked the beer because the tipped the glass up and almost emptied it in one drink. "Is there another lady in your life now?"

I hesitated as I tried to come up with an explanation of my relationship with Anna. Bill knew about her and me and had never passed judgement in any way. How could I explain to a stranger who had twenty years of marriage under his belt that I was having a serious relationship with a married, albeit legally separated woman. Like water, I took the path of least resistance and simply told him that I was seeing someone. He accepted the abbreviated explanation, and I was spared questions when his steak arrived, and he immediately attacked it.

He gave his attention to his meal for the next ten minutes and only commented on the quality of the steak and to order another beer. I'm sure he and I knew there was a dark cloud hanging over us that had to be recognized at some point and we were rapidly approaching it.

After carefully wiping his mouth with the cloth napkin the restaurant provided, he placed his utensils on the plate, took a drink and settled back in his chair. "I know from speaking with your friend, General or if you prefer, Bill Hart that you are a competent investigator, so you must be curious as to the level of interest from my government in the death of one of our citizens."

"That thought had crossed my mind," I said as I pushed the small amount of the bowl of clam chowder I had for lunch aside. "But I also knew that if you wanted to share the information with me, you would."

"Allow me," he said as he reached into his jacket pocket and extracted several pieces of folded paper and slid them across the table. "This is a recap of the annual value of the tulip industry to the economy of the Netherlands. As you will notice, a great deal of the revenue comes from tourists who visit for the sole purpose of seeing the tulip fields when they are in full bloom." He motioned toward the field outside the restaurant. "Much like what you have here, but these fields produce income that is primarily local to the area and the state. I don't think you get many visitors from Europe or Asia, unlike the Netherlands,"

He stopped talking and gave his attention to a large fishing boat as it made its way to a fishing or crabbing area someplace farther away. "Imagine if you will, if a local grower announced that he had re-created a strain of tulip that has not been seen in over three hindered years. A tulip with a color so vibrant that the only record of it is in literature and several paintings."

I had a feeling I knew where this was going. "Let me guess. Dirksen had or was about to have that re-creation?"

He pulled another paper from his jacket. "I'm sure you've never heard of the Simper Augustus."

I shook my head.

"Few people outside the industry have and most of them think it something like the Holy Grail or your Bigfoot monster." He finished his beer. "But unlike those two examples, I can assure you that it did exist, and Professor Jacob Dirksen appears to have found a way to bring it back to life."

*   *   *

Frank Richardson was sweating like a boxer after a ten-mile run. Even his hands were so wet he could hardly hold the handset to his phone as he punched in the numbers on the black instrument sitting on his desk. It was answered on the third ring. "I don't know why they call them rings," he said aloud as he listened to the buzzing sound of a European phone system.

"Why are you bothering me in the middle of the night?" Andre Verhoeven was not happy to get Richardson's call.

"I just had a visitor...no, two of them. One of them had been in before but this Van der Beck was from your government. I don't like that. You said you could cover everything..."

Verhoeven cut him off. "I said I would take care of everything, but you must do your part. Now, tell me exactly what they asked and how you answered."

For the next thirty minutes Richardson replayed the conversation and listened while Verhoeven gave him advice on what to do going forward. By the time they finished the call, both were satisfied that they had a plan that would keep the police, both local and the investigator from the Netherlands at bay and get them the information they needed to replicate the elusive Simper Augustus.

*   *   *

We were half-way back to Seattle when Van der Berg dropped another bomb on me. I readily admit I had no knowledge of the Simper Augustus and probably couldn't pick one out in a one-tulip police line-up, but if that was what got Dirksen killed, it was something I needed to follow-up with along with what now seemed to be my partner from Holland.

"We found out Dirksen was very close to having discovered and replicated the virus that created the original tulip, so several governmental agencies took an interest in his research. Along with his professional life, we discovered some interesting aspects of his personal life, as well."

I glanced over at Van der Beck with a feeling I had an idea where this conversation was going. "And what did you find out? I mean with his personal life?"

"I also checked on you when I found out you were working, in a round-about way for us, and I know you spent several years of your Army career in Europe." He had turned to partially face me.

"And...?"

"And like most Americans and all military personnel who had the opportunity, you visited some of the famous red-light districts in Amsterdam." Before I could respond, he continued. "Not that you actually partook of any of the goods on display, but you came like many do, out of curiosity."

"I did visit once, but my wife at the time went with me." The traffic began to get heavier as we approached Everette, the largest city between Seattle and Bellingham on the Interstate. Fortunately, we were heading south and most of the traffic was in the opposite lane as Seattle belched forth its workforce living north of the city.

"It seems Dirksen was a frequent visitor to an establishment that had a particular specialty."

"And that would be?" Before he could respond, a motorcycle blew by me in the far-right non-lane running at least ninety. I was doing seventy-five and I watched him weave in and out of traffic.

"The workers in the house were in a transitional mode. Most had been born male but for reasons known only to them, felt more comfortable identifying as female. The more popular ones were in the process, or already had undergone surgery to complete the transition." He looked at me for a reaction. When he didn't get one, he assumed I understood. "I can only assume that there are similar establishments in your Seattle. Have you run across this aspect of his life yet?"

I knew if anyone could answer that question with any degree of authority, it was the taxi driver I had on retainer. "I think I may have run across that inadvertently, but I have not confirmed it to my satisfaction, but I know who can assist us."

Van der Beck was staying at one of the better hotels in the city. I hoped his government had a more liberal per diem policy than the one the Army used when Bill and I were traveling all over Europe. Even being as frugal as we could, we always lost money when we left our home command. I dropped him off and we agreed to meet the next morning for breakfast. I left him promising I would call Patrick and arrange for him to drive us.

I made it back to Edmonds and my place a little after sunset. On the days when I am in the city at sundown, I always marvel at the last rays as the sun settles in over the Puget Sound and eases its way across the Pacific. Several times, I went to a deli just off the traffic circle downtown, picked up a couple of sandwiches or something light, a bottle of wine and

Anna and I found a place at the waterfront park and just sat and watched the sunset. The only one that I have ever seen that rivals an Edmonds sunset is what one sees in Key West, Florida. Unlike Edmonds where only Anna and I watch it, sunset in Key West is a community event. Tourists as well as locals flock to the pier to see it. Mixed in with the crowd are street musicians, jugglers, mimes and others who come to work the crowd. The last time I was there, I paid a young man dressed in full Scottish regalia complete with bagpipes to play Scotland the Brave as the sun disappeared.

I parked on the street and headed for my front door. I was met by my next-door neighbor, Dan, a retired tugboat captain. "Evening, Max. How's it hanging?" He had half an unfiltered cigarette hanging from his lip on the right side of his mouth.

"Low, Dan. Mighty low. How 'bout you?"

He flipped the cigarette into the yard and watched it spray sparks when it landed. "Used to hang low till I got my doctor to write me a prescription for those little blue pills." He laughed.

I went into the living room and turned to the television, not because I was remotely interested in anything playing, but for the noise. I did not like the quiet of my quarters without some type of noise. I slept with the television on all night unless Anna was beside me. The sound of the television, even on a very low volume setting helped to mask the ringing in my ears. If Anna was sharing my bed, it seemed to go away, or I didn't notice it. I think we made enough noise to mask the sound of a jet aircraft passing overhead sometimes.

I pulled a frozen entre from my freezer and prepared to have a bachelor's dinner. If I was not meeting Van der Berg the next day, I would have made arrangements with Anna to take her up on the offer of spending several days together, but I wanted to clear things up with both Van der Beck and Dirksen and Getz and his insurance scheme, so when she and I had the time together we could enjoy it without my business interruptions.

A plate of almost recognizable and edible Mexican food, a cup of coffee and a G and T afterwards and I had the remainder of the evening to do anything I wanted. I decided to read a little of the book I had been trying to finish for longer than I could recall. I selected one of the uninterrupted music channels on my television and settled in.

I had been reading and, I think, nodding off for a while when my cell phone rang. It was almost ten, so my first guess was that it was a mistake since I didn't recognize the number. "Max here. Who is this?"

"Max, it's Patrick. I got your message that you want to put me back on the payroll tomorrow. Right?"

"I thought you were a taxi driver and not a mercenary. Do you always work for the highest bidder?"

"No, I work for the person who actually needs me, and since I know more about your professor friend than you do, you fall into that category." I heard him chuckle.

"Okay. There will be two of us for a while," but I quickly added before he could ask, "the price is still the same. You don't get paid by the passenger. Only by the day."

"And night."

"That too, and there may be a lot of that for the next few days."

"Okay. Where do you want me to pick you up?"

I gave him the name of the hotel where Van der Beck was staying, and we agreed to meet the next morning. After ending our conversation, I closed the book, put it on the end table by my chair and headed for the bedroom. It was always a crapshoot when I went to bed as to whether I'd have some of my less welcome nighttime visitors. It made me want to stay awake all night on occasion.

The next morning, I met Van der Beck in the hotel coffee shop where he was already seated and finishing a cup of coffee and an English muffin. "Good morning, Max. Please join me," he said as he folded his napkin, placed it on the table and stood. He pointed to a chair across the table. "Have you had your morning coffee, yet?"

"I think I have time for another cup while I let you know what I have in mind for us today." Both of us sat down.

By the time I finished my coffee, I had filled him in about my relationship with Patrick and by extension, his relationship with Dirksen. "Do you think he will be able to shed some light on exactly what transpired to cause the professor's life to end in a tulip field?" He stalled for a minute as he fingered his napkin. "I'm not totally convinced the Simper Augustus was the entire cause of his demise."

"That's interesting," was all I could muster for a reply.

"You see, we found a great deal of his lab notes when we determined he was missing and of course, we had to assume that it had something to do with the Simper."

"But?"

"But some of our most knowledgeable scientists in the field, assured me that he was close to a breakthrough on replicating the bulb, he was not quite there yet...but...perhaps he did not realize it."

I tend to think in any instance where the law is broken in anything other than a traffic violation, the easiest path to the truth is to follow the money. "So, let's say he came to Seattle and then to the Skagit Valley to sell the formula, if that's the right word, on how to recreate this long gone and elusive tulip."

Van der Beck nodded his head in agreement.

"And let's say for the sake of argument, that the person he approached either wanted to be the only one who had the process or else he tested the formula and found out it didn't work and thought Dirksen was trying to rip him off."

"I can see why you were assigned to work on this case. Your theories are sound."

"So far, Richardson is the only one I would consider a person of interest. Your thoughts on that?"

"I like that term, person of interest. I quite often hear it on the American television shows or movies we get. So yes, I think we can consider him in that manner, but I want to reserve judgement until we meet your taxi driver friend."

He had hardly finished his thought when I saw a taxi pull into the circle drive and park. Patrick emerged from the driver's seat and headed to the entrance. "Our driver just pulled into the drive." We stood and Van der Beck placed several bills on the table, and we went to meet Patrick.

Chapter 35

Patrick came around to open the door for Van der Beck and me. "Morning, Boss. Getting an early start today?" He stepped aside while I let Van der Beck crawl across the back seat and settle in behind where Patrick would sit.

"Yes, we have some new ideas and want to check them out." He closed the door and went around the car and got into his seat. As soon as he got in and pulled out of the hotel's driveway, I leaned forward. "Patrick, this is…" I hesitated as I didn't know what to refer to him by. I knew he was a member of some sort of the government, and I suspected it had a title, but so far, he had not shared it with me. While I considered the way to introduce him, he saved me the trouble.

"My name is Van der Beck. Unlike many names you are probably used to, to properly address me, one would use all three words."

Patrick spoke without looking back, although I did see him glance in the rear-view mirror. "So, you're Mister Van der Beck. Right?"

"As I said, that would be the proper manner in which to address me."

"And if I did not want to be proper, what would I call you?"

"I doubt we would reach that point in our relationship," Van der Beck replied with no emotion.

Patrick laughed aloud. "I like your friend, boss, but I think we'll stay on a formal basis." He turned half-way in the seat to face me in back. "Where to?"

"Let's go to that coffee shop in the University district. I think we need to come up with a game plan."

We parked on the street almost directly in front of the coffee shop, got out of the taxi and went inside. After getting coffee for me, the concoction that Patrick ordered, and a cappuccino for Van der Beck, we selected a table mid-way to the back, but still overlooking the street. It was early enough that the sidewalks were filling with students and others heading for the University of Washington campus. The dress of the day was anything that the wearer could put together. Several girls passed in what I assumed were pajama pants. I saw two who had on blue jeans with so many holes in them I wondered is there was enough fabric remaining to hold them together. Skateboards were the mode of transportation of choice for male and female alike and small groups of them whizzed by the window. As each passed, Van der Beck shook his head.

"Have you ever tried to ride one of those?" he asked.

"Only once for me. How about you? Are they as popular in the Netherlands as they are here?"

"I think they're a world-wide conspiracy perpetrated by surgeons so they can get more patients." He took a sip from his cup. "I know the one my daughter went to was making a small fortune from those things."

That was the first time he had said anything about his personal life. I did not pursue the conversation and figured if he wanted to talk about his family, he would do so when he was ready.

"Yeah, I tried one time and busted my ass in the process. My son rode them all the time when he was growing up. Never broke anything but he took some serious ass bustings," Patrick added

It was time to get serious.

"Patrick, Mister Van der Beck has come from Amsterdam to find out more about the death of Professor Dirksen. I've told him all I know and that you probably can give us more information." I waited to see if I got any reaction from Patrick. He nodded as if he not only agreed but had more information as well. "He's given me some information that may have an impact on why he was here and what he was doing that may or may not have gotten him killed."

Patrick took a long drink from his cup and finished what was left of the coffee. "Why do I suddenly get the feeling I'm not working for you as a taxi driver and guide and am now the third member of a team investigating what could be a murder?" He looked at Van der Beck for an answer.

"I understand that you are on the payroll of Mister Maxwell when you are driving him. I am prepared to pay the same amount and offer a bonus for any additional information you can provide that will assist me in my efforts." Now it was Van der Beck's turn to be quiet and see what happened.

Two young women came into the coffee shop. They were dressed in torn jeans and sweatshirts. One shirt was a souvenir from a concert and dated several years in the past. The other sweatshirt was a University of Washington one and was about three sizes too large for the woman who wore it. It hung loose from one shoulder and from the amount of skin exposed, it was obvious that she was not wearing a bra since there was no shoulder strap visible and nothing across the back to indicate one. I took a longer than I should have look at them, but it was nothing to the stare-down they got from Patrick. He watched as they ordered and then moved to a nearby table to await their orders. I thought I was going to have to rap on the table to get his attention back to the reason we were there.

"I don't know how much more I can tell you other than what I have told Max." That was the first time he called me by my first name.

"I am most interested in his activities at night. Where you took him. Who went with him? Anyone you saw him with." Van der Beck pulled out a silver cigarette case and snapped it open. Before he could take out a cigarette, I stopped him.

"Can't smoke inside in Seattle." He nodded in understanding, closed the case and waited for Patrick to respond.

"I already told Max, that your man was into some kinky shit. I took him to a couple of clubs that aren't on the Chamber of Commerce list of places to see in Seattle. He had one place he seemed to like more than any of the others. I took him there three or four times."

"Did you go in with him or see anyone he met there?" Van der Beck gave Patrick his full attention.

"I never went in with him. I doubt they would have let me in if I tried, but after the first time, he always had a woman with him."

"A woman?"

Patrick looked at me. I had a feeling I knew where he was going with the answer.

"I think it was a person who was either a woman or one who wanted to be and may have been well on the way to becoming one."

Both Patrick and I sat quietly while Van der Beck absorbed what he had just been told.

"That seems to have been a particular interest of his when he visited certain establishments in Amsterdam. I'm not shocked that he continued to pursue it here." He leaned forward. "Tell me. How did he discover those…uh…women after being here for such a short time?"

The two women went back up to the counter and picked up their order. They noticed Patrick openly staring at them and it did not affect them as they passed by our table and completely ignored him.

"The first night, we got into a conversation about some things he wanted to see and do. I told him I could probably steer him to anything he wanted...no matter what it was. To be honest, I was thinking of a couple of ladies of negotiable affections that I am acquainted with. They're clean and safe. Much better than picking up someone and something off the street or in the hotel bar. I'm not a pimp, but I do them favors and when they need a taxi, they call me."

"Can you take me...us...to the same places, and do you know how to reach the person he went with?"

"Yes, to both of those, but not in the middle of the day. Since I'm on the payroll, why don't you let me take you around and show you some of the better...and more normal things we have here in the area?" Without waiting for an answer, Patrick stood and waited for us to do the same.

When we got to the taxi, I waited for them to get in before I spoke to Patrick. "I think I'll be better served taking care of some other business today rather than being a tourist. Take me back to the hotel and I'll meet both of you at seven. That'll give you time to freshen up or take a nap or have a drink once you've seen all you want to in the city." Van der Beck thought for a moment before responding.

"I think that's a good idea. We can meet for dinner at a place of your choosing." He leaned up and put his hand on Patrick's shoulder. "And you will be a part of anything we do tonight, not as a taxi driver but, as you said, a third member of an important investigation."

Patrick took me back to the hotel and dropped me off. I got my car from the parking lot and went back to my office. I had something I needed to do. It was time to check in with Getz.

As soon as I got back and opened my office door, I saw a pile of mail on the floor beneath the mail slot.

I pushed the pile aside with my shoe and continued to my desk.

I wanted to start the coffee pot first and then I'd go back and pick up the mail and toss it. I put water in the pot, added the proper amount of coffee to make it as strong as I had grown used to in the Army and placed a mug beside the pot.

When I picked up the mail, I found one letter of interest. It was from a former client who wanted to hire me to check out one of his employees who he was certain was stealing from him. He had a shop in the nearby mall, and I had identified an employee in the past who was running merchandise out the back door when no one else was working the sales floor on her shift. I placed it on the desk with the intent of calling him later. Whether I took the job or not depended on the outcome of my looking into the death of Dirksen.

The coffee pot light indicated I could pour a cup, so I filled my mug and took it to my desk. I took a couple of sips and punched the number for Getz in my cell phone. He answered on the second ring, although I guess cell phones don't really ring anymore.

He must have caller ID on his phone, since he didn't answer with the name of his company but rather by greeting me by name. "Max. How the hell are you?"

"I assume since I'm not under arrest or in jail, I'm doing okay." The fake burning of the house had been scheduled for three days ago. It was not a newsworthy fire and with any luck, no one had died or been injured in it. I had scanned the newspaper and the local news and did not see anything about it, so either it never happened, or it worked without a hitch. I was rooting for door number two.

"You got nothing to worry about. It went like clockwork. I had the arson investigator on site when the torch arrived. We caught him in the act of rigging the electric panel so it would burn. Seems he had a propensity for doing this in the past and when he was confronted with the possibilities of a long time in prison, he saw the error of his ways and we couldn't stop him from talking." He began to laugh aloud. "I tell you it was one of the best nights I've had in a long time. You should have been there."

"I don't think so."

"Yeah, I guess you're right. When he gave us the names of the contact at the management company, it would not have been good to have you along when the sheriff knocked on their door."

I took a long drink and an even longer sigh of relief that all had gone well and a professional arsonist and the company that utilized his services were going to be out of business for a long time. All that remained was for Getz to pay me and I was about to ask about that when he cut me off.

"Hey, I know I owe you for this job…"

I cut him off. "If you're about to say you can't pay and want me to wait, forget it. I did my part, now you do yours."

"Are you this cynical with all your friends?"

"You're a client. We're still working on the friend part."

"Okay, I can live with that. What I was about to say is my underwriter was so impressed with what we did and especially you, since I told him it was your idea, that he wants to put you on retainer. You interested?"

This was the second job I had done for Getz. He paid well and more importantly, on time, so it was an offer that I should seriously consider. I had enough of a tie-down with Bill Hart so I didn't want another boss, even though I would still in control, for the most part of what I did and when.

"Tell your underwriter that I appreciate the offer, but I'm going to pass. I don't mind having an occasional lunch with you and even working with you sometimes, but I don't want to be obligated to anyone. I like my independence."

"Thought you'd feel that way, but I told him I'd run it by you...but don't be shocked when you get a call from him with a job offer."

Getz said he was sending me a check and we ended the conversation. Afterwards, I spent the remainder of the afternoon doing almost nothing. I did break down and call the shop owner and talk to him about his employee. I agreed to stop by sometime in the next few days and see if there was something I could do. After that, I went home, took a long hot shower, an even longer nap which is something I haven't done in longer than I can remember and when I awoke, I dressed for dinner and a night of who-knows-what as we followed the footprints Professor Jacob Dirksen left in Seattle.

Chapter 36

Van der Beck was waiting in the hotel coffee shop when I arrived. He was dressed in a conservative dark suit and had a metal tea pot in front of him on the table. The tea pot was part of a three-piece set which included the sugar and cream pitcher. A teacup and saucer rather than a mug, held a tea bag with the tag hanging out. He looked up and waived his hand indicating I was to join him at his table.

"Good evening, Max. Please join me. Do you drink tea?"

Tea was not high on my list of beverages, but I liked to drink it in the winter if I felt a cold or sore throat coming on. I'd fix a large mug, put in a generous amount of honey and an even larger amount of brandy. I don't know if it helped but it was a good cold weather drink. "I appreciate the offer, but I think I'll pass," I said as I pulled out a chair and took a seat across the table from him.

"I think we may well have a very interesting evening ahead of us if we are able to find some of the places Dirksen went and see some of the people he met." He pulled the tea bag from the cup and put in a spoonful of sugar and a splash of cream.

"Patrick should be able to help with all of that. He seems to be the key to what Dirksen did in Seattle. Between him and Richardson, we should be able to backtrack his every move."

Before Van der Beck had a chance to respond, I looked up and saw a man approaching our table. It took a second look to recognize Patrick. From our first meeting he had worn clothes that befitted a taxi driver. He did not dress up, but he wore clothes that would be comfortable. Now he wore a shirt with a collar, a dark sports jacket and charcoal grey pants. "Good evening, gentlemen. Am I interrupting?"

Van der Beck did a double-take and when he recognized Patrick, invited him to join us. "I was just telling Max that I think we have an exciting evening ahead of us. Do you agree?"

"I guess only time will tell how exciting it is or will be, but I'll do my best to make it happen."

We left the coffee shop and went outside in anticipation of getting into Patrick's taxi, but it was not in the driveway. He stood beside us and handed the valet a parking ticket. "I thought since we were going to be doing this together, it might look better if we pulled up in something other than a taxi."

While we waited, Van der Beck commented on the city at night. "I have been in many cities throughout Europe and a few in your country, but I have to say this is a most interesting skyline at night." We were in the center of the city and surrounded by office. There were no clouds, so every building was visible and any lights they had on shimmered in the darkness.

"I really enjoyed the tour that Patrick took me on today, but I think it must pale in comparison to one that can be taken at night."

"I think you'll find tonight equally interesting and perhaps a little more exciting," Patrick offered as the valet pulled up in a new four-door Japanese sedan. After handing the man a folded bill, Patrick got in the driver's seat, and I opened the front passenger's door for Van der Beck.

"Sit up front with Patrick so he can point out some places you may have missed today."

After making several turns on one-way streets, I realized that we were leaving the downtown area and heading for the University district. We were on

271

Broadway when Patrick pulled to the curb. "This is the place he wanted to go most often." He looked at Van der Beck. "How much do you know about his...uh...his personal life?"

"I don't think you can show or tell me anything that will surprise me about Professor Dirksen, if that is your concern."

Nighttime in the University district is a cornucopia of mixed sights and sounds. The streets were alive with college students, locals out for a drink or a walk and the ever-present Seattle staple: the panhandler. Even from where we were parked, we saw several supposedly homeless, hungry or otherwise down-on-their luck, people with a variety of signs indicating they were hungry, would work for food, needed a beer or were homeless veterans. The latter group was the ones who really bothered me since there was a multitude of agencies willing to assist any veteran who really wanted help.

Patrick pointed to a large, two-story Victorian house across the street. "That's where we need to start. I brought him here a night or two after we met, and he confided in me about what he was looking for."

"And what would that be?" Van der Beck asked.

"Like I said, he was into some kinky shit. I didn't pass judgement, I just helped him find someone to scratch his particular itch."

While we watched, the front door opened and two people left and walked to a waiting taxi. The man appeared to be in his mid-fifties and from what I could see, the other person was clearly eye-candy for him.

"After the second time we came here, he had a favorite. I heard him call her Dianna once. A couple of times I picked them up, took them to a club and then came back a couple of hours later and dropped them off at his apartment."

"He had an apartment?" Van der Beck was surprised. "I didn't expect him to be here long enough to make that practical."

"Maybe he planned to make his stay permanent," I said.

"That would fit in with the Simper Augustus, assuming he planned to sell the plans to someone here in the area."

"Richardson?"

"That would be my assumption."

"I don't know what you guys are talking about but If you want to see if..." he hesitated. "I don't want to keep trying to come up with something to describe him and his date, but his woman wasn't. This is a specialty house that provides escorts. Most of them are real women and some of the best-looking ones in Seattle, but they also have some who are about to become women and that was what he was interested in."

After he said it, Patrick sat back to check for responses.

"I am aware of his sexual interests from my background check on him. He was known to frequent a similar operation in Amsterdam, where, if you know anything about the city's reputation, you know that one can get anything from the standard and simple to what some would call extreme or even perverted."

"Never been there, but I've heard stories." He looked toward the house. "How do you want to play this? I've brought people here before your man, and they always went in by themselves. I don't think we would get a very welcome greeting if we all went together. They might not do gang bangs."

I nodded in agreement. "I think you're right, Patrick. Why don't you go in first and tell them you're a friend of Dirksen and he recommended the place," I said to Van der Berg. "Try telling them a lady named Dianna came highly recommended by Dirksen. If you get her, call a taxi and come back to the hotel. We can follow you."

Van der Beck sat in silence as he thought about what I said. Finally, he reached for the handle to open the door and leave us. "I'll do my best, but I have to tell you I'm not entirely comfortable going into a place such as this." He let that comment hang as he walked away.

We watched him walk up the sidewalk to the front door of what was once a high-end mansion for some of the old Seattle money. It had gone through several transformations over the years and was now probably back to what it was in its prime. Houses like this, if they survived the depression of the nineteen thirties, were converted to boarding houses for the military during World War Two when Seattle and Boeing were booming. Like all good things, that came to an end and the city settled back to a normal post-war economy. There had been several boom and bust periods and the city, the neighborhood and the house had weathered them all. Now it was back to boom times and the house showed it.

While we waited, I had not noticed a light rain had begun to fall. Rain in Seattle is like no other place. It usually starts with a mist, but Seattle mist is heavy and hard. I looked out the side window as Van der Beck walked and saw that the mist was rapidly turning into rain. Fortunately, the front door was covered with a small overhang that protected him as he rang the doorbell and was let inside. It was now up to him.

While we waited to see what was going to happen with Van der Beck, Patrick and I swapped stories. I told him a little about my military service since his son was on active duty and he wanted to know what he might face. I didn't tell him about my having been wounded or my assignments as a military police investigator or my intelligence work. He took great delight in relating some of the things he had seen in the back seat of his taxi over the years. He had seen all manners of sexual escapades, some of which seem to require two gymnasts and not everyday passengers. He had two occasions when women went into labor in the taxi, one delivering in the driveway of the hospital while still in the back seat. He laughed and said he only charged for two fares for the lady and her husband and did not include the baby boy she delivered.

Patrick had the motor running and the windshield wipers on high when we saw Van der Beck open the front door, look at the downpour and gather enough courage to make a run for the car. I opened the door and he rushed inside.

"I heard about your rain in Seattle. Reminds me of Scotland although I doubt we'll be heading to a pub with a peat fire burning in the hearth."

Patrick put the car in gear and pulled away from the curb. "There's some napkins in the glove box if you want to dry off a little." He reached over and pushed the lock to open the compartment.

Van der Beck took several large paper napkins and carefully dried his face and hair. "Quite the experience in there, if I do say so. I've had the occasion to visit several of our establishments…in an official capacity, of course…and I think yours are far more pleasing to the eye than most."

"Are we talking about the architecture or the residents?" I asked.

"I would say both, but I did not stop to survey the woodwork."

"Did you see Dianna?" I asked as I tried to be serious again.

"No, but I got some very interesting information about her." He leaned toward Patrick. "Can you take us to Swedish Hospital?"

"The hospital? You didn't catch something in there already, did you?"

"No, but it seems our Dianna is a patient."

Now he had my full attention. "A patient? What's wrong with her?"

"Let me start from the beginning, but first can we stop and get a cup of tea to warm me up?"

We went to the same place we had visited in the past and after ordering, took a seat at a table near the back. Van der Beck seemed to relax once he had his fresh cup of tea. "When I entered, I was questioned quite extensively about why I was there, how I knew about the place and who recommended it to me. Evidently my answers were sufficient and the Madam or lady in charge asked me what I wanted. I explained that my friend had recommended Dianna and I would like to have her company for the evening." He stopped and took a cautious sip from the paper cup. "When I mentioned the name, she immediately tried to dissuade me from Dianna and offered several other choices. I could tell she was nervous about my asking about her, so I pressed the issue. Dianna or nothing, and I was prepared to pay well for her company."

"Did that work?"

"No, and I was assured that Dianna was not, and would not, be available for some time. I was about to leave when one of the other ladies slipped up to me and we had a hasty, whispered conversation. She liked my accent and said Dianna was enamored with Dirksen and his accent as well. She said if I wanted to see her, I was to go to Swedish Hospital room 523."

"Did she say what was wrong?" I was really interested now.

"Suicide attempt."

Chapter 37

The rain was coming down like we were in a tropical storm by the time we left the coffee shop. Seattle is known for its rainy climate, but this was a rainstorm on steroids. We ducked as best we could and ran to the car. Once inside, Patrick headed down Broadway to the main entrance for Swedish Hospital. The complex is on what the locals call Pill Hill. It occupies several blocks across Broadway from Seattle University. On the drive we decided the best approach was to go to the main entrance and ask for her room.

"I can think of one thing that might cause a slight problem," I said as we approached the entrance. "We don't have a last name and I'll bet a bucket of red ants that Dianna isn't on her birth certificate."

"Yeah," Patrick said as he turned to look at Van der Beck. "And it's a good thing they don't have a men's ward and one for the ladies. We wouldn't know which one to ask for."

"That did cross my mind when the other…uh…person I spoke to said she was in the hospital. I asked if she was there under her real name and she said I was to inquire about Lois Kennedy." I detected a bit of a cockiness in his voice as he spoke.

Patrick had to wait for an ambulance to pass us on the way to the emergency room two blocks from the hospital. Seattle installed a system that recognizes a signal issued from emergency vehicles which turns all traffic lights green in the path of the vehicle. That way there is less chance that another vehicle and the EMT, fire or police will get t-boned in the middle of an intersection.

When we were able to get back on the street, Patrick pulled into the circle drive in front of the entrance. "I'll let you out here and I'll go to the underground parking lot. By the time I find a slot, you should have a location for her. I don't know if there is a room 523 in each of the buildings, but if there is, we could spend all night looking for the right one." He stopped behind a taxi with the back door open. A woman with a newborn baby in her arms was seated in a wheelchair next to the taxi. After making certain the wheels were locked, a nurse assisted her into the back seat. The only man there was the taxi driver. I don't know if either Patrick or Van der Beck noticed or even gave it a thought, but it made me wonder if there was going to be a father in the kid's life. But that was not my problem.

We watched as Patrick left us and finished the circle and headed for the underground parking lot. The covered entrance kept us dry as we walked to the entrance. Once inside we stood in a short line at the information desk as other people inquired about a patient's condition or location.

When the lady in the pink striped dress recognized Van der Beck and asked if she could assist, he stepped forward. "We're here to see my... Lois Kennedy." I noticed the hesitation when he tried to decide if he should as for a female or male relative. Asking by name was a safe bet. "I was told room 523. Is that correct?"

"Let me check," she said as she pulled up a computer screen. I knew instinctively that if Lois was here for an attempted suicide, room 523 was in or close to the psych ward. After searching the screen, she returned to Van der Beck. "You can go to the floor, but you must stop at the nurses station. They'll let you know if you can visit."

Van der Beck thanked her, and we left and stood by the door to await Patrick. When he entered, we went across the lobby to the elevators and waited for it to take us to the fifth floor. When it reached the floor, the door opened, and we stepped out and held the door for two men dressed in scrubs to enter. The nurse's station was down the hallway to our left. As we made our way down the hallway, I noticed that unlike most hospital hallways, no patient's door was open. Each one had a sign on it indicating that all visitors were to be escorted to and from the room.

We were almost to the nurse's station when we were challenged by a young woman in a white coat with a stethoscope hanging around her neck. She looked far too young to be a doctor and I immediately felt my age. "Can I help you?" She had half a smile on her otherwise stern face. A young, attractive woman destroyed the Norman Rockwell image of the old family doctor.

Van der Beck stepped slightly forward. "Yes. Will you please direct us to room 523?" It was a variation on an interrogation technique. Keep the ball in his court. It was not a response that left anything in doubt. Pro-active. No doubt that he knew why we were here.

The doctor hesitated for a second. "Follow me." We did.

At the nurse's station, she checked what I assumed was the chart for Lois on the computer. Satisfied that she could have visitors, she closed the page. "Down the hall, then turn left. One of the nurses will escort you as soon as one is free." She looked at all of us. "Only one in the room at a time and only for five minutes each." I almost snapped to attention and saluted.

We waited less than five minutes, but during that time we saw a new patient being wheeled down the hallway and into a room. From what I could see, it was a man but that may have been just an assumption on my part. The patient had bandages wrapped like a turban around his head from just above the eyes. Several bags filled with different colored fluids, one clearly blood, hung from poles attached to the bed. Each bag had a length of plastic tubing running from the bottom of the bag to someplace on the patient. My first thought was a failed gunshot attempt. I had investigated several in the Army. When that happened, I always thought the person would probably have been better off if the attempt has been successful. Most of the time, what remained of the victim was in terrible shape and was destined to remain in that shape forever. If their life was so bad as to want to end it before, they surely would not want to spend the remainder of it as a vegetable.

A young nurse came up to us. "Follow me, but only one of you at time can go in. You are family, right?"

The three of us shared a look that was clearly one of "who wants to handle that question." Neither the lady at the information desk, nor the doctor who challenged us asked if we were family. Van der Beck answered. "Yes, I'm her uncle. I came over from Amsterdam when I heard about the terrible tragedy." He looked at us. "And these are her cousins."

That must have satisfied the nurse because she led the way down the hallway to the room where the person we knew as Dianna, and was listed as Lois Kennedy by the hospital, was a patient. The nurse pushed the door open and eased inside after motioning us to remain in the hallway. I heard her speak to the patient telling her she had a visitor. I did not hear a mention of it being family members, but I guess it was assumed that any visitor fell into that category.

When she came out, she pointed to Van der Beck. You can go in but only for five minutes. Remember, only one at a time." She left us on the

280

honor system and returned to her station. Big mistake.

The room was situated around the corner from the nurse's station, so unless they were in the hallway and knew we were supposed to go in one at a time, we felt we were safe when Van der Beck and I both went into the room.

The person in the bed had shoulder length blonde hair, skin that looked like it was silk lightly stretched over bone, lips that had clearly been enhanced but not overly so and arms that had bandages from wrist to elbow. Evidently Dianna, if that is who she wanted to be, had watched too many movies and television show about an attempted suicide by cutting her wrists. In the movies, the person cuts across the wrist. That causes a severe loss of blood but generally not enough to cause death. If the person is serious, the cut is done along the length of the vein. Either she was not serious or had made a mistake.

She looked up when we entered but did not say anything. Perhaps she thought we were doctors or other medical staff, although I'm sure the nurse indicated visitors and not medical personnel. The room was typical hospital, with the exception of anything that could be used to harm oneself. Electrical cords were securely fastened to all equipment. Only two leads were attached to her to monitor heart and blood pressure.

"I'm sorry. I don't know you. You must be in the wrong room. The nurse said you were family. I don't have any..." Van der Beck interrupted her before she could finish.

"I'm sorry, but that is the only way we could get to see you." He spoke in a soft, calming voice much like one would do if talking to a wild animal. "I'm a friend of someone I think you may be acquainted with." He walked to stand beside the bed. "His name is Jacob Dirksen. He's a professor at a university in the Netherlands. Does that sound familiar?"

281

The person in the bed looked at Van der Beck and then at me. "He's dead, isn't he?"

With complete disregard for the five-minute rule or for Patrick left standing guard outside the door, we listened for over twenty minutes as we found out what happened to Dirksen. Midway through her explanation, she burst into tears. I watched the monitors to see if her emotional state set off any alarms. When everything stayed normal, I asked her to continue.

"He was so nice to me. Much more than most of the men I meet. Non-judgmental and no embarrassing questions. He accepted me for who I really am." She hesitated as she collected her thoughts. By this time, I was fully convinced that I was looking at and speaking with a woman. "I meet a lot of men, but he was different from the first night. It was crazy, but I felt a connection…almost like love at first sight and I think he did as well."

"How did you happen to meet?" I asked.

"Frank Richardson set it up. He was dating my friend Venus. He called and told us to meet them for lunch in La Conner. Jacob took me back to Seattle and we went out that night. We were together every night until…" She choked back what could have been a serious outbreak of crying.

"Why do you say they killed him and who are they?" Van der Beck was ready to cut to the chase.

"I knew he had something special to do with the tulips and whatever it was Richardson wanted it. He's connected with some serious money in the flower business, and I think they are the ones who put him up to it."

I knew we were pressing our luck, both with our questions and with the time we were in the room, so I tried to hurry her along. "How do you know Richardson killed him?"

"Richardson invited us up for dinner one night. We met him and Venus and after dinner he said he

282

wanted to show Jacob something in one of the fields. Jacob had taken me up there twice and we walked through the blues at night. They were his favorite color and whatever he has was supposed to make a better tulip or color or something. I never really understood." She stopped and looked at us. "I had nothing to do with it. You must believe me."

Van der Beck's background as an investigator came out at that moment. He did not make any commitment to believe her or not. "Please continue."

"The four of us went back to Richardson's place. We had another drink and Richardson suggested we all take a walk and look at the tulips. I knew Jacob would jump at the chance so we went to one of the largest fields of blue tulips they had." She stopped talking and pulled a tissue from a small box on a bedside table. "After we got to the field they started talking about formulas and stuff and I had no idea what it was."

"What was the mood that Richardson was in?" Van der Beck asked.

"They started to argue, and Richardson told me and Venus to go back to his office. I didn't want to because I had seen Richardson get mad in the past. He can get out of control."

"Did you leave them in the field?" I was curious when she said he could get out of control. It was sounding more and more like the death in the blue tulips was not an accident.

"Yes. We went back and waited. I was really scared."

Van der Beck went to the door and opened it to check on Patrick. "Has anyone come by looking for us or said anything to you?"

"No. One nurse came by, but she just kept looking at a chart she was carrying."

When he came back in, he stood by me and whispered. "I think we are pressing our luck in several manners. If the doctor we met comes by and sees two of us in here, we may never get a chance to speak to her again."

"And?"

"And you have the Miranda decision and I think we may be getting very close to something what will stand up in court if my suspicions are correct."

"You think Richardson killed Dirksen?"

"I would bet on it, but we have to prove it according to your laws." I agreed with him and knew we had to make our move.

"Please tell us what you think happened while you and Venus were waiting for them," Vander der Beck said as he moved closer to the bed.

"We waited for about an hour. When Richardson came back, he had dirt and mud all over his shoes and pants and Jacob was not with him. When I asked what happened and where he was, he slapped me and told me to go back to Seattle and forget about Jacob and anything that had happened since I met him." This time she could not hold back the sobs. "Later on, Venus told me that Richardson told her Jacob fell in the field and hit his head on a rock and that he was probably dead."

We now knew what happened and who did it. All we had to do was prove it. As soon as we left the room, I called Bill Hart. If anyone could help us at this point, it was him.

Chapter 38

"Are you certain that he was killed?" I had Bill on the phone as Patrick drove us back to the hotel where Van der Beck was staying.

"We're both convinced that he was murdered, and Richardson did it. We just spoke to the woman that Dirksen spent most of his time with here, and she presents a very good case." I knew Patrick was listening, but I had little choice but to talk to Bill. If he agreed to do what I was about to ask, we would be able to button this one up. "She's scared and she was probably in love with Dirksen...." Bill interrupted me to question about her falling in love in less than two weeks.

"I know it sounds crazy, but you haven't seen some of the things we have seen. I think, under the circumstances that it's highly likely love would blossom almost immediately with anyone who was understanding to the plight of this person." Once again, I had to listen to him rail about getting between two people's personal feelings. We were in a business where we were supposed to be insulated against personal feelings. It didn't work too well for me and for Bill when he met Lannette, so I had to accept the fact that it didn't work for Dirksen and Dianna as well.

I heard Bill take a long breath and let it out. I had awakened him in the middle of his night, so I knew it would take a little longer for him to come around to what I wanted.

"Okay, it's the middle of the night here in DC, so give me a few hours and I'll see what I can do. I think I can make it happen with one of two agencies that owe me a favor. I'll cash it in for you, but it'll cost you." He laughed, knowing I was already in debt to him so far that another favor would not make any difference. "You should have something tomorrow by about noon your time. Call me later." With that, he hung up on his end.

"Is he going to assist us?" Van der Beck had been listening to the conversation, and like Patrick, only heard one side of it.

"If anyone can do what we talked about, it's him. He has his finger in everyone's pie in the District.

"All we can do now is wait." Van der Beck looked out the window as Seattle at night unfolded around us. "You do have a beautiful city," he said as he stared at a light fog settling atop some of the taller skyscrapers.

"What do you want me to do, or where do I take you now?" Patrick spoke up as we crossed over the Interstate.

"Take us back to the hotel. We can all go get some rest and I'll call as soon as I get something from Bill in the morning. I don't think there is anything more we can do tonight."

I drove back to my place from the hotel. By the time I got on the Interstate heading north, the traffic was as light as it ever gets in Seattle. I keep waiting for the completion of the light rail system that is supposed to run from north of the city to the airport. I don't know if I'll ever use it, but I'd like to see it completed, if for nothing else but to cut down on traffic, unless everyone felt the same was as I did.

When I got home, I fixed a cup of coffee and settled down into a large reclining chair in my living room. I started to fix a gin and tonic instead of the coffee, but I hate to drink alone. I looked at my watch and decided that although it was late, I'd take a chance and place a call to Anna.

She answered almost immediately. "Hi," she breathed into the phone, knowing full well that that one word was enough to make me want to roll over and smoke a cigarette.

We talked about mostly nothing for over thirty minutes and ended by agreeing to meet the next night for dinner. She knew I was involved with Bill and consequently I may have to cancel at the last minute, but we made the plans, nonetheless.

I finished my coffee, went to the bathroom and brushed my teeth before climbing into bed, thinking about what may happen the next day.

I had grabbed a cup of coffee and a Danish at the bakery around the corner from my office prior to my opening the door. After going in, picking up and checking the mail that was on the floor beneath the mail slot in my door, I settled in at my desk and waited to see if Bill was going to come through. I didn't have to wait long.

My desk chair has a squeak that I keep planning to oil, but I keep forgetting to bring a small can with me. I have almost lost the ability to hear it, since it is now such a part of the sound of my office that I surprised myself when I heard it. I had leaned back to make it squeak again, when I saw my front door open and a man walk in.

It was not hard to see that he was either military or law enforcement. Both groups have a look that, if you have ever worked around either, it's like a secret handshake. You recognize it immediately. I pegged him as law enforcement. He was in his mid-thirties, a little over six feet tall and if he wasn't careful, he was going to have the beginning of a beer-gut. Too many celebrations for a job well done with his teammates will put on unexpected pounds. His haircut was from a barbershop and not a stylist and it was starting to go grey around the temples. Like the beer-gut, it was the result of too many close calls, late nights, seeing things one should not see and not being able to understand or discuss them.

"You Maxwell?" he asked as he passed through the outer office and came into mine.

"Since I'm the only one here, my guess would be that I am."

He pulled out a leather folder and flashed a badge and an identification card with the logo of the US Marshal's Service on it.

"I don't know who you are or who you know, but we got a call this morning from the head of the Marshal's Service in Washington about you." He stopped as if he were searching for a way to say what was on his mind. "Please stand up."

"Excuse me?"

"Stand up. I can't swear you in if you're sitting down, so stand and raise your right hand."

He administrated an oath. I signed three documents and was handed a cred pack with a badge and a Marshal's Service Identification with my name on it. "You're now a Deputy US Marshal. Whoever you are, don't fuck up and don't embarrass us." He turned to leave and then stopped. "Here's my card. When you get in over your head, give me a call and I'll try to help."

As soon as the marshal left, I took the time to examine the badge and the credentials. The badge was a star in a circle and looked exactly like the ones I had seen on old western marshals in the movies and television since I was a kid. The credentials, or cred pack, had an identification card with my name and, strangely enough, a photo of me as well. The photo was a recent one, but I had no idea where or when it was made.

Satisfied that Bill had come through with my request, it was time to see if it was what we needed. I picked up my cell phone from my desk and called Van der Beck. He had purchased a burner cell phone when he got to Seattle to use when he did not want to use his official, but European based cell phone.

"Max? Is that you?" He asked when he answered the phone. I didn't know if the burner had caller ID on it or he had not given his number out to anyone else.

"Yes. I got what we spoke about. I think we need to meet prior to heading out tonight to work out a game plan."

"Excellent idea. Where shall we meet?"

I looked at my watch. It was heading for mid-afternoon and soon the roadways, no matter if they were surface streets or the Interstate, would begin to clog with traffic. I wanted to avoid as much of that as I could. "I'll meet you in the coffee shop at your hotel in an hour. Does that work for you?"

"I shall be awaiting your arrival."

I noticed on occasion that he used the most proper English and I wondered where he had been schooled. I made a mental note to ask.

In my back room, I have several pieces of equipment I have purchased over the years that I occasionally use in my PI business. I pulled down a small briefcase, checked to make sure what I needed was inside and took it with me as I left the office.

Edmonds Way is the main artery leading from the downtown area to the Interstate. I took it and, on the way, I was stopped at a traffic light when I saw Mayor Valentino. He and I had not spoken since we had our confrontation in my office, so I watched to see if he was going to pick up a rock and throw it through my windshield or something. All he did was look at me long enough to let me know that he recognized me. We locked eyes and only the light changing from red to green allowed me to break contact. I knew then he was not a man to forgive and forget.

Just prior to taking the entrance ramp to I-5, I was passed by an Edmonds firetruck. It continued on its way to assist somebody in need. I gave a silent thanks that it wasn't me.

The remainder of the drive was uneventful, and I parked in the underground lot at the hotel. We had agreed to meet in an hour, and I was about ten minutes early so I took my time and did not use the elevator but took the stairs to go from the parking lot to the hotel lobby.

From the lobby, I looked across the room to the coffee shop and saw Van der Beck seated at a table where he could watch the door. His selection of the gunfighter's seat was a natural for anyone who was involved in what I assumed was his line of work. It was also my seat of choice, but he was here first, so he got it.

He stood when he saw me enter the coffee shop. "Max!" He
waved. " Over here."

As soon as I was seated, a waitress appeared to ask what I wanted. I asked for a cup of coffee and Van der Beck got a refill on his.

"I get the impression that this Bill Hart friend of yours is a miracle worker of sorts." He sprinkled half a teaspoon full of sugar into his coffee.

"Where would you get that impression?"

"When I was told of this assignment, he was the first name I was given. It appears his reputation is more far-reaching than perhaps you realize." He glanced over the rim of the cup he held to his mouth. "Or perhaps you do know more about his background and his current position than you have shared with me."

"I've known and worked with him in the Army in Europe and after we both retired. We have a long history, but that doesn't mean he shares all his secrets with me."

We were at the beginning of the day's happy hour, so the lobby was beginning to get more foot traffic as men and women came in from a day's work and headed for the bar. "I find your concept of waiting for a certain time to begin social drinking a unique custom. Something I hope never to catch on in Europe. I don't like to be bound to the clock any more than necessary." He watched a group of three men and two women take a table in the bar. "Do you think that there will be a pairing of two or more of those five at the table before the night is over?"

One of the men was clearly making a play for the woman seated next to him. He was laughing at something, and she forced herself to join him. His hand was intermittently touching her arm as he spoke, and she did nothing to dissuade his actions.

"I think the man in the light blue shirt in the dark suit and the woman next to him on the right are clearly playing the game."

"That would be my assumption as well, but we didn't agree to meet to judge who will be with whom for the evening, did we?"

The briefcase I brought from my office was on the floor beside me, so I picked it up and placed it on the table. I turned it so it opened so he could see the contents.

"I think our best chance is to get Richardson to confess to Dianna. If he does, we'll probably be able to make a deal." I pulled out the cred pack and showed him the card and the marshal's badge. "I can't offer him a deal, but I can Mirandize him and I have arrest authority. If we play it as an international investigation with federal involvement, we may get him to tell us what happened and how Dirksen actually died."

"All we have to do it to get Dianna to agree to the plan, get her released from the hospital, and somehow get Richardson to confess to killing Dirksen." He placed his cup on the table. "Perhaps we should get started."

Chapter 39

Patrick picked us up at the hotel and we drove to the hospital. This time he found a parking place across the street and pulled into it. "Looks like this may be our lucky day. Finding a street side parking place around here is something I haven't done in months." He put the car in park and we walked to the front entrance of the main hospital.

This time we didn't have to ask information for Dianna's room number, so we went directly to the elevators and heading to the fifth floor. The elevator stopped on the third floor and two men in scrubs, complete with shoe coverings and something on their head got on. No one spoke, but it was safe to assume that they were either coming or going to something more than visiting a patient. They were still on and still silent when the doors opened on the fifth floor, and we exited.

We bypassed the nurse's station and went directly to Dianna's room. We only passed one person who was a part of the medical team, and she was pushing a cart loaded with cleaning supplies. She and Patrick exchanged a polite nod in passing and we continued on our way.

The door to Dianna's room was closed, so I gave it an easy push to open it. Dianna had raised the head of her bed and was sitting up. Unlike on our other visit, she had managed to put on make-up, fix her hair and put on a gown that was not hospital issue. The bandages that had previously covered her arms from wrist to elbow now were replaced by two square bandages applied across each wrist. Fortunately, she smiled when she saw us instead of reaching for the nurse call button.

"Good morning, Dianna. It's good to see you looking so much better." I did not inquire as to whether she would welcome us in since it didn't matter. We were there and we had a mission.

"Yes, thank you. I'm feeling much better. I think I may be released in a day or so…" She nervously pulled at a length of hair hanging down on the right side of her face. "Although they want me to come back to see a…a specialist…but I don't have insurance, so I don't think I'll be coming back."

That gave me the opening I wanted. I moved closer to the head of her bed. "Dianna, there's something very special and important we need to talk about."

"Jacob?" she asked.

"Yes. Jacob and what happened to him. We are interested in the way he lost his life, and you can help us. I think you know more than you've told us, and I also think you may be the key to answering the question." I hesitated. The look on her face indicated that I had not frightened her away, so I continued. "We want you to talk to Richardson and see if he will tell you how Jacob died."

"I'll tell you. Richardson killed him." A tear was about to ruin her eye make-up.

"I know you say that, but we need to hear Richardson say it, and tell you how he did it. Will you help us?"

"If it will put that son of a bitch in jail for killing Jacob, I'll do anything. But how do you get me out of here?"

I patted her arm. "You let me worry about that. In the meantime, tell Patrick what you need in order to leave."

The hallway outside her door led to a right turn which I remembered from our last visit took me to the nurse's station. There were several nurses and other hospital workers at computers throughout the area. I saw three men in their thirties, dressed in suits with stethoscopes draped around their necks and one older woman in a pants suit whom I assumed were doctors. Two of them had charts in their hands and the woman and one man were speaking to a nurse. I stood in silence for a minute before one of the nurses recognized my presence. "May I help you, sir?"

"Yes, I'd like to speak to the person in charge of Lois Kennedy's care." At the mention of her name, one of the males wearing a stethoscope turned in my direction.

"I'm Doctor Harris. Are you a relative?"

I moved closer to him to add emphasis to what I was about to say. "I'm not a relative, but I'm here to check her out."

"I'm afraid that's not possible. She has an appoint this afternoon to…"

I cut him off and pulled out my marshal's badge and ID card. "I'm afraid I must override that decision. "She is the key to an important investigation and time is of the essence, so unless she is in mortal danger, I'll take full responsibility for her release. If you want to prescribe any medication or further treatment, please do so now, otherwise we will be vacating her room in the next ten minutes." I waited to see if he was going to call anyone to check on my story, and if he did, would it hold up, but after giving me a long look and an even longer sigh, he turned to a nurse.

"Please prepare the release papers for Lois Kennedy. She will be leaving AMA."

"AMA?" I asked.

"Against medical advice." He turned and went back to his computer.

Unlike most patients who are released from a medical facility, Dianna was not given a wheelchair and an orderly to escort her out. She walked out between Van der Beck and me with Patrick bringing

294

up the rear. When we got to the lobby, he left us to go retrieve the car. There were already two taxis in the circle drive so Patrick pulled in behind them and waited for them to load prior to stopping at the front entrance. I didn't know if he was being polite and waiting his turn, or if he had been one of the taxi drivers picking up patients in the past and was extending a professional courtesy. Once we were in Patrick's car, Dianna looked at me. "Do I want to know what you did to get me out?"

"We'll explain everything as soon as we get to the hotel."

"You're taking me to a hotel?" There was no mistaking the fear in her voice.

"Not for what you think. We need to talk, and we can do it there and not be disturbed." I tried to reassure her. "Don't worry. You're safer than you have ever been."

We stopped by the restaurant and had dinner sent up to Van der Beck's room. I know we turned some heads when three men and one woman walked through the lobby together, stopped at the restaurant and ordered room service dinner.

We spent an hour talking to Dianna and explaining what we needed while we had dinner. The first thing we needed was for her to make a call to Richardson and we wanted her to do it from the room.

She called him on her cell phone, put it on speaker and the four of us listened. "Frank, it's Dianna. I talked to Venus, and she told me what you did to Jacob."

He came in loud and clear over the speaker. "What the hell are you talking about? You don't know shit. And don't you ever…"

She cut him off. "I know more than you think. I know you did it and I know why." She hesitated and looked at us for concurrence. "Jacob told me about the formula he had for the new tulip and that you wanted it. You killed him for no reason. He gave it to me to keep for him. You can talk to me, or I can call the sheriff and you can talk to him. It's your choice."

"You crazy bitch. I'll kill you for this."

"I'm going to come up to your office tomorrow and we'll see who you want to talk to." A smile spread across her face as she spoke. "You took something very special from me and you're gonna make it up to me."

With that, she ended the call and began to weep.

We sat in silence as what she said registered with us. Neither Van der Beck nor I had said anything about the tulip formula, but evidently Dirksen has discussed it sufficiently with Dianna that she was able to convince Richardson she had it. This was a most welcome addition to what we planned to do.

We got Dianna a room at the hotel and Van der Beck put that one, and separate ones for Patrick and me on his government credit card. Ours were on either side of the one for Dianna. We had her sandwiched in, so we could listen in case she wanted to bail during the night. We were guests of the government of the Netherlands that night.

Van der Beck and Dianna had breakfast the next morning, and we agreed to meet back at noon. Patrick and I needed time to go home and change clothes and clean up a bit. Before he left, Patrick drove Dianna to her apartment and waited for her to do the same.

By the time we met again, Van der Beck had rented a car for himself and Dianna. I had my 4 Runner and Patrick was still driving his personal car, so we had a small convoy as we pulled out of the city and headed north on the Interstate. Van der Beck called me on my cell as we were passing through Everette and told me that Dianna had set up a meeting with Richardson for three that afternoon. The meeting was to take place at an equipment shed in one of the fields. We knew that if he got Dianna into an isolated location, she would suffer the same fate as that of Dirksen. He gave her the directions and we decided that she would take the rental car to meet him. In the meantime, Patrick in his car, and Van der Beck and me in mine, would do a roll by to see the best way to protect Dianna.

The field he selected was bordered on two sides by freshly plowed fields, being made ready for a second or winter crop of whatever they planted in the non-tulip season. We could see a shed on the north side, so that was where he planned to meet Dianna. Near the shed was what appeared to be another farm. This one had a small herd of cows grazing not far from the place where they were to meet. A dirt track led from the hardstand to the pasture and a barn. The barn was close enough for us to do what we needed to do, so all we had to do was ask permission, or just go in and if we were caught, beg forgiveness.

I had to make one more call prior to our settling in to see if she could get a confession. After everything was set, we contacted Dianna and told her to proceed.

We watched Dianne drive slowly up to the shed. She was five minutes early, but Richardson had arrived fifteen minutes prior to that. She parked and eased her way across the field to the entrance to the shed. The door was closed, but she pushed her way in without hesitation.

As soon as she pushed the door open, I activated the recorder on the seat between Van der Beck and me. We had Dianna agree to wear a wire to record Richardson's conversation. We knew it would be sketchy evidence if he had a good lawyer, but with it on tape we hoped we could get a formal admission.

The first sound we heard was Richardson. "Well, little Miss half-way-there herself." The voice got louder, and we felt that he was getting in her face to talk. "What secrets did you and your little fuck buddy share?"

"He told me about the new kind of tulip he developed and how much it's gonna be worth and that you wanted to buy it."

"No, I didn't want to buy it. I wanted to make him a deal. My partner, Andre Verhoeven, in Amsterdam was willing to pay a lot for it. We could have all made a lot of money, but he wanted a bigger piece of the pie."

"And you didn't want to give it to him?"

"When he got greedy, I knew we couldn't make a deal, so…."

"So you killed him for it?"

As soon as she said that all of us held our breath. Ricardson was being steered to confessing to murder.

"No, I didn't plan to kill him. We went out to those precious blue tulips he liked to walk through at night, and I tried to reason with him. The little bastard wouldn't listen to reason or to any deal I offered…"

"Is that when you killed him?"

"Damn right. I hit the little shit and I thought he'd buckle, but he fought back. Used some kind of martial arts, but he was no match for me, and he should have known it. I tried to reason with him, but he kept saying no. I got so pissed thinking of what he had and wouldn't give me that I went kinda crazy. I had him down and then I found a rock and finished the job. There's so many kids and homeless that pass through here that there's no way anyone would suspect me." He stopped speaking. "Except for you." We heard the distinct sound of a slap.

"Who's going to believe a freak of nature like you? I'm gonna put you into the ground in one of my fields, and plant blue tulips on you, just to piss off your boyfriend."

The last part of the conversation recorded while we sped to the shed. I kicked the door open with my badge in one hand and my .45 automatic in the other. I was followed by the county sheriff who had reluctantly agreed to accompany us. "Do more than blink and I'll blow you to hell." I pointed the weapon at Richardson's head.

The sheriff was also covering him.

"Who the fuck are you?" Richardson was holding onto Dianna's arm. If he tried to pull her in front of him as a shield, I was prepared to put a hole in his forehead.

"US Marshal. You have the right to remain silent..." Before I could finish, he shoved Dianna aside and pulled a Glock 40 from a holster he had in the small of his back. I made my promise to him a reality as I fired.

Chapter 40

The next month was a tornado of activity. First, the county sheriff was not happy that a US Marshal had come into the county unannounced and in effect, reopened a case that he had closed. The only thing that satisfied him was the fact that he was with us when I took Richardson down. The next day the local paper gave him and his office full credit for solving the murder. I heard from the Supervisor of the US Marshal Service in Seattle who threatened to pull my credentials if I "ever got out of line again." I let him ramble on, since both of us knew that as long as I had Bill Hart in my corner, his immediate chain of command did not reach sufficient heights to have that done. I did promise to keep him informed of any future use of my position, if possible.

The sheriff's office and the state crime lab had to review the circumstances to include the taped conversation. The state gave us its blessings, and the sheriff was happy to concur.

Van der Beck contacted his office, and an investigation was initiated into Verhoeven. He said the best charges he could come up with was a conspiracy of some sort, possibly leaning more to the tulip formula than to the murder of Dirksen.

After a week of extensive meetings, Van der Beck suggested we take a cruise through the San Juans. He chartered a boat for a Friday sunset departure. I assumed it would be just Van der Beck, Anna and I but when I got to the dock it looked like a family reunion. Van der Beck was standing beside a stunning red-haired woman I had not seen before.

We were about to make introductions when Patrick walked up with a woman on his arm.

Van der Beck sensed the confusion and raised his hand for quiet so he could speak. "My good friends I wanted to do something special for all of you. Perhaps this will be a weekend that you can put in your memory bank under pleasant." He looked at the woman beside him. "Now I think we should make some introductions. This is Hema. She works at the consulate's office in Seattle. We have been friends on the phone for several years but until I arrived. I never realized what an attractive face went with the voice." He turned to Patrick.

"This is a very special lady I have been dating for three years. We've talked about a cruise like this in the past, but we just never got around to it."

"Max?" Van der Beck looked at me.

I was holding Anna's hand as I realized this was the first time I was going to have to introduce her as …what…friend….girl friend…FWB?

"This is Anna." I hesitated as I felt her grip tighten on my hand. "She is a part of me that I can't imagine living without. She is a partner in every sense of the word…and…and I…I love her very much." I felt my voice crack before I finished.

"And now Dianna?"

"This is Venus. My friend." With that, she ended the introduction.

"My friends, we are the guests of the Government of the Netherlands for the next twenty-four hours. I suggest we make the most of it. The boat is fully stocked with food, alcohol and I've even had some Dutch chocolates sent here for us. If there are no questions, I will instruct the captain to take over."

Dinner at sunset was Dungeness crabs, a Caesar salad and the best white wine I have ever tasted. The ladies had champagne, and the men had mixed drinks or imported beer and Cuban cigars, which we had to promise not to talk about. Just as I fired up mine, Dianna reached over and pulled it from my hands. "I think I can handle a good Cubano, if you don't mind." That was enough to make any dark clouds that may have been lingering over the group roll away. The remainder of the evening was spent drinking, smoking, telling some risqué stories and then leaving in pairs to go to our individual rooms

Anna and I had spent the night on a sailboat once when we did a mission for Bill that required us to bring a boat across the Puget Sound to Seattle. When we got to our room, it was small as was to be expected, so I watched as Anna slowly slipped out of the clothes she wore. When she was nude, she closed her eyes as she spoke. "I've given you everything I can and never looked back. You know I love you and I've never asked you to say the same." She raised her head and opened her eyes. "Did you mean what you said tonight? Do you love me?"

Before I could respond, she placed her finger on my lips. "No. Don't answer. Let me keep what you said without reservations." She eased beside me and crawled into bed. "Make love to me."

The next morning, we docked, and had breakfast at a little place on Lopez Island. Too soon the day ended, and we were back at the dock where we began. As we were leaving, Van der Beck called us all on deck. He had a bottle of Champagne and after pouring for everyone, he cleared his throat. "I have an announcement if you will indulge me. My government as well as the university where Professor Dirksen worked had established a reward fund for bringing the death of the professor to a satisfactory conclusion. I would say that the group, here assembled, was responsible for that. I have arranged for a monetary payment to be made to Patrick, but I suspect there are things in this world that are worth more than money." He looked at Dianna and raised his glass. "Dianna, I have taken the liberty to arrange for any surgery you require to be accomplished at the university hospital in appreciation for your help." He waited for a second. "I hope I have not overstepped my boundaries."

He got his answer when Dianna completely broke down in gut-wrenching sobs while Venus held her.

"And for you, Max, I have arranged for air passage and a week's stay at one of our better hotels in Amsterdam. I do hope you and Anna will contact me when you arrive."

An hour later, it was like taking your hand out of a bucket of water. There was no indication that it, or in this case, we had existed.

Anna and I went back to Edmonds and to my place where we spent the night in each other's arms without asking questions.

The End

Please leave a review.

Help this Author Catch More Readers

Also published by BWL Publishing Inc.

Operation Thunder Strike

Paul has a BA in Criminology and an MFA in Creative Writing from Antioch University, Los Angeles. He is a published novelist and a People's Choice Telly Award winning screenwriter with eight feature films produced from screenplays he wrote. He has two mystery series in print from Black Opal Books. He is a retired Army Lieutenant Colonel with two combat tours. He served as the Army Liaison to the TV and Film Industry in Los Angeles for five years. He was the Technical Advisor on such films as TRANSFORMERS 1&2, I AM LEGEND, GI JOE, THE MESSENGER, TAKING CHANCE and numerous other feature films and television episodes.

His film work is listed on IMDB

bwlpublishing.ca

Made in the USA
Columbia, SC
25 May 2022